"What's the matter?"

Ben smiled. "I lied."

"Is that right?" As if she didn't really care one way or the other, Sierra continued to eat with a very healthy appetite. "About what?"

Ben pulled his own chair close to hers, turned it around, and straddled it. He crossed his arms over the back and propped his chin there, watching Sierra with the sun-kissed skin, the luscious mouth, the smiling eyes.

Softly, feeling wolfish indeed, he said, "About wanting you."

She went still, not even chewing. Suddenly she choked, sputtered. Ben reached around to pat her on the back, but her eyes widened and she leaned out of reach.

She swallowed hard, wheezed, then choked out, "Uh . . . what do you mean, *wanting* me?"

Knowing she was about to bolt, Ben pushed to his feet, and Sierra pressed back in her chair, watching him warily.

Another telling reaction. He lifted one brow. "Not to worry, Sierra. You made yourself real clear. Not interested, right?"

He propped his hands on his hips and stared down at her, more than ready to give her some of his own honesty. Her eyes locked on his, her pupils expanded.

"The thing is, I've been looking for a challenge." His voice lowered even more. "And guess what?"

"What?"

Ben whispered, "You're it."

More from Lori Foster

LORI FOSTER

NEVER TOO MUCH

ZEBRA BOOKS
KENSINGTON PUBLISHING CORP.
www.kensingtonbooks.com

ZEBRA BOOKS are published by

Kensington Publishing Corp.
119 West 40th Street
New York, NY 10018

All Kensington titles, imprints, and distributed lines are available at special quantity discounts for bulk purchases for sales promotion, premiums, fund-raising, educational, or institutional use.

Special book excerpts or customized printings can also be created to fit specific needs. For details, write or phone the office of the Kensington Sales Manager: Attn.: Sales Department. Kensington Publishing Corp., 119 West 40th Street, New York, NY 10018. Phone: 1-800-221-2647.

Zebra and the Z logo Reg. U.S. Pat. & TM Off.

First Brava Books Trade Paperback Printing: October 2002
First Brava Books Mass-Market Paperback Printing: December 2003
First Zebra Books Mass-Market Paperback Printing: December 2008
ISBN-13: 978-1-4201-5268-5
ISBN-10: 1-4201-5268-8

ISBN-13: 978-1-4201-3661-6 (eBook)
ISBN-10: 1-4201-3661-5 (eBook)

20 19 18 17 16 15 14

Printed in the United States of America

Chapter One

The damp, sultry night air felt thick with the threat of a violent storm. Not a single star glimmered through the ominous gray clouds gently crowding the dark sky. It was the type of night that stirred a man's blood, made him think of warm mussed sheets and a warmer mussed woman.

Ben Badwin needed a woman, and he needed her now. Tonight.

Taking slow, deep breaths, Ben let his mind wander to the carnal image of uncontrolled sex, of raging lust. His muscles tensed as he dredged up several female possibilities, but he dismissed them all as not quite right. A muggy breeze ruffled his hair, drifted against his heated skin through the open collar of his shirt. Ben turned his face up to the night and smiled. He knew what he wanted.

A challenge.

Lori Foster

Lately, the thrill of the chase, the chance to seduce, had been missing in his life. But he was a man, and damn it, he *liked* the chase. He liked testing himself and coming out the conqueror. He liked being a dominant male.

Tonight, the bar and grill attached to his motel was packed. Not only were registered guests eating, playing pool, or drinking, but a lot of truckers had stopped in, as well as some locals who often frequented the bar.

For the most part the crowd remained friendly and free spending, allowing Ben to take a moment to himself. He stood just outside the entry door and surveyed the parking lot. Flood lamps lit the area, showing a collection of shadowed cars and trucks. Business was good, booming even. On that level, at least, Ben was very satisfied.

On another, he burned with edginess.

A little way down, in one of the ground floor rooms, a door opened. Two attractive, chatty women, probably in their early thirties, emerged. They laughed together as they moseyed toward the bar along the covered walkway. From all indications, they'd already been drinking. They neared Ben, and the one with short, stylish blond hair winked and gave a three-finger wave.

Ben smiled back, typically polite, charmed as always, yet uninterested. "Ladies."

A leggy brunette cocked her shapely hip. "Helluva night to be hanging outside." She eyed him up and down and up again with lascivious significance. A long scarlet fingernail touched his naked chest just inside his open shirt. "You should come on in and let me buy you a drink."

Wishing he felt even a spark of interest, Ben raised his arms in mock regret. "An offer that sweet is hard to refuse, but refuse I must."

She leaned forward, showing an impressive bosom to advantage. "I promise not to bite."

Ben couldn't help grinning. He adored women and their antics, how they flirted and the games they played— the games he *always* won. "Sweetheart, I don't believe that for a second."

The woman laughed in delight. "You sure you don't want to join us?"

The blonde added, "It'll be fun."

"Can't." Ben shook his head, and lied. "My time is already taken."

"Your loss."

"I'm sure it is."

They went inside and promptly found new game. Amused, Ben crossed his arms over his chest and leaned back against the clapboard wall. He enjoyed the business; he definitely enjoyed the female attention.

But these days he simply needed more, and he refused to settle for less.

A low rumble, probably thunder from the approaching storm, stirred the air. Ben looked to the sky for lightning, but saw none. The rumbling increased and seconds later the headlights of an ancient truck came around the curve, briefly flashing into Ben's face before swerving into the landscaping business directly across the street.

A few weeks ago Ben had noticed that the shop, after being abandoned for several months, was turning operational again. He'd noticed new paint, repaired shutters, a clean sweep of the cluttered gravel lot. Truckloads of mulch and plants had been delivered and arranged into neat rows.

Ben watched the old battered truck come to a jarring halt with grinding gears and a spattering of the loose rock and dirt. The headlights died, followed by a slamming door. He stared through the darkness, strangely alert.

Inside Ben's bar, someone started the jukebox, and the rousing tune of "Bad to the Bone" emerged. The base was low and thrumming, reverberating in his chest, in his head.

That's when Ben saw her.

She came out of the shadows and started across the street toward him. Spellbound, Ben watched as fog seemed to part around her, giving her an ethereal appearance. Somehow her steps, slow and rhythmic, matched the beat of the music, and the beat of his heart.

The reflection of a streetlamp glinted off her reddish-brown hair. It was tied into a high ponytail that might have been neat at one point during the day but now straggled loose and messy around her face. A fringe of bangs, stringy with sweat, hung half in her eyes. She wore a dusty white sleeveless shirt under a pair of coverall shorts with unraveled hems and a pair of brown lace-up work boots over rolled gray socks.

Ben wouldn't call it feminine attire, but maybe fetish attire? Whatever. She sure got his attention.

He couldn't help but wonder what kind of panties a woman wore under a getup like that.

Despite it being midnight and hotter than Hades, her stride was long and sure and fluid, matching that provocative music—*Bad to the Bone*.

She had the walk of a satisfied woman, and it turned Ben on. He'd always found confidence to be very sexy.

Because he stood in the shadows, she didn't notice him until the last moment, when she was a mere three feet away. Their eyes met; their gazes caught and held.

She faltered, then slowly, intently, surveyed him. Her lips parted in surprise.

Ben didn't move, didn't alter his relaxed pose against the building. But inside, interest roiled, kicked up his heartbeat and sent his senses—and his equipment—on full alert.

Knowing he looked too enthralled, Ben managed a more casual nod.

At his acknowledgment, the woman inched closer, but now her every step seemed weighted with caution and curiosity, as if she didn't want to look at him, but couldn't quite help herself. When she was directly in front of Ben, her wide lush mouth tilted and her eyes smiled. She shook her head, as if bemused.

Or disbelieving.

"You ought to be illegal." Her laughing comment, low and throaty, broke the spell. "It's a good thing I have a stout heart."

With that strange, yet provocative remark, she strode on past and into the building.

A little amazed at his aberrant reaction, Ben realized he hadn't said a single word, hadn't taken advantage of the situation or her comment, hadn't even introduced himself. He turned to view the back of her and his interest expanded. Her ass looked great in the coveralls, soft and cuddly and rounded just right. A nice handful. Her legs were strong, shapely with smooth muscles, lightly tanned.

The rousing music faded away, but the scent of heated woman touched by the damp outdoors remained. Ben grinned in acute anticipation.

Oh yeah, this was what he'd been looking for. *She* was what he'd been looking for.

The chase was on.

Feeling like a bull in rut, he trailed into the bar after her. Impatiently, he waited while she looked around, located a booth at the back of the room, and headed in that direction.

With one nod, Ben let the waitress know he'd take care of this particular customer. He followed along and when she slid into the bench seat, Ben propped his hip on the table. He tried for a nonchalant smile of welcome, but he knew his eyes were glittering, that his smile was more wolfish than not. He couldn't help that; he hadn't felt this sexually alert in a long time. "Hi."

She glanced up, saw it was him, and pinched off her automatic smile in an effort to keep her expression impassive. "A Coke please. Plenty of ice."

The interior lights this time of night were dim to accommodate all the drinkers. Ben couldn't see the color of her eyes, but the shape was exotic, tilting up on the outsides, heavily fringed with dark lashes. Ben studied her face and attempted to determine what it was about her that lured him.

Her mouth looked sinful, and very soft.

Her freckles looked playful, a bit impish.

Her body . . . Well, it was hard to tell in her sloppy clothes, but he sure as hell intended to find out.

Even with his obvious perusal, she looked away, reached for the menu, and effectively dismissed him.

Ben's interest escalated. Oh yeah, she was good at this, at playing the game. So, she wouldn't make it easy for him? Good. He nearly rubbed his hands together in anticipation of the coming night.

Feeling challenged and loving it, he straightened away from the table. "I'll be right back with your drink."

She didn't reply.

Taking her at her word, Ben filled a glass with crushed ice and then poured in the soda. She had her head propped up on a fist, her exotic eyes closed tiredly when Ben returned.

Her nails weren't painted. They weren't even clean. Wherever she'd worked today, it had been a dirty job, and the stains on her fingers proved it. But that didn't bother Ben. He was too pleased to make note of the lack of a ring. Not married, not engaged.

Perfect.

He set the drink down and waited.

Very slowly, her eyes opened. She had a sexy, full mouth, which stretched wide in a yawn before she mumbled through her hand, "Thank you."

Her voice was smoky and deep, her expression orgasmic. Or maybe exhausted. Hard to tell when he was so aroused.

Rather than take a drink, she lifted the icy glass to her forehead and sighed at the cool touch. "It's so hot outside tonight."

It was hotter than hell inside, too.

A drip of condensation rolled down the frosty glass, fell onto her upper chest, and trickled down between her breasts. Ben held his breath.

Damn, everything about her seemed devised to push his buttons. Only he couldn't ever recall a bedraggled, sweaty woman in work clothes turning him on before now.

In an effort to diminish the lust and further his association, Ben cleared his throat. "You work next door?"

A proud, friendly smile lit up her eyes. "Yeah. I'm the new owner. We've spent the past couple of weeks getting the place into shape. But today we finally started business."

She owned the business. She'd be close by.

Damn. Any woman who would constantly be so close could be trouble. Starting something that would be difficult to end due to proximity would be plain foolish. He had to be cautious, to consider all the possible problems . . .

Using two fingers, she fished an ice cube out of the glass and sucked on it.

Ben drew in his breath. *To hell with caution.*

He held out a hand, anxious to touch her even in a platonic way. "Welcome to the neighborhood. I'm Ben Badwin, and I own this motel."

She looked at his extended hand. "Is that right? Wow, great place." She swiped her fingers across the top of her thigh, on the coveralls to dry them, then took his hand and pumped twice in a mannish way. "Sierra Murphy. It's nice to meet you, Ben."

Sierra—an unusual name for an unusual woman. Her hand was small, slim, warm. And callused. She looked far too young to own a business, and far too appealing to be working in the dirt. Reluctantly, Ben released her. "You're out late."

"Yeah." That deep satisfaction was back, somehow as tantalizing as a woman's natural perfume. "Working on the condos around Parker's Point."

"By moonlight?"

She shrugged strong, feminine shoulders, bare beneath the sleeveless shirt. She appeared sleekly muscled all over and that had Ben's brain in a cramp, trying to picture her naked. There wasn't anything masculine about her figure, but despite her small stature, she wouldn't be a weak woman either.

She took a long drink, then slouched back in her seat with a genuine show of tiredness. There was nothing posed about her posture, nothing deliberately enticing, and Ben appreciated the natural picture she made.

"I unloaded a lot of stuff so we'll be ready to go bright and early in the morning. Getting a job that size was sheer luck. I don't want to do anything to blow it."

Her candor surprised Ben.

At his expression, her smile turned playful and she wrinkled her narrow nose.

Her freckles were *really* very cute. Was she freckled anywhere else?

"I'm excited about it all," she admitted, "and knew I wouldn't be able to sleep anyway. Figured I might as well get some work done."

He had a cure for sleeplessness that beat the hell out of work anytime, but the timing wasn't right just yet. Sierra chatted with him, but she wasn't in any way coming on to him. Other than her beguiling comment out front, there were no signals, no "come and get it" signs. She was friendly, but only friendly.

Improvising, Ben made the only offer he could think of to extend their introductions. "You look hungry, Sierra. Can I get you something to eat?"

Her arched brows disappeared under her bangs. "Your menu says you stopped serving food at midnight. That was ten minutes ago."

"True. The kitchen is closed and the cook has gone home. But we're neighbors, so I'll make an exception for you." And hopefully some headway.

She sat back in surprise. "Thank you."

"You'll have to eat in the kitchen though, so no one else starts ordering up." He grinned his most engaging grin, the one that made females flutter and giggle. "I close up at one, and I don't want any delays."

Sierra didn't flutter, giggle, or even appear to notice his grin. She pursed her mouth, tilted her head, and stared him right in the eyes. "No way will I argue with food right now. I'm starved and too tired to cook for myself."

"I'm glad to be of service." *In any way you might need me.*

"But I've got to make sure you understand, it's only a little food I want."

Ben blinked at that additional dose of bluntness. "Beg your pardon?"

"What I said out front? When I first saw you?"

"What about it?"

She lowered her thick lashes, hiding her eyes. "I don't want you to make too much out of it. That was just shock talking."

"Shock?" It had sounded like interest to Ben. Very welcome interest. Reciprocal interest, damn it.

"Mmm. You really took me off guard, just showing up like that." She gestured somewhere around his midsection, up and down and back again. "Not every day a woman sees a man like you, especially in the dark that way. And I guess I'm just tired enough that I spoke without really thinking."

Ben stared at her, hoping he displayed a man in ultimate control of himself. "A man like me?"

She laughed. "Yeah. Gorgeous? Sexy? A stud?"

He had no idea how to reply. For the first time in his life, he found himself speechless with a woman.

"Oh, come on. I'm sure you're aware of how you look, right? I imagine women throw themselves at you all the time."

Ben crossed his arms over his chest and nodded slowly. This game was new, but he was catching on real quick. "Yeah, leaves a horrible mess around the diner. All the fallen bodies, you see."

She laughed again. "No doubt. Probably trips up the waitresses, huh?"

He didn't answer. He just waited to see what else she'd say.

She smiled up at him, as if to soften her rejection. "The thing is, I'm plain not interested. In fact, I'm one hundred percent disinterested. So if your offer to feed me is a come-on, I'll just go home and try to find some cheese crackers or something to eat."

Remaining speechless, Ben pondered her. He'd never met a woman who spelled things out so candidly. The jury was still out on whether he liked it. Such honesty in bed would be great. But in the middle of the diner?

Sierra lifted her shoulders and her expression was apologetic. "Just trying to make sure we start our neighborly association off on the right foot, since my comment out front could be misleading."

Well, hell. She sounded too damned sincere. Could she really be that unaffected when he was *very* affected? He couldn't remember the last time a woman had captured his attention like this. He felt . . . alive. On the prowl. Anxious and turned on.

At the moment, she had the verbal upper hand and she knew it. But no way would Ben let any woman, not even a woman who intrigued him this much, keep the upper hand. It wasn't natural.

He drew a deep breath and made his move to take control. "Have you seen a mirror lately, Sierra?"

Her confident smile slipped a notch. "I . . . uh . . ."

"You're pretty much a sweaty mess." His gaze roamed over her. He reached out to flip her bangs with his fingertips, and despite himself he felt a smile tug at his mouth. "And dirty."

She ducked her hands under the table and glared at him. "It's hard to get the ground-in dirt out from under my nails without soaking them. But I *did* wash, of course."

Stung by guilt at her embarrassment, Ben girded himself and continued. "Maybe you clean up real nice, hard to tell, but at the moment you don't look all that beddable, so I think we're both safe, don't you?"

Her face colored, her sweet mouth opened, then incredibly, she laughed. When Ben frowned at her, she wiped her eyes and chuckled some more. "Oh, you're right of course. How conceited I must have sounded. It's just that you have 'wolf' pulsing off you. I figured any guy who looked as good as you do had to always be on the make." She smiled up at him. "Nice to know my new neighbor is more discriminating than that."

There was that disconcerting honesty again. Her every word seemed to push Ben closer to the edge. She had him pegged.

Sierra eased out of her bench seat and saluted him with her half-empty Coke. "Is the offer of sustenance still open?"

Standing in front of her, Ben realized how petite she was, how delicate regardless of her strength. He had the urge to pull her close and see how she fit him, to feel her against his body.

Ben forced himself to behave. "Yeah, the offer stands."

"Great. Then lead the way. I'm faint with hunger."

Ben had expected her to be insulted by his comments on her person, not amused. She wasn't an average female, to be amused. But then he hadn't wanted an average female.

Finding himself at another loss, Ben led.

A few people looked up as they crossed the floor toward the kitchen, but for the most part no one paid them any mind.

Ben was very aware of her strolling behind him, physically close but emotionally distant, sexually disinterested. He stepped aside until she'd passed him, then let the doors flap shut behind them. Muted noises from the outer area drifted in, but they were now afforded a small bit of privacy.

He flipped a wall switch and bright fluorescent lighting flickered on to illuminate the kitchen. Being furtive, he glanced at her and finally saw the color of her eyes.

Green. But not just green, sort of a soft green with deeper flecks of blue and gold. Nice.

"Horace, my cook, always leaves something edible in the fridge for me. Let's see." Ben opened the gigantic refrigerator and peered inside. "There's a sub sandwich, pie, soup . . ."

"The sandwich sounds great if you're sure you don't mind sharing. Thanks."

Ben took it out and unwrapped it, using the time to gather himself, to rethink his position. He'd helped out in the kitchen many times and, in fact, had worked every job in the motel and bar. He liked staying busy.

He put the sandwich on the large cutting board, cut it in half, and put it on a utilitarian plate. After forking a pickle from the enormous jar on the counter and adding some chips from a large airtight bin, he turned back to Sierra—and caught her staring. At his ass.

Ah-ha.

She glanced up, looked startled, and frowned at him, as if it were his fault she'd ogled him.

Ben was a gentleman, so he didn't remark where her gaze had strayed, but it was a real relief to know she wasn't as disinterested as she'd claimed. "This way."

He made a point of leading her into the employee lounge, affording her the chance to cop another peek, if she was so inclined. When he looked at her, her expression was blank, so he couldn't tell if she'd been checking him out or not.

She took the first chair and dropped into it with a groan of weariness. She stretched out her legs, crossed her booted feet, and blew her bangs from her face. For a moment, her eyes closed tiredly and she looked very vulnerable.

Ben eyed her limp form, the weariness etched into her bones, and shook his head. He was horny, and she looked ready to pass out. "You're really exhausted, aren't you?"

Her head lifted. "Yeah, but it feels great." She accepted the plate he handed to her and took a large bite of the sandwich.

"You like getting dirty, do you?"

Her nose wrinkled. Around the mouthful of food, she said, "Beats working in a stuffy office any day."

"Agreed." Ben wanted to keep her talking just to hear her. She had a throaty voice that reminded him of a purring kitten. "But any business will have some office hours, too. God knows I put enough of them in here."

"True, but right now the paperwork is minimal because we're doing only on-site jobs, which keeps me out in the sun and fresh air during the day. At night, I do the paperwork."

Which would make for long hours. No wonder she looked so tuckered out.

She ate several chips before continuing. "If I can get ahead in a year or two, I'd like to sell summer flowers and plants, maybe Christmas trees in the winter, mums in the fall . . . You know, have someone always on the lot during business hours. There's a lot of call for seasonal stuff. If that ever happens, I'll probably hire someone just to keep the records."

If she was doing it all by herself right now, she had a heavy load to handle. "Being your own boss isn't always easy."

"I know, but I'm working for me, not for anyone else. That's makes the hard work worthwhile."

Because he shared those sentiments, Ben nodded. Above the pulsing lust, he was aware of a strange affinity toward her, and a stronger sense of anticipation. His body was tense with basic awareness, and his blood felt hot, pumping thickly through his veins. He was a man on the prowl, and it felt good.

He wanted her. But he also wanted to sit down and converse with her more because they had a lot in common.

Strange.

It was time to get things back on track. He waited until she'd eaten half of the sandwich, ensuring she wouldn't starve on him, then gave her his full attention.

She caught him staring and must have seen the heat behind his gaze because she blinked. She looked down at herself, apparently checking that nothing showed, then she looked behind her. Finally she frowned at him. "What's the matter?"

Ben smiled. "I lied."

"Is that right?" As if she didn't really care one way or the other, she continued to eat with a very healthy appetite. "About what?"

Ben pulled his own chair close to hers, turned it around, and straddled it. He crossed his arms over the back and propped his chin there, watching Sierra with the sun-kissed skin, the luscious mouth, the smiling eyes.

Softly, feeling wolfish indeed, he said, "About wanting you."

She went still, not even chewing. Suddenly she choked, sputtered. Ben reached around to pat her on the back, but her eyes widened and she leaned out of reach. The rest of her sandwich dropped to the plate and fell open.

She swallowed hard, wheezed, then choked out, "Uh . . . what do you mean, *wanting* me?"

Now this was a reaction he could understand but hadn't really wanted. "Strange, huh? Part of what I said is true, you are a little on the raw side right now." He looked at her body again, this time with his thoughts clear on his face. His voice dropped, became husky. "I can smell you, Sierra."

She looked horrified.

"You smell good, sort of warm and soft. Hell, maybe that's even it. Woman *à la naturale,* ya know?"

Bright color rushed into her cheeks and spread out. Ben hadn't thought the little barbarian could blush, not with her confident swagger and outrageous conversation. But boy, did she ever.

So, he decided, her confidence didn't extend to sexual matters. How interesting was that? What a little paradox she was proving to be.

Obviously stunned, Sierra's gaze moved from his, to her sandwich, and then around the isolated room. It was as if she'd only just then become aware that they were alone.

Knowing she was about to bolt, Ben pushed to his feet, and Sierra pressed back in her chair, watching him warily.

Another telling reaction. He lifted one brow. "Not to worry, Sierra. You made yourself real clear. Not interested, right?"

She looked far from reassured by his words.

Did she think he planned to attack her? He propped his hands on his hips and stared down at her, more than ready to give her some of his own honesty. Her eyes locked on his, her pupils expanded.

"The thing is, I've been looking for a challenge." His voice lowered even more. "And guess what?"

She stared in disgust at the remaining food on her plate. "What?"

Ben whispered, "You're it."

Chapter Two

Sierra was hungry damn it, and now he was forcing her to leave. He stood far too close, but still she stood, sighing with annoyance and regret. The sandwich had tasted delicious. Beyond that, Ben had seemed so nice, so easy to be with. "I guess that's it then."

"What's it?"

She rolled her eyes. Ben Badwin could be called a lot of things, not all of them complimentary. But not dumb. He knew exactly what she meant—he just wasn't used to hearing it. He probably expected her to jump at the chance to be with him.

Strangely enough, it wasn't a distasteful proposition. But it was totally out of the question all the same. "I'd say pretty much everything."

"Everything?" He looked a little more alert now, with determination darkening his sinful eyes. His lashes were thick and girlishly long, but there wasn't anything girlish about him. The man pulsed with testosterone.

Not for a single second did Sierra think he really cared if she left or stayed. In the scheme of things, her interest—or lack thereof—wouldn't matter to him at all.

When they'd walked through the diner to the kitchen earlier, Sierra had noticed all the females present, from the customers to the waitress, staring after him. She'd be willing to bet he could have his pick, so why bother with her?

That business about her being a challenge was absurd.

She snagged a chip off the plate and turned to go. "Everything as in the free meal, the proffered friendship, the neighborliness." She gave him a look. "You know, I meant it when I said I wasn't interested. I wasn't flirting."

He caught her arm to halt her retreat. His hand was very warm, very big, his hold gentle. He tipped his head, watching her intently. "Huh. You didn't strike me as the cowardly type."

Ben was a big man, lean but hard, naturally dark. He had an athletic build with long legs, muscular forearms, thick biceps, and an extremely sexy butt, which she'd made note of earlier. It still surprised her that she'd noticed because she simply didn't pay any attention to most guys.

But there was a big difference between Ben and other men, and it wasn't just his looks or great physique. He had a sort of throbbing sex appeal, an engaging wit and a concentrated way of giving his attention that no woman could ignore, not even Sierra.

But while she was aware of it, she wouldn't spare the time to explore it. She couldn't.

And so she stared at his hand on her arm until he released her, then she met his gaze. "I'm not a coward." *Not anymore.* "But neither am I an idiot. You're on the make. I don't have the time to fend you off. Sticking around would be dumb."

He crossed his arms over his chest and leaned back on the edge of the long table. His abdomen was flat, his hips narrow. And beneath his fly . . .

"Maybe I wasn't clear. I would never force you."

Sierra jerked her gaze up to his face, appalled at herself and her wayward attention. She blushed again and wanted to kick herself. "There's force, and then there's force."

His eyes narrowed with an intuitiveness that unnerved her. "You know something about that, do you?"

His tone had altered, gone soft and gentle, and if she didn't know better, she might have thought it was concern that brought the change. Ridiculous. He didn't even know her.

Sierra dredged up a dose of nonchalance and shrugged. "I'm twenty-four, so yeah, I know about pushy men. You, Ben, with your good looks and better body, are probably pushier than most."

"Thank you." He didn't smile, but satisfaction oozed from him at her compliments. "I like to think I'm not so predictable, though. Besides, I was being up-front with you, letting you know my intentions—since you'd been so up-front yourself."

Was he mocking her? Sierra wasn't sure, and she stiffened. These days, she refused to let any man intimidate her in any way. Ben had been bold, so she'd paid him back in kind. Maybe he hadn't liked it, but that was his problem, not hers. "I appreciate the warning, really I do."

"It wasn't a warning, just a little notice. You don't know me yet, so I wanted to reassure you."

She felt far from reassured.

"I believe in being fair." He smiled. "So now you know what I want. But you don't ever have to worry about force from me, of any kind. Okay?"

She'd believe that when pigs flew. Not that she thought he would physically harm her—as he'd said, she didn't know him well enough to make a judgment like that. But Ben had already tried to force his will on her, and that just naturally made her rebel.

"Where's the harm, Sierra? Sit down, eat your sandwich, chat with me. You'll see I'm harmless."

She gave him an incredulous look, and he laughed. But calling him harmless was too funny.

"I own a reputable business, Sierra. Everyone in the area knows me. I can't be too bad or I wouldn't have any customers, right?"

He made her feel foolish, as if she'd overreacted. And perhaps she had. There were still customers in the diner, within shouting distance—not that she expected to shout. But still . . . she'd spent so much time avoiding situations like this one, she'd forgotten how to handle it.

"I'm not going to harangue you, I promise. Stay, please."

Oh, he personified appeal with that seductive voice. Sierra would be willing to bet he could coax a woman right out of her shorts with very little effort. That image almost made her laugh.

After a long day of working outdoors, her shorts were so dusty and dirty she was amazed that he had any interest in them at all. Amazed and . . . beguiled. Much as

she'd like to deny it, the woman in her was very complimented by his persistence.

And that might prove dangerous.

She sighed. They would be neighbors, so she couldn't
avoid him forever. It might be better to get things straightened out now. She glanced back at her plate, where food
still waited.

She could almost hear that thick sandwich calling her
name. Her belly rumbled, and to her embarrassment, he
heard.

He pulled out her chair again. "C'mon, Sierra. Be
neighborly." His smile teased. "Let me feed you."

"You expect me to just eat, knowing you'll try to seduce me?"

His mouth curled at the old-fashioned term. "Seduce?
Yeah, I'll try to seduce you. By showing you what a nice
guy I am, by letting you see how good it'd be. But I won't
push, I promise. And since you're forewarned of my interest, and you have no interest yourself—well then,
there's no problem, right?"

If she'd truly been uninterested, she might have agreed.
Unfortunately, that wasn't the case. It was beyond stupid,
and not something she was used to anymore, but she could
feel herself reacting to him.

Her stomach rumbled again, making up her mind for
her. "Oh, all right." She pulled the chair out of his hand
and plopped down. "Fine, but the second you get pushy,
I'm outta here."

He laughed at her ill temper, as if she amused him.
"Agreed." Ben reseated himself, a man at his leisure now
that he'd won. "So why landscaping?"

Sierra took another big bite before answering. She was
so hungry she shook.

Or maybe she was shaking because she'd just given in to a devastating man who claimed to *want* her. Gads. She finished chewing and swallowed.

Talking about work would keep him from talking about seduction. She thought about it a moment, tried to remember all the reasons she'd wanted to become a landscaper. "Fresh air, physical labor, nature. I like digging in the dirt, mixing soils, and then seeing things grow. I have a green thumb, an eye for color and textures."

"Is it something you always wanted to do?"

"No." Sierra had no intention of telling him the foolish plans from her youth. They were long gone. "But I worked for a landscaper for a while and realized I loved it and had a knack for it."

"A summer job?"

She shrugged. "A way to pay for school and rack up experience."

"You said you like physical labor?"

He sounded puzzled by that. "Yeah, don't you enjoy using your muscles?" She eyed his upper body. "You've got enough of them."

He smiled lazily. "Thank you."

Sierra caught herself. She'd sort of meant that as a gibe because with his open shirt and posture he all but flaunted himself and it kept distracting her—but it had come out as a compliment.

She sighed, giving it up. "You're welcome."

"I take it you enjoy using your muscles, too?"

"That's right. I'm small but strong, and I like staying fit." To change the subject, she said, "Tell me about your motel." If he talked, that meant she could eat, and she wouldn't say the wrong thing again.

"All right." Hooking another chair with his ankle, Ben

pulled it around and propped his feet up. "This place was a real dive when I bought it. Run-down, dirty, fights every damn night. There's still the occasional brawl, but it's better."

"You ever in those brawls?"

His eyes glittered. "When necessary."

This time Sierra did laugh. "No doubt you enjoy yourself."

He shrugged but didn't deny it. "I repaired the built-in pool for summer use, added a game room with two pool tables, a jukebox, some coin games. It's been a challenge getting it in order, making a profit. No way in hell am I going to let a rowdy drunk tear stuff up."

"Sounds like a lot of work." Sierra guessed his age to be somewhere in his late twenties. He'd accomplished a lot, and her admiration expanded.

"True, but it's been fun for the most part."

"You like a challenge." He'd already labeled her his newest challenge.

"Guilty." His smile promised she'd like it, too. Sierra looked away, and he continued. "I had to hire a lot of new staff, but I started with an excellent evening cook. My brother runs an upscale restaurant, among other things, and he taught me how important it is to give customers good food. Horace may look like a mean son of a bitch, but he's a whiz in the kitchen. Customers are always surprised by the quality of the meals."

"The sandwich is great." She eyed it, considering. "It doesn't taste like a regular old sandwich. There's something different about it."

He looked pleased that she'd mentioned it. "Horace buys a special kind of bread, bakes it here, then uses his own sauce as a condiment; something he whips up when no one is looking. The recipe is real secret stuff. Even I don't know what he puts in it. The customers love it. He's training the morning cook, a younger guy, to do some special things with bagels and doughnuts and croissants."

Sierra nearly groaned. "Doughnuts are one of my weaknesses."

Ben gave her a casual, calculated look. "Is that right? Stop by in the morning and I'll feed you again."

"More neighborly offerings?"

He lifted one broad shoulder. "Could be the best way to a woman's heart is through her stomach."

Sierra waved a pickle slice at him, determined to hold her own. "You don't want my heart."

He laughed, and even his damn laugh was appealing. "True," Ben said. "But if food can seduce the heart, maybe it can seduce the body, too."

"Need help with that, do you?"

"Just trying to find a shortcut. I'm . . . impatient."

Oh, the way he said that. It made her impatient, too. Sierra forced a look of nonchalance to hide her turmoil. It was the absolute worst time for her to start flirting. "I know you don't know me well, Ben, but let me clue you in. It'd take more than a doughnut to get me into bed."

"Ah, more challenge."

Sierra barely covered her laugh. He was a shameless rogue, and if she weren't careful, she'd end up doing something really stupid.

She needed to get away from him now.

With her hunger mostly appeased, Sierra became more aware of her exhaustion. She stood and stretched. "Do all men in Gillespe move so fast?"

Ben stood too, much taller than she, much more powerful. "And here I thought I exemplified patience. After all, I've known you"—he glanced at the watch on his thick wrist— "almost forty minutes now and despite a powerful desire, I've held myself in check."

Sierra snorted at that idiotic remark, then stuck out her hand. "Thanks again for the meal and the . . . warm welcome to the neighborhood. I appreciate it."

Ben took her hand, but rather than indulge in a friendly handshake, he enfolded her fingers in his own and held on. "Doughnuts tomorrow?"

Would it really hurt anything? She was new to the area, and she'd noted the convenience of his diner right away. Since she wasn't much of a cook but loved to eat, it'd be handy to have a friendship with the owner.

Still feeling undecided, she warned, "I have to start working by eight."

"We'll be open. A lot of truckers come in early."

Still she hesitated. He allowed her to tug her hand free, holding to his promise that he wouldn't push her. At least not too much.

"Sierra?" He leaned down to see her. "Stop by and I'll have some coffee ready, too."

She hadn't even unpacked her personal things yet, much less her coffeepot. She had a hard time starting the day without coffee, and she'd intended to drop into a coffee shop somewhere anyway . . .

At least, those were the reasons she gave herself, and damn it, they were good reasons.

"All right." She turned away, determined to make her escape before she found another excuse to linger. "Now I really need to get going."

Ben fell into step beside her. As they reentered the bar, he took her elbow. Most of the customers had left and only one waitress remained. The place was now quiet and subdued and it felt as if those still in attendance again made note of Ben's stroll across the floor. Sierra thought of how she was dressed, her messy hair and dirty hands and sweaty face. She wanted to cringe.

Amazing, that Ben—such an incredibly handsome man—claimed to want her. When she cleaned up and wore makeup and had her hair fixed, she supposed she made a nice enough appearance. But it had been ages since she'd bothered because it had been ages since she'd had the time or inclination to worry about attracting a man.

She shook her head. She wasn't interested in attracting a man now, either.

Ben glanced at her. "What?"

They stepped through the door into the humid night air. "I was just thinking it must be a full moon, even though it's so dark I can't see the moon." She stopped, which forced Ben to stop.

"Why do you say that?"

"No reason." She wasn't about to explain that she felt different, sort of unsettled. Because of him. She forced a smile. "Well, good night."

He looked down at her, his expression enigmatic. Somehow, he shifted closer without seeming to move. "I'm walking you to your truck."

Sierra felt his nearness in the gloomy night, and it felt different than a mere physical positioning. It was . . . warmer, almost static.

"I'm not going to my truck."

One brow rose high. "No? Then how do you expect to get home?"

She looked across the lot and into the darkness toward her new home. "I guess I didn't explain that part. I live in the small house next to the shop."

"Small house?" Ben turned, too, to peer through the darkness. A flood lamp in her parking lot barely lit the surrounding area. "You mean that . . . hut? I thought that was just a building to store flowers or something." He turned back to her with a frown. "You can live in there?"

Because that had been her first reaction, Sierra didn't take offense. In fact, the original owner had intended the building as a mere convenience for the workers, not as living quarters. But it had a fully functioning, if minuscule, kitchen, complete with phone hookup, and an apartment-size stove and refrigerator. The bathroom had a shower stall, and there were two other rooms that had been used for storage but would now be her living room/office and bedroom. That is, if she ever got unpacked.

"It's small, but it's not a hut. Actually, it's kind of nice. And cozy. And I'm only one person, so I don't need a lot of room."

Not quite convinced, Ben shook his head. "I'll walk you to your door then."

"Not necessary." She gestured at her legs. "Everything is operational. I can make it there all on my own."

Just as she finished speaking, lightning flashed close by, making them both jump. The accompanying thunder was loud enough to shake the ground.

"Wow."

Ben took her arm. "Come on. We better get going before we get soaked." When she hesitated, he sighed and said, "Okay, have it your way. I'll just follow behind to make sure you get inside okay."

"You intend to follow me?"

"You make me sound like a stalker." He chucked her chin. "I'm not that desperate. It's just that my mother raised me as a gentleman."

"And you think to protect me from—what? The rain? There's no one out here but us."

A gusting wind that was both refreshing and a bit alarming in its ferocity swallowed up her words. Sierra felt a fat raindrop hit her nose, then another and another until they were spattering the ground all around her. Not willing to get caught in a downpour, she started away, leaving Ben to do as he pleased.

The rain started in earnest and she broke into a jog. She could hear Ben trotting along behind her, resolute in his gentlemanly purpose, despite the downpour.

They reached the shelter of a large elm that shaded her front door and the small overhang on her new home. Ben crowded in close to her, trying to get out of the rain. They were both soaked and breathing hard.

Sierra fished her key out of her pocket, got the door open, and reached inside for the light switch. A dim, bare bulb glowed, lighting the small stoop.

Feeling safer, she turned back to Ben—and stalled. His raven hair, now wet, hung over his brow and stuck to his forehead and temples. His black lashes were spiked from the rain, his shirt clinging to his chest, shoulders, and upper arms.

He was so appealing he took her breath away.

Not even trying to hide his curiosity, Ben leaned toward her—nearly stopping her heart—but he only peeked inside her new home. Boxes sat everywhere, nearly hiding the unmade twin bed that had been placed temporarily against an outside wall, directly under a large window. The bed was the only thing she'd set up so far.

His gaze came back to hers. "Cozy, huh?"

"Good-bye, Ben." To her chagrin, her voice sounded like a croak. But she could smell him, musky and sensual and male. She could feel his heat and his vitality. It shook her.

Of course, Ben noticed. A slow smile curled his mouth as he looked down at her. "Damn." His voice was low and deep. He brushed a wet tendril of hair away from her cheek, and his hand lingered, his fingertips rough, warm on her skin. "I want to kiss you, Sierra."

Rainwater dripped from her nose. She swiped it away with an impatient hand.

"I don't understand it," he continued, sounding almost as confused as she felt. His hand opened, cupped her head. "I barely know you, and it's not like you're trying to turn me on. Hell, you're not even being all that nice. But you're making me nuts."

The look in his eyes, the things that he said, nearly undid her. Sierra believed he wasn't trying to seduce her with words, but rather telling her truthfully how he felt, spelling it out. He'd been open about his intentions since meeting her—and that wasn't something she ever expected from men.

She swallowed hard. "This isn't a good idea."

"Just one small kiss?" His voice was hot enough to turn the rain to steam. He leaned closer. "A peck. Very brief." Closer. "I promise it'll be over with before you know it."

His provocative words faded away into the storm, and then his mouth touched hers. Sierra went still, holding her breath, her body hot with a riot of sensations.

Oh damn, he smelled so good.

And his mouth was so warm . . .

"Sierra?"

Devastated, she blinked and saw his small smile, the intensity of his expression. Well, shoot. He was right.

It had ended before she realized. "Hmmm?"

He drew a breath. "See you in the morning."

And like the walking temptation she now knew him to be, Ben strolled away. He seemed unconcerned with the rain that pelted him and the wind that tossed his hair. Sierra thought she even heard a faint whistling.

She stepped inside and slammed her door. *Damn, damn, damn.*

Ben walked into the bar, soaked to the skin and sizzling with sensation.

He was frankly dumbstruck.

One tiny kiss, not even worthy of a grade-school kid, and he was hard. Unbelievable. And exciting.

But if that one tiny, almost avuncular kiss had burned so much, what would it feel like to get on top of her? To feel her hands on him, her mouth on him?

It would be incredible, and he could hardly wait. He understood her game of advance and retreat, and now he was positive that he'd eventually have her. But waiting was going to be pure hell. He closed his eyes and tried to regain his control.

Molly, a female truck driver who also happened to be one of his best customers, strolled up to him. "It takes a real reprobate to be out fooling around in that storm."

Ben cocked one eye open. He thought all the customers had left. "I wasn't fooling around."

"Uh-huh. Honey, I've seen that look on more male faces than I care to remember."

"'S that right? And what look would that be?"

"The look of Lust, sweet cheeks, with a capital *L*."

"Unrequited lust, Molly." Though no music played, Ben caught her hands and swept her into a formal dance, gliding her across the floor, around the tables.

The waitress dodged them, smacking at Ben's behind with the dishcloth she'd been using to wipe off the tables, so she could go home for the night.

Molly was easily fifty-five, very hard edged, and what could only be called sturdy. But she laughed like a schoolgirl, and her eyes twinkled at Ben's attention. He loved women, all ages, all kinds—and they knew it.

She batted her eyelashes at him. "Say it ain't so, Ben. You've actually been turned down?" She rolled her eyes and patted his chest. "The girl is a fool."

"The girl is . . . different." Ben dipped Molly back, laughed, and then kissed her cheek. He straightened them both.

Molly tugged her extra-large T-shirt back into place. "Different, as in odd?"

"Different, as in unique." Ben rubbed his hands together. "Very unique."

Molly said, "Ah, I see. Different, as in special."

Ben froze. "Did I say special?"

"You don't need to."

Ben felt momentarily stunned.

The place was now empty except for the waitress who applauded them both on their dancing skills. She said, "Why don't you go call your special, unique new girlfriend so I can get the hell out of here?"

Thankful for the distraction, Ben saluted her. "Yes ma'am. But take an umbrella. It's raining like hell and I don't want you to melt."

"I'm not sugar, Ben."

He winked. "Close enough."

Molly shook her head at him. "I gotta get on the road."
She peeked outside, squared her broad shoulders and
shouted back to Ben, "See you in a week or two, honey."

"Take care, Molly. Don't run over any possum." He
pushed in a few remaining chairs. The waitress came out,
bundled in a slicker, umbrella in hand. "Go on," Ben told
her. "I'll lock up."

"You sure?"

"Yeah." He wasn't ready to settle down yet. He was
still charged, still tingling from that pathetic little kiss. A
unique kiss but not special. He scowled and held the door
open. "Drive careful, hear?"

"Of course, Ben. Don't worry about me." She patted
his chest, then disappeared out the door.

Ben watched till she made it to her car and got inside—as he'd told Sierra, he was a gentleman—then he
went about securing all the locks.

Like Sierra, he lived at his business. His living quarters connected to both the diner and the motel, located between them. It had taken a little time to get used to the
noise, the lack of privacy, but it was a lot cheaper than
trying to maintain a separate residence and with all the
improvements the place had needed, cheaper definitely
meant better.

He went through the back door of the diner, secured it,
and stepped into a hallway leading to the front desk. Two
clerks were on duty, Wendy handling some paperwork,
Gary talking on the phone. Ben gave them both a wave
before unlocking the door to his suite.

Unlike the rest of the rooms, he had a regular key
rather than a key card. He'd learned the hard way that

some of his female employees liked to surprise him by making use of the key cards and waiting in his bed. Naked.

Ben grinned, just remembering. It had been a hell of a shock, one he didn't want to repeat. Not that a naked woman was a bad thing, and he'd definitely enjoyed the show. But as far as he was concerned, employees were off-limits. Besides, he preferred to choose who would be in his bed, rather than have the matter taken out of his hands.

Before deciding to convert the rooms into his living space, they'd been two separate rentals with a connecting door. Ben had removed twin beds from one room and added a sitting area, a television and stereo unit, a very functional desk and computer system, and a tiny kitchenette where the bathroom used to be. The kitchenette housed a microwave and small fridge for the sake of convenience, which was all he needed since he generally took his meals in the motel kitchen. He'd also had a round table and chairs moved in.

It wasn't a spacious mansion, such as his grandmother enjoyed, or posh like his brother's new home. But it was his, and for Ben, that was all that mattered.

He stripped off his wet shirt and tossed it into the bathroom toward a hamper. He was briskly drying his hair when suddenly every window lit up with a blinding flash of lightning. Almost at the same time, the motel trembled from a thunderous roar.

Had they been hit by lightning?

Ben cursed and started toward the window, intending to look for any damage in the lot. He'd just pulled aside the curtain when the overhead lights blinked and went out. A thick curtain of inky darkness fell all around him.

"Shit." Ben moved back across his room to the hall-way door. The storm was accommodating, sending strobes of light to guide him. He jerked the door open and saw only impenetrable blackness. "Where the hell are the emergency lights?"

He no sooner asked it than the dim lights over the exit doors and elevators came on. His two employees stood frozen behind the desk, their eyes round in an effort to see. "Don't move," Ben told them, and ducked back inside for a flashlight.

Wendy called out to him, and she sounded nervous. "The lights are off everywhere, Ben. The whole street is dead."

"Great. Just great." Ben took the large utility flashlight off the wall in his kitchenette area and flicked it on. He got the other smaller flashlight from his bedside drawer. He heard a few late-nighters mill into the lobby and wanted to curse. Just what he didn't need.

Frustrated and tired, Ben directed Gary to retrieve the other flashlights from the inner office and to turn on the battery-operated radio.

"Our electricity is out," a young man complained, and the woman beside him bobbed her head. Though the walkways from the rooms were covered, they were both damp from the blowing rain.

"The whole street is out," Ben explained. "The lightning must have hit a transformer or something."

"We'd only seen half the movie." The man drew the woman closer into his side and she gave a vacuous grin. "You won't charge us for it, will you?"

No doubt an adult movie, given their flushed faces and disheveled appearances. Ben hid his grin. "No, you won't be charged. Just remind the desk clerk in the morning that your show got interrupted. We'll listen to the radio and if the storm worsens, you'll be notified, but in the meantime, there's nothing to be done."

The two left the lobby, fondling each other. Maybe it was a full moon, as Sierra had suggested. To Ben, that sounded like a more plausible excuse for his extreme infatuation than anything else.

He hoped like hell that's all it was.

He turned back to his employees. "If anyone else feels the need to venture out in this weather, remind them that the key cards might not work after a time. They could end up locked out of their rooms."

"Will do." Wendy's voice sounded ominous in the otherwise silent motel. "But what do you want us to do?"

Ben shrugged. He could see through the front lobby window that Sierra's lot was black. Sudden worry for her coursed through him. She was new to the area, unfamiliar with the house. A woman alone.

He smiled at Wendy. "Play cards, make out, hell I don't care. Just hold down the fort." He started out the door. "I'll be back in a little bit."

Gary snickered, then Ben heard Wendy mutter, "He was kidding Gary, so forget it."

Still shirtless, Ben stepped out into the storm. No reason to dress when he'd only get soaked again. The rain was stinging in force, the wind howling and so hard he had to lean into it to get across the street. The narrow beam of the flashlight barely penetrated the gloom.

Already debris littered the road, and when Ben finally made it to Sierra's front door, he saw that a large limb had broken from the tree, crashing against the front of the house. Her door was blocked by it, and the front window was shattered.

It was late, the night black and the storm ferocious. He was worried, damn it. Ben flicked the flashlight around the stoop while calling to her.

He didn't get an answer. He stepped over the limb and pounded on the door, but still got no reply.

Without a second of hesitation, he picked up a smaller branch and knocked the rest of the broken glass out of the window, then climbed inside, being careful not to cut himself or step on her bed with his wet shoes. Not that it would matter—her mattress was already damp.

Over the roar of the storm, he heard a muffled sound and followed it down the short hall. He had to step around packing boxes and crates and pieces of furniture.

"Sierra?"

Behind a closed door, Ben heard a loud thump, then a low curse. Alarmed, he jerked the door open, bounced the flashlight beam around—and found Sierra sprawled naked on her backside, just outside the shower stall.

Ben stared hard. He didn't really mean to, but . . . his gaze wouldn't budge. She had a towel in her hand, but it didn't cover a single inch of her bare, wet body. Ben forgot to breathe. Her work clothes had hid a very sweet little figure.

Sierra looked up at him and her green eyes, in the glare of the light, snapped with fury. "Out!"

Still a little dumbfounded, Ben turned his back. He didn't want to. Hell no, he didn't want to. He swallowed and tried to collect his wits, but he just kept seeing her, her legs straight out, her round breasts glistening with water. And her belly. Jesus, she had a sexy belly.

She looked even better out of her clothes than in them.

"Sierra?"

"If you look, I swear I'll kill you." She had a mean voice when provoked.

But her warning was too late. He'd already looked. Her image was permanently emblazoned on his brain. Lust coiled inside him. "It might be worth it," he suggested and heard her horrified gasp. Women could be so funny about nudity. Ben shook his head, and relented. "I'm teasing, so don't shoot me. I won't turn around until you're covered."

He heard her moving, heard her grumble. *She was naked behind him.*

Ben cleared his throat. "Did you hurt yourself?" With concern motivating him—*uh-huh*—he started to peek.

"Ben." She growled his name like a bear.

"All right, all right." God, his awareness of her as a desirable woman, a woman he wanted, was so acute it hurt.

There were times when he cursed himself for being a gentleman. This was one of those times.

"Here, this might help." Without turning, Ben held the flashlight back to her and felt it snatched out of his hand. He braced himself, half expecting her to bludgeon him with it.

A few seconds passed without movement, and Ben grew impatient. "You aren't decently covered yet?"

There were a few more seconds before she admitted in a small, yet defiant voice, "I don't have anything in here except the towel."

Just a towel. Ben locked his thighs against temptation and barely swallowed his groan. "I'd offer you my shirt, but as you can see I don't have one."

"I noticed." The flashlight moved over him. Slowly. "Why is that?"

Did her voice sound deeper? What game was this now?

"I was getting ready to shower when the lights went out." He shifted, on edge. "Once I realized you were in total darkness, too, there didn't seem to be much point in getting dressed again."

Ben could feel her stillness, and her disbelief. "So you rushed over here to help me?"

"Why else?" He grinned despite his desire and attempted to reason with her. "I didn't know you were naked and in the shower, you know."

He sensed her moving closer and made a magnanimous offer, all things considered. "Tell me where your pajamas are and I'll get them for you."

More silence. Maybe she'd decided not to get dressed. Maybe she'd decided to just take advantage of this very propitious moment . . .

"I don't have any pajamas."

Ben's eyes closed and his hands curled into fists. Oh, she didn't just tell him that, didn't just admit that she slept . . . naked. He shifted again, trying to ease the sudden constriction in his pants. "No?"

"All right, this is ridiculous." She sounded very put out, even with herself. "We're both adults, right?"

Ben had no idea what she was getting at, so he answered cautiously. "Right."

"Then I guess you can turn around. But don't you dare leer at me."

Ben slowly turned. She had the flashlight in his eyes so he couldn't really see her. "Tough to leer when you're blinding me."

She lowered the light to her side, shining it on the floor, leaving them both heavily shadowed. "I heard a crash right after everything went black. Did you break in?"

"No." Despite his best intentions, Ben looked her over

and felt the increased acceleration of his heartbeat. The towel was white and showed up in the darkness. "A tree limb came through your window. I just knocked a few pieces of broken glass out of my way so I could get in without cutting myself to ribbons."

"You snuck in through my window?"

"Sort of. I called your name and you didn't answer."

"And you were . . . worried? About me, a total stranger?"

She sounded so disbelieving. "Exactly. By the way, your front door is blocked by a big tree limb. You should have that elm trimmed right away before one comes through your roof."

She groaned, then shoved her way past him. Now, with her back to him, Ben indulged his need to absorb the sight of her. Her pale shoulders looked very feminine and smooth. The towel hugged her round bottom and put those shapely legs on display.

One little tug, Ben thought, and the towel could be relegated to the floor. His hands twitched—until he heard her gasp.

"Oh, no." She moved the light over her window, her bed, the surrounding boxes. Rain sprayed in, soaking the mattress, forming a puddle on the floor. "Damn, I didn't need this."

She sounded utterly defeated, beat down with exhaustion. Her shoulders, which had been so straight a moment ago, now slumped. Watching her, something stirred inside Ben, something he didn't recognize.

He decided it was a new form of lust.

Using her woeful voice as a reason to touch her, he lightly laid his hands on her slim shoulders—and shuddered with reaction. God, he was a goner. *He* had shoulders, for pity's sake. Not soft and sleek and narrow like hers, but hell, it wasn't like he'd touched her breasts or her sexy belly or . . . between her thighs.

Just thinking that made him shake.

He had to clear his throat twice to speak, whereas Sierra seemed almost oblivious to him. "It'll be all right," he told her. "I'll block the window to keep anything else from being ruined, and help clean up this mess."

"No, that's okay." She sighed, then rubbed her forehead. "Go on back to your place and get some rest. I'll take care of this."

Annoyance prickled. "I insist."

She glanced at him over her shoulder. "You do, huh?"

The way she said that made him shift uneasily. "I'm a neighbor, Sierra. I want to help." Then, cajoling, "Let me help."

She dismissed him without replying, and moved the flashlight over the window again. "My bed is soaked."

Mother Nature must love him, Ben decided. He squeezed her shoulders. "You can sleep at my motel."

Now she stiffened. "I beg your pardon?"

As she slowly turned to face him, Ben dropped his hands. His eyes were quickly adjusting to the dark, and here, near the window, the lightning made it easier to see. The towel covered her, but it was still just a towel, with her naked underneath.

And he knew what she looked like naked.

Convincing arguments crowded his brain. "Be reasonable, Sierra. You can't stay here. As you just said, your bed is soaked. Unless you've got a mattress in one of those boxes, you don't have anywhere to sleep. Besides, it's not safe with the window out. And who knows how much worse the storm might get?"

She crossed her arms under her breasts and scowled.

Her hair was wet, hanging in sodden ropes over her shoulders and onto her chest. She wasn't overly endowed, but breasts were breasts and he could see the upper swells of hers.

Her legs were . . . Well, they were the stuff of fantasies and he was already having a few. She shivered as she watched him and Ben concentrated on looking innocent, on wiping all lascivious intentions from his face.

With a continued frown, Sierra turned to survey the damage again, offering Ben another opportunity to view her perfect behind in the very short towel. About two inches, and he'd be able to see her cheeks.

When he finally got her naked and willing, he fully intended to spend a prolonged amount of time on her lovely tush.

"Do you promise to behave?"

No. He asked, teasing, "Do I have to?"

Exasperation exploded from her. "Fine. Just forget it."

She started to stalk away—to where, Ben couldn't guess—but he caught her shoulders and brought her back around to face him.

"Ben!" She panicked and made a fast grab for the towel, which had almost come loose.

He waited, but she held it secure. Shaking his head at himself, Ben apologized. "Okay, okay. Bad joke. I'm sorry."

Her eyes glittered in the darkness. "Was it a joke?"

Ben tipped his head back and stared at the shadowed ceiling, contemplating the advantages of lying. But he decided against it. If he wanted her trust, he'd have to be truthful.

"You know I want you." Using his thumbs, he stroked

the soft skin of her shoulders, up to her throat, and watched her eyelids go heavy, her lips part.

Amazed, Ben realized how quickly she'd gone from ill humor to warm awareness. She'd done that earlier, too, when he'd kissed her on the stoop. He hadn't wanted to push then, but he'd seen the smoldering heat in her eyes.

He wondered if this was another part of her game. With any luck, he'd find out tonight. "I won't do anything to you that you don't want me to do. Cross my heart."

She seemed so undecided, so uncertain about what to do that Ben wanted to comfort her. He gently began easing her closer so that her body touched his. Just as she would have been in his arms, her eyes widened and she scowled.

"Fine." She shoved the flashlight at his chest, and in the process forced some space between them. "I want it to go on record right now that no matter what I might say later . . ."

Ben's eyes widened. "Damn. What do you plan to say later?"

She ignored his interruption and raised her voice to talk over him. "I do *not* want to have sex with you."

"Ever?" Ben asked, needing her to clarify that much or he'd never get through the night.

Her mulish expression faded. She looked down at his naked chest, breathed a little harder, then shook her head. "Tonight."

His knees almost gave out. He sucked in air until he knew he could talk without choking. "All right." He touched her chin, lifted her face so that she had to meet his gaze. "No sex—tonight."

But he made no promises about the morning.

Chapter Three

Somehow, Ben's promise didn't sound all that reassuring to Sierra. She hoped his willpower was better than her own. Ben Badwin in wet jeans and a naked chest was tempting enough, but when he poured on the charm and freely gave assistance, he was too tempting to resist.

But resist she must.

She'd set up new priorities for her life, and she had to stick to them. So far that hadn't been a problem; she knew what she wanted and she'd gone after it with single-minded purpose.

Granted, she hadn't counted on Ben in the equation, but she'd just have to get over her attraction.

She was trying to convince herself that might be possible when Ben stepped closer to her back and she felt his warm breath on her temple. She'd been alone too long, she reasoned, or something so simple wouldn't seem so tantalizing.

His left hand rested easily on her waist while the right held the flashlight. Even through her thick towel, she felt his touch like a brand. His voice was a low, teasing growl that he no doubt knew to be effective.

"I can't believe I'm saying this, but . . . do you want to get something to wear? Not that I'd insist, because Sierra, you look incredible in a towel. But since you'll have to walk through my lobby . . ."

"Yes." Sierra stiffened her resolve. "I definitely want something to wear." Sleeping naked was out of the question now. It wouldn't be easy to sleep in clothes since she'd gotten used to going without them. She'd started the habit as an act of freedom and had quickly discovered it was more comfortable.

She turned to wave a hand at the boxes on the floor. "My clothes are in one of them."

Ben looked at her, waiting, and she rolled her eyes. "I can't very well . . . bend over, now can I?"

His slow grin did funny things to her, but luckily he didn't say a word, just turned with the flashlight and hunted around. Finally, he hefted up a box. Thankfully, it was dry. "Here you go."

He held it out to her while she kept the towel secure with one hand and rummaged inside with the other. She located panties, which he hummed over, then a T-shirt and loose cotton shorts. She stepped away from him and wondered where she should change.

Ben cleared his throat. "I suppose you want some privacy."

"Absolutely."

He nodded. "All right. I'll run across to my place to get something to block the window."

"There are long sheets of plastic out back. We use them in landscaping to stop weeds. They'd probably work." She rubbed her head. Much as she disliked imposing on him, she needed his help. "I don't have any nails or anything though."

"Sierra?"

She looked up.

"It's not a problem, okay? Quit fretting."

How had he known she was fretting?

He touched her chin. "I'll grab a staple gun and be right back."

"Thank you." For some ridiculous reason, she hated to see him go.

He hesitated, then crowded nearer and looked down at her with a direct gaze that seemed to see right through her. "Will you be all right for a minute?"

His concern, his flirtation, felt both nice and bothersome. Nice because she hadn't felt it in far too long. There'd been few men in her life who ever showed her concern.

But it was bothersome because she was independent, and she intended to stay that way—despite the unfortunate circumstances of the night. She was emotionally and physically depleted after the long day, but she managed to dredge up a credible sneer. "What's the problem, Ben? You expect a little female like me to be afraid of a storm? Or do you think I'll trip in the dark and crack my head open?"

Rather than take offense at her surly tone, his gaze dropped south of her belly. "I dunno. You did fall once already, and I'm not sure how bruised you might be." He grinned, making her belly flip-flop. "Not that you don't have a nice cushion there on your backside, but it still had to hurt."

Sierra wasn't sure if he'd insulted or complimented her.

"Want me to check it out?" he offered. "Maybe kiss it and make it better? We could play . . . doctor."

She almost laughed. But she'd encouraged him enough for one day so instead she gave in to a yawn. "I'd prefer to get done so I can get to bed."

"You always have the best ideas."

"Alone."

He surprised her by leaning down and placing a gentle kiss on her forehead. "Be right back."

For a man she'd only just met, he was too forward, always touching and kissing her.

But she stupidly went weak in the knees every time he did.

It was another hour and a half before they had the window covered and the boxes moved and partially unpacked. Ben helped her spread things out around the small building so they would dry by morning. All the while he was there, he chatted with her, asked her questions about her business, laughed with her. He pitched in without complaint and seemed happy to do so.

Sierra didn't know what to make of him.

The rain continued to rage down on them. She got a headache thinking of how far behind the weather would put her. She couldn't very well plant in the pouring rain, so unless it let up real soon, and the sun really came out in force, her first few days on the job were doomed.

Add to that the additional expense of replacing a window and trimming the enormous tree, and she knew her finances were going to be very tight. For now, she wanted to sleep and save her worrying for the morning.

Ben had removed the large branch blocking her front door, and they left the house together. He'd not only slipped a slicker over her head, but he shielded her with an umbrella too. As they crossed back to his motel, she aimed the flashlight and saw that her yard, orderly and neat just that morning, was now littered with fallen debris. She prayed the storm hadn't damaged any of her nursery stock.

Ben tightened his arm on her shoulders and led her around a large puddle in the road. Sierra gave him a sideways look, but he appeared to be concentrating on where she walked. His touch now was . . . protective.

She had the feeling he'd have treated any woman in her position the same way. He'd have given assistance without complaint, never mind that he'd put in a full day already, and it was now the middle of the night. And he'd have been just as protective whether she was nine or ninety.

The big difference in her situation was that he'd also told her he *wanted* her. She couldn't quite get over that.

At least he'd put on a shirt when he'd gone for the staple gun. Once she'd gotten over the shock and humiliation of being found naked, she'd absorbed the sight of him. Ben, shirtless, had left her in a stupor. He was naturally dark, but also tanned. His shoulders had looked sleek and strong. She'd had to fight the urge to touch him. Crisp hair lightly spread out from the center of his chest, then angled in a thin line down his muscled abdomen to disappear into his pants.

She could have looked at him for hours and not minded in the least.

"You're eating me up with those eyes, honey, and it's making me nuts."

Sierra started, and felt her face heat. *Eating him up?* She went on the defensive and said, "Don't call me honey." Then, because she felt compelled to apologize, she added, "Sorry."

"I kind of liked it." They stepped into the lobby, scattering any attempt she might have made at replying. Two employees looked at them with identical expressions of curiosity.

"Gary, how about a key for an empty room?"

The young man shrugged in apology. "As you predicted, key cards aren't working as of about half an hour ago."

Sierra groaned. She was dead on her feet, aching to be in bed, and she wasn't at all certain she could make it back across the street, even if she could find a place in her new home to nest. She'd been up since four-thirty, almost twenty-four hours now, and she desperately needed some rest.

She considered sleeping in her truck, but one look at Ben and she knew he had other ideas.

He nodded to his employee. "No problem. Thanks." He kept a hold on Sierra's arm and led her around the desk. Sierra felt both employees watching after them with interest.

"Do you do this often?"

"What's that?"

"Scandalize your employees by dragging women here?"

"I live here, so yeah, they see me with the occasional woman. But I don't *drag* them." He looked down at his hand on her arm. "Am I dragging you?"

"No." She imagined most women would be more than

willing to go with him. More likely than not, they dragged him off to bed. "But in about another two minutes you might be. I'm shot."

Ben smiled at her. "I'll carry you if I must, but if you can manage a few more steps, I'll have you to a bed."

It was iffy, but she'd try. "Whose bed?"

"Mine." He pulled a key from his pocket and unlocked a door, then motioned her inside. "My humble abode."

Sierra peeked in, saw nothing but shadows, and balked. This whole night would have to go into the files of not-to-be-believed, but this was a little too much. "Do you have two bedrooms?"

"Yes." She started to relax when he added, "But I turned one into a sitting room."

Oh boy. One bedroom. Probably one bed.

And one devastatingly handsome man.

Sierra considered her options, but as usual, there weren't any. She needed to sleep, and unless she wanted to drive out of the area and try to find an empty motel that hadn't been affected by the storm, she was stuck. "Lead the way."

Ben chuckled softly to himself as he steered her inside. "No reason to look like you're headed to the gallows. I have a nice roomy couch I'll sleep on—if you insist."

"Of course I won't insist," she said around another yawn.

He was dragging a little himself, but at her words, his heart skipped a beat in anticipation.

"I'll sleep on the couch."

Well, damn. He closed the door with a firm click and turned the lock. Sierra was so tired, she looked wilted. He didn't like it. It made him feel that strange, elusive emotion again. It was something like lust, but softer, deeper.

"Here. An extra flashlight for you." He would control himself, damn it. "I'll show you around."

She trailed next to him, using the flashlight to briefly explore as he showed her the way to the bathroom, the phone, the tiny kitchen.

"It's small, only the two rooms."

"It's wonderful." She saw the couch and made a sluggish beeline for it. Ben caught her elbow to sidetrack her and headed her toward the bed.

Her eyes, barely visible from the expanded glow of the flashlight, stared at him in exasperation.

"Just hush, Sierra. You're in no shape to argue with me. My place, my rules. And I say you sleep in the bed." *In my bed.*

She surprised him by agreeing. "Fine. Whatever." They reached the unmade bed and she dropped to the edge of the mattress, then almost toppled over the side when she bent to remove her sneakers.

Amused, Ben went to one knee in front of her. "Let me."

She did a double take, then shook her head as she watched him remove her ratty-looking sneakers. "You're too much, you know that?"

She sounded drowsy and warm and he wanted her. "It's no big deal."

She watched his every move as if fascinated. "No one's taken my shoes off since I was a baby."

"Yeah?" He encircled her slim ankles in turn, slipped her shoes off her feet, and then swung her legs up into the bed. "Consider it a new experience. Maybe one of many to come?"

Chuckling, Sierra sprawled back on the bed, boneless, and then just lay there, her attention fixed on his face. Was this a come-on? An invitation? Ben wished like hell he could see her better, to judge her thoughts. "You've really had a long day, haven't you?"

She continued to scrutinize him as she answered. "Too long. I'm used to hard work," she explained, her tone defensive, "but I guess the excitement of starting the business was wearing, too."

"Plus just moving in," he offered, willing to give her her due.

"Yes. Normally I'm in bed long before now. I like to get up early. I guess that's why I fell getting out of the shower. I'm not really clumsy. But it was dark and my feet were wet and the noise from the storm startled me." She shrugged.

Ben touched her bare foot on the bed. It was small and cool and he was beginning to feel like a pervert, getting aroused over a damn foot. "Anyone can slip, Sierra. I wouldn't call you a klutz." Just the opposite, she moved with a very fluid, relaxed grace, a woman comfortable with her body and aware of her feminine strength.

She sighed and rolled to her side, then reached out and set the flashlight on the nightstand. She clicked it off, adding to the shadows, intensifying the intimacy of the moment.

It took all Ben's considerable effort to lift the sheet over her. "Good night, Sierra."

"Night."

Ben was so horny he could barely walk, and it appeared she was already half asleep. He watched her snuggle into his pillow, and he swallowed a groan. Her shape made interesting swells beneath the sheet—the length of her legs, the rise of her hips, the dip of her waist . . .

It was the first time he could ever remember tucking a woman into his bed when he didn't intend to join her.

Best to get out of the room now, while he still could. Without really thinking about it, he bent and pressed a kiss to her temple. She was curiously still, her breath held until he straightened away. He went to the window and pulled the drapes, then headed toward the adjoining room, stripping off his shirt as he went. At the last second, he decided to leave her door open. She was in an unfamiliar place and might wake disoriented. He could sleep in his pants for one night. It wouldn't kill him.

"Ben?"

He paused with one hand on the door, one on the doorframe. So she wasn't asleep yet. Maybe her silence had been more thoughtful than slumberous. "Yeah?"

"Thanks for everything. I really appreciate it."

"No big deal."

He heard the mattress shift with her movement and knew she'd turned her back again. "No really, it is. I . . . well, if I've seemed ungrateful it's because you aren't what I'm used to."

Ben crossed his arms and lounged in the doorway, wondering what type of man she was used to. "Meaning?"

Long seconds passed, filled only with her uncertainty. "I'm not thinking straight," she finally said. "I'm too tired to make sense and I don't want you to think I'm coming on to you."

Now a statement like that was just too damn provoking to ignore. Ben sauntered back into the room, moving slow to avoid colliding with anything, and sat beside her on the bed. She stiffened as he did so but didn't move away.

He filed away that small reaction to his nearness, along

with everything else he'd learned about her so far. "We made a deal, remember?"

"We did?"

"Yeah, so no matter what you say now, I won't go back on my word. You said no sex, and that's that."

With the drapes drawn, blocking out the lightning, the inky blackness was impenetrable. Ben couldn't see a thing. But the darkness only made his other senses more alert to the fact of a desirable woman in his bed. He knew just where Sierra was beside him, how close his thigh was to her hip, where her shoulders would be. Where her breasts were.

But it was the feel of her vitality, her warmth, and her anxiety that had his muscles all tightening.

"You really mean it, don't you?" She sounded a little awestruck, as if the idea of a man keeping his word was foreign to her. "You really wouldn't take advantage of having me here?"

"For as long as you know me, Sierra, you can trust that I'll always keep my promises." This particular promise might kill him, but he began thinking she wasn't playing a game at all. She'd meant it when she said she didn't want to get involved sexually. Not because she wasn't interested; she'd been clear on the fact that she found him attractive, and Ben had seen the reciprocal awareness in her pretty green eyes whenever she looked at him. But she was confused by him, and apparently she expected the worst just because he was male.

He wondered what experiences had given her that perspective on men. He'd known women who'd gone through nasty divorces, who'd had men cheat on them or otherwise mistreat their feelings. Most were venomous in their complaints; they liked to talk and because he adored women, he listened.

But he had the gut feeling Sierra would be different in this too, that she'd never share her burdens, past or present. She'd told him she wasn't interested, but she wouldn't tell him why.

Perversely, that only made Ben more determined to get her to open up.

He reached out and found her elbow, trailed his fingers down to her wrist, then to her hand, and entwined his fingers with hers. Her hand remained stiff in his. He could feel the rough calluses on her palm and fingertips, testimony to the hard work she did.

"When I kissed you at your door, you liked it."

Though he couldn't see her clearly, Ben knew her chin had lifted. "I imagine you know women well enough to know I did."

"Don't be cynical," he chided. "All women are different, and it's safe to say I've never met a woman like you."

She snorted, disbelieving, then went on to say, "It doesn't matter."

"What doesn't?"

"That I . . . liked it."

"No?" They were in his bedroom, in the darkness, in a bed, and he was touching her. Of course it mattered. "How come?"

Rather than answer, she shook her head and started to pull away.

"I know we've only just met, but I like you—and you like me a little too, don't you?"

She hesitated a long time, lacerating his ego before finally saying, "It's strange, but I do."

He managed to swallow his laugh. "What's so strange about that? I'm a nice guy. Lots of people like me."

He felt her restless movement. "You mean lots of women like you."

She tried to edge her hand away from him again. Ben pretended not to notice and she gave up. "What are you thinking, Sierra?"

"That this is too damn awkward."

"Why?" He rubbed his thumb over her knuckles, hoping to help her relax. "I won't take advantage of whatever you tell me."

He could feel her warring with herself. So much caution, he thought, further intrigued. She was so gutsy and outspoken one moment, but now very timid.

Everything she did, from the way she walked and her brash honesty to her shyness now, struck him as sexy. "Come on, Sierra," he urged her, eager to know her thoughts. "It's dark, quiet. I promise you can trust me."

She drew a deep breath, as if for courage, then blurted, "I'm sort of . . . excited."

Totally misunderstanding her stammered admission, Ben asked, "About what?"

The bed shook as she snickered nervously. "You."

She wanted him? His first thought was *thank God,* and then desire pierced him. "Ah." He lifted her hand and pressed a kiss to her palm, smiling to himself, relieved. "That's good."

"No, no it's not. Not for me and not for you."

Heart beating too fast, Ben murmured, "You want to tell me why, Sierra?"

She shook her head. "No, not really."

He locked his jaw over her continued stubbornness. "Tell me anyway."

With a long annoyed sigh, she said, "The reasons are obvious. For one thing, we barely know each other."

"But we will."

That made her laugh in exasperation. "You are so damn pushy."

"I don't usually need to be."

"I can believe that!"

Ben wondered if it was the darkness that had made her less inhibited. Or maybe it was the fierceness of the storm, the natural forces of nature. Maybe the overwhelming chemistry that gripped him had taken her as well. Whatever the reasons, he relished this moment to get closer to her.

Her humor faded into the gloomy darkness and she groaned. "This is nuts."

"It's sexual chemistry, that's all." But it felt like more, damn it. No. Ben shook his head. "It happens all the time. You'll get used to it."

She yanked hard and got her hand away from him. "It doesn't happen to *me* all the time and I don't want to get used to it. I didn't want to feel it in the first place."

Her disgruntled tone almost made him smile. He could count on Sierra to give it to him straight. "You know, this is the strangest conversation I've ever had with a woman, especially with a woman in bed."

He could almost hear her mind working. "My life is just too complicated right now."

Suspicions rose, and Ben braced himself on stiffened arms at either side of her hips. Though she hadn't worn a ring, she could still be involved with someone. He never poached and despised men who did. But if she was involved, he'd . . .

His sudden flare of anger was out of proportion to the

amount of time he'd known her, yet he couldn't seem to rein it in. In his mind, he'd already laid claim. He wanted her and refused to be thwarted now. "You're not wearing a wedding ring, Sierra."

She stilled at his growled statement, and he could feel her confusion. "No." She put her hands against his chest, as if bracing him away. "I don't wear any jewelry."

Her nonanswer made him want to explode. "Damn it, are you married?"

She shook her head. "Divorced. And don't curse at me."

That threw him—and relieved him. He settled back, thoughtful, aware that her attention on him now was more wariness than interest. He didn't understand himself. "The divorce is final?"

"For a while now."

Damn, had she been a child bride? The thought didn't sit well with Ben. He waited for her to share the barest details, to give a clue about why she'd gotten divorced, how long it had been. He waited for her to be like so many women he'd known.

He wasn't really surprised when she remained silent.

Her hand flattened on his chest, tentatively, then with more confidence. Unable to help himself, Ben bent toward her. "One more small kiss, okay?"

He took her silence as agreement and touched her mouth with his, easy, gentle. Her lips were warm and so damn soft, he slid his tongue over her, not entering her mouth, just tasting her.

She made a small sound and angled her head slightly away from him. Her hand kneaded his chest and her voice was low, sincere, breathy. "You are about the sexiest man I've ever seen. I can't believe I even noticed because I never do, not really."

More brash honesty. Ben wasn't sure what she meant by that, but she was touching him, so he didn't move, didn't interrupt her.

"Now that I have noticed, it's hard not to keep noticing." Her hand slid up, almost to his shoulder, idly stroking him. "You make me feel . . . funny."

"Good funny?"

"I suppose. But there's a lot going on in my life. I have things all planned."

His laugh sounded strained even to his own ears. Damn, she only touched his chest, not any place vital, not any place sexual. But he liked it. A lot.

Insanity.

"I'm not asking to take over your life, Sierra." Yet he knew that he'd already considered all the ways he intended to get involved with her.

"I know. But it's complicated."

"What could be less complicated than sex between two consenting adults?"

"For you maybe, but not for me."

"Why don't you let me show you how uncomplicated it could be?" Ben waited, tense with anticipation for her answer.

"All right."

Her agreement took the wind out of him, and he shuddered.

Then she added, "One night of sex. I suppose I can handle that."

"One night?"

"Yes." She touched him again, her small hands moving over him, up to his shoulders then around his neck. "Who knows when I'll feel like this again? Nothing today seems real anyway. And you're right, how complicated can one night be?"

No, hell no. Ben didn't want one night. He wanted . . . well, more than one night, damn it. "There's a problem here, Sierra."

"What?"

"I made you a promise, remember? No sex."

"But . . ."

"Uh-uh. I'm not letting you change your mind now. You'll blame me in the morning."

She stiffened. "I take responsibility for my own actions, Ben Badwin."

He could believe that. Ben knew firsthand that she had a hard time sharing with anyone, even when she desperately needed a helping hand.

"I know." He kissed her again, this time as he wanted, slow and deep, then deeper still, giving her his tongue and feasting on her mouth until she was breathless and clinging to him, her fingers tangled in his hair, holding him close. They were both panting.

Damn, she turned on so fast, he felt singed.

She wanted him now, and he wasn't above using her natural sensuality against her. Forcing his mouth from hers, Ben said against her throat, "I'm going to offer you a really workable solution. Okay?"

She tipped her head, making it easier for him to kiss her there. "What solution?"

Moving slowly so that he didn't startle her, giving her time to refuse him, Ben stretched out next to her. He drew her close, aware of her trembling excitement, her wildly beating heart. He was shaking, too. It wasn't every night that he met a woman who pushed all his buttons. It wasn't every night that he hopped into bed with a stranger either. But Sierra didn't feel like a stranger and he wanted her too much to quibble over what was or wasn't proper.

She was so skittish with him, this might be his only opportunity to prove a point, to show her that when he gave his word, it meant something. It'd test him to his limits, but he could handle it.

"Ben?"

He nuzzled her temple, felt her still damp hair, her silky soft skin. He wanted to strip her naked, to move atop her and slide deep.

Instead, he murmured against her ear, "Let me help you. You're tired, and you need to sleep, but sleeping isn't easy when you're aroused."

Predictably enough, she went rigid and tried to put some distance between them. "What are you talking about?"

He pulled her closer. "I'll take care of you." He kissed her earlobe, nibbled on it. "Give you an orgasm."

She gasped. "But I want . . ."

"To have sex? Nope." He continued to touch her, encourage her. "That is, we won't have intercourse, which is what you didn't want, right? But there are other ways for me to make you feel good, Sierra."

She held herself still with uncertainty, doubt, and what felt like shock. He waited for her to be sarcastic, to get angry.

Instead she whispered, "You really think you can?"

Everything male in him expanded. Determination, excitement. He levered up on one elbow and gazed at her in the darkness. "Damn right." He'd make her feel *very* good—so good, she wouldn't be able to stop with just one measly night.

Her small hand on his chest contracted, fisting in his shirt, tugging him closer. He wanted to feel her hands on his bare flesh.

Ben said, "Let me get this off," and levered away from her to remove his shirt.

When he cuddled her close again, her breath came fast, heating his skin. "So what do you say, sweetheart?"

She gazed up at him with a look of consternation. "What about you?"

Ben kissed the tip of her nose. "I'll consider it a gift."

Low and shaky, she said, "I don't know. That doesn't seem fair."

His fingertips found her chin and he turned her face toward him. Even without light, he could see that her eyes were wide, curious, and cautious all at once.

Foreign emotions clamored inside him, turbulent and wild and overwhelming. He touched her lush mouth and felt his cock throb with need. "The thing is, I want you so much it's making me nuts. I don't understand it, but it's true. But I want you to want me just as much."

She made a sound that was part confusion, part disbelief. "I do."

"No, not yet." But she would. He kissed her mouth, teasing her with gentleness, with light touches that made her strain toward him for more. "Let me make you feel good, okay?"

Ben could feel her shaking and knew it was with arousal now, not anxiety. Her scent was stronger, intoxicating, making him shake, too.

"We'll go one step at a time." He smoothed his fingers across her nape, feeling the baby-fine curls there, stroking until she tightened against him. He shifted to the fragile bones of her shoulder, then slowly to her upper chest. He held his breath, waiting, but she didn't complain, didn't tell him to stop.

Her T-shirt had a loose scooped neck. He splayed his fingers just above her breasts. She wasn't wearing a bra and the soft cotton of her tee tantalized him.

His voice went hoarse, deep. "If I do anything you don't like, you'll tell me. We can stop whenever you say."

Shifting subtly, she nestled her head between his neck and his shoulder. Her breasts brushed his chest, his wrist. Her legs tangled with his, her hips snuggling closer to his groin. Her upper thigh pressed his erection, inciting him further. "Sierra?"

He felt her very tiny nod of agreement and wanted to shout with his relief. "Good." He kissed her forehead, her temple. "That's good."

She shifted again, trying to get his hand on her breast. Ben was in no hurry; in fact, he intended to do a fair amount of sensual teasing. Women loved it and he sure as hell had no complaints. He wanted to drive her wild, to make her as uncontrolled as he felt.

Opening his mouth against her throat, he kissed her, wet, hot, sucking her skin gently against his teeth to deliberately mark her. When she looked in the mirror, he wanted her to remember this night, this moment. He wanted her to know that whatever was between them, it wouldn't go away in one damn night.

"Ben . . ."

With a light stroke, he teased her upper chest, back and forth, dipping into her cleavage, trailing away. Her skin was so warm and satiny. He slipped his fingers just under the neckline of her shirt and brushed the edge of her left nipple. She inhaled sharply, released a ragged moan.

With some surprise, Ben registered her reaction. How long had it been for her? Already she trembled all over and he'd barely touched her. "You really are on the ragged edge, aren't you, honey?"

Her teeth sank into his shoulder, not hard, but definitely hungry. She nodded.

Oh, this would be fun.

Feeling like a magnanimous conqueror, Ben dismissed his own frustrated need to concentrate on hers. Gauging her every response, he cupped her left breast fully, squeezing gently, caressing her. Sierra gave a throaty purr of wonder and lifted into him. Ben moved his palm over her nipple, again and again, then caught her nipple and lightly pinched.

With a broken gasp, she twisted against him.

Ben pushed her onto her back and bent over her, kissing her throat, her chest, finally settling his mouth on hers. She tasted incredibly good and returned his kiss just as wildly. He continued to taunt her nipple, tugging, rolling. Her back arched as she devoured his mouth.

Panting, Ben lifted his head. "It's too damn dark in here." Her form was a murky shadow, indistinguishable to the eyes. He wanted to see her, but he had to hold her hands down so he could move away. "Just a sec."

He reached to the nightstand and turned on the flashlight. He wasn't cad enough to shine it right on her, though he wouldn't have minded stripping her naked and exploring her in detail. For whatever reason, she fascinated him, from her forthright manner and sexy mouth to her unbridled sensuality.

Ben swallowed a groan and quickly set the flashlight upright on the nightstand, removing the temptation to scrutinize her small body in detail.

The mellow glow of light filtered out to the corners of the room, falling in selective places and glinting off Sierra's auburn hair and her pale skin.

The flashlight didn't help as much as Ben had hoped, considering he saw everything in a red haze. He reached for Sierra, voice shaking, hands trembling. "Let's get this shirt off you."

"Wait." Dim light slanted over her cheekbones, the bridge of her nose, a shoulder, the rise of a breast. Her eyes remained mysteriously dark with her long lashes leaving feathery shadows on her cheeks.

Blood thundered through Ben's veins. He held the hem of her shirt in both hands. "What is it?"

"I haven't been with anyone except my ex."

Would she forever take him off guard? Ben worked her words over in his mind, trying to decipher her meaning. "You're saying you're not real experienced?"

"It's not just that."

"What else?" When she didn't answer fast enough, he leaned down and kissed her, his mouth moving warmly over hers, firm but brief. Full of urgency. "Tell me."

He could hear her breathing now, her reaction again swift and hot. "I'm not very good at . . . at coming either."

Her words were so stimulating, Ben groaned. God, he'd wanted a challenge . . . Well she was that, a constant bundle of challenges. Trying to sound as serious as she had, he whispered, "It'll be fine, you'll see."

Her trust washed over him seconds before she released the shirt. "All right. If you're sure."

He touched his nose to hers and smiled into her mesmerizing eyes. "Just close your eyes, relax, and leave it all to me."

Chapter Four

There was so much promise in the way Ben said that, how he looked at her, that Sierra couldn't get a single word out.

She hadn't thought about sex much in the past few years. There hadn't seemed any point. She'd been busy trying to survive, making efforts to get her life into some kind of order. Men, and sex, had gone way down on her list of priorities. But Ben . . .

He literally took her breath away. In a secret little part of herself, she was thrilled with how things had worked out. Not that she wanted or needed the added hassle of damage to her property. She'd have her hands full getting the repairs taken care of.

But the whole situation had necessitated that she be here in Ben's bed, and now he was touching her and kissing her and wow, the man was potent. His every look, his every word, made her feel things she hadn't even known existed.

He wanted to give her an orgasm. Not have sex with her, because that would mean breaking his word. But he looked more than capable of accomplishing the deed, of doing all kinds of things, really. The idea made her nervous, made her heart race.

It excited her unbearably.

Despite what common sense told her, despite her sense of propriety, she wanted him to touch her. And so she did as he asked and trusted him.

His hands were so large, so rough and dark, that seeing them lift her shirt was an enticement in itself. She closed her eyes as her breasts were bared and prayed she wasn't a disappointment. She just didn't know about such things, what a man like Ben might expect sexually, physically. She was healthy, lean, her build average as far as she knew. But she was proud, and she hated the idea that she might be less than he expected.

"Lift your head."

Keeping her eyes shut, Sierra raised up and the shirt got swept up and over, then tossed aside. Ben's hands closed on her bare waist and he just sat there, not doing anything, not touching her in any other way. He wasn't even breathing hard.

He didn't seem overcome with lust at the sight of her naked breasts. In fact, he seemed calmer, more controlled now that he'd gotten her upper body bare.

The suspense of not knowing what he thought wore on her so she peeked up—and saw him devouring her with his gaze. His shadowed face looked hard, the set of his jaw exaggerated by the slanted light. His nostrils were flared, his naked chest rising and falling.

Without a word, he slowly bent down and drew her left nipple into his mouth.

Heat. And wet suction.

And soft, luscious strokes with his velvet tongue.

With a shuddering groan, Sierra felt the insistent pull of his mouth everywhere, in the pit of her stomach, in her trembling thighs, between them. She caught his head, holding him to her, letting him know without words how much she liked it.

Ben kissed his way to her other breast and treated it to the same attention. To Sierra, he didn't seem to be in any hurry but already her every nerve ending jangled. *"Ben?"*

He rose up and took her mouth, plunging his tongue in, stroking deep, sucking at her tongue. At the same time, he cupped both breasts in his hands, thumbing her wet nipples, rasping them. It was like sensation overload and Sierra tried to tell him with her kiss, with the movement of her body, that she wanted, needed more.

He whispered, "Hush, not yet," and went back to kissing her. Long, deep, eating kisses that drugged and provoked her and made her ache. A liquid warmth coiled inside her, drawing tighter and tighter until it seemed she couldn't bear it. And still he didn't do anything else, just played with her breasts and kissed her in that mind-numbing way.

She hadn't realized a kiss could be so consuming, so effective. But the more his mouth moved on hers, the more she wanted it. Breathing became secondary to his taste, the connection such a kiss provided. She'd forgotten, or she'd never known, that there was so much pleasure in a man's hungry kiss.

Her breasts swelled, her nipples felt unbearably sensitive, but he didn't relent. Every so often he left her mouth to kiss her throat again, the joint of her shoulder. She felt so sensitized in so many places that everywhere he touched sizzled with awakened nerve endings. He raised her arms and licked lazily at the inside of her elbow, down to her wrist, where he gently drew on her pulse. Sierra writhed. He pulled her to her side to face him and his hand went to her behind. Fingers spread wide, he cuddled one round cheek.

"You have such a sweet ass," he rumbled roughly while squeezing and kneading, urging her closer, and Sierra was thrilled with the blunt compliment. "Wanna take your shorts off now, too?"

She nodded, anxious to be naked so he'd touch her more. She felt on the verge of something truly wonderful, something explosive, and was anxious to get there.

Ben's laugh was husky with triumph. He sat up to untie the loose drawstring that kept her shorts in place. After rolling her shorts down, he tugged them off her ankles.

"Beautiful legs," he murmured.

She was naked except for her panties and she started to hook her thumbs in them too, wanting to experience it all.

"No, there's no rush."

She started to insist otherwise, but then Ben looked up at her face—and cupped his hand over her sex.

"Mmmm. Nice and hot."

With his big fingers pressed there, it was all she could do not to squirm against him. She inhaled a shaky breath and parted her thighs just a bit.

He watched her, his awareness so keen she felt caught in his gaze, unable to free herself.

"Wet, too." His fingertips teased gently. "You're en- joying this? You want more?"

It took two breaths and a lot of concentration to nod. "Please."

He pressed his palm against her, heard her broken moan, and said, "I want you to open your legs just a little more for me, okay?"

Heat rushed over Sierra, making her face hot, her body hotter. All shyness melted away, and she widened her thighs.

"That's nice. Now, how does this feel? Be honest." He very lightly trailed his fingertips over the crotch of her nylon panties, tracing the triangle of hair beneath, dip- ping down low, coming up to her belly button.

Sierra tipped her head back and bit her bottom lip.

"Tell me, honey."

"It feels like—"

His fingers went low, pressed between her lips, and rose again to one ultra-sensitive spot. "Yes?"

Sierra shook her head. "Stop it," she said, then quickly explained, so he wouldn't misunderstand, "Stop . . . try- ing to make me talk. I can't." She closed her eyes and tried to control the trembling that racked her.

"You wanna just concentrate on how good that feels? Here? And maybe here?"

The groan erupted, broken, low. *"Yes."*

Idly, Ben used his other hand to return to her breasts. It was the strangest thing for Sierra, to be lying there in the bed, all but naked, her legs spread, while an incredibly gorgeous man who was also a stranger, sat beside her, pleasuring her with single-minded purpose.

It was also the most exciting thing to ever happen to her. One night, she thought. She deserved this one night.

"You're getting wetter," he told her, then in a rush, "All right, panties off. I want to feel you."

He startled her with that abrupt decision and before Sierra could gather her wits, he had stripped her underwear down her legs, leaving her naked. Hands resting on her thighs, he bent to kiss her knee, her hipbone, her inner thigh. It was the most provocative sensation, the touch of his silky cool hair, his beard-rough jaw, in forbidden places.

With his mouth pressed to the tender flesh in the crease of her leg, he looked up and caught her gaze. His eyes slowly closed and he turned his face inward to draw a deep breath. She heard him growl softly.

In the next second, he stretched out next to her and pulled her close into his side. His hand tangled almost painfully in her hair and he kissed her hard, crushing her mouth under his, stealing her breath. His jeans-clad leg thrust between hers, opening her more. Sierra clung to him, felt the iron steel in his shoulders, the way his muscles corded and flexed.

"God, I want you . . ." he said into her mouth. His hand pressed between their bodies and now there was no hesitation as his fingers glided over her, once, twice, spreading her slick wetness over swollen, sensitive flesh. "Put your leg over my hip, I want to . . ."

She did as he asked and he sank his middle finger into her.

"Ah, yeah. How's that?"

Sierra lurched, but his hand on her skull held her from moving away. Surely, he didn't expect a reply, she thought wildly.

He leaned over her, pressing her to her back, pinning her down. His finger moved slow and deep until she moaned and her back bowed trying to bring him closer.

"Shhh," he said against her lips. "You're so hot, so wet." Watching her closely, he slid another finger in, then a third and she knew it was too much but she couldn't escape his iron hold and wasn't even sure that she wanted to.

"Ben." Even to her own ears, she sounded weak, soft. She felt stretched, full, but not in a bad way. There was discomfort, but it fed into other feelings of satisfaction. She wanted to be full. She wanted him.

His arm slid from her head to her back, forcing her breasts up so he could clamp down on one throbbing nipple, sucking strongly, ruthlessly. Sierra twisted as the feelings intensified, burned. She cried out, her hips pumping against him without conscious thought, seeking relief.

"Here we go," he whispered so softly against her breast she barely heard him. And he used his thumb to touch her clitoris, a gentle touch at first, barely brushing, teasing, allowing her to assimilate the rush of concentrated feelings, then with more insistence, his touch demanding, consistent, pushing her.

She broke on a moan of disbelief, her thighs taut and shaking, her belly pulled hard, wave after wave of heat rippling through her.

Ben's mouth on her nipple softened, his touch eased, slowed, until finally she lay spent, stunned, perspiration cooling her body. Sierra wasn't sure she could move, even if the storm blew the motel over. It had been a long time since she felt so sated, so drained. She concentrated on calming her ragged breathing, on fighting off the tears of relief—and the bubbling laughter.

Astounding.

His fingers still inside her, Ben levered up to his side and propped his head on his fist. She knew he was looking at her, but she felt too astonished to meet his gaze. Her nipples were still wet from his mouth, still tight and sensitive and the crisp hair on his chest abraded her, made her shiver.

He was a stranger, but he knew her body better than she did.

Ben kissed her open mouth, and she felt his arrogant smile. Against her lips, his damn fingers still pressed deep, he asked, "You wanna sleep now, or talk?"

Her mind felt numb with pleasure—and with questions. How had he done that so . . . so *easily?*

Would he be able to do it again?

Gads. Appalled at herself, Sierra said, "Sleep." It seemed the wisest choice. She had a lot to consider, and besides, what would they talk about? She supposed she could thank him for what he'd done. To her. So very, very skillfully.

No, that could wait till morning, when she didn't feel so shattered. She could tell him good-bye, thank him, and make her escape.

Taking his time, Ben removed his hand from between her thighs. Silence stretched her nerves to the breaking point, and she opened her eyes to see him put his wet fingers in his mouth. Dumbstruck, she watched him suck her taste from his hand, saw his eyes close in pleasure.

She must have made a sound of surprise because Ben looked at her, his eyes so burning hot that she almost melted again. He touched his damp fingers to her cheek and growled, "You taste incredible." He turned her face up, lowered his mouth to hers and slipped his tongue past her lips.

Shocked, Sierra tried to pull away but he didn't let her. His tongue moved against hers, sharing her taste and she was both startled and a little turned on by the carnality of it. He left her mouth with a licking kiss and a smile.

"Next time," he promised, "I'm going to taste you the way I want to."

Next time? Her eyes widened at that awesome thought.

"Do you think you'd like that, Sierra?" He pecked her mouth, nibbled her bottom lip, almost as if he couldn't stop kissing her. "Would you like to feel my tongue on you? In you?" The words were deep and rough. "I'll suck on your clitoris, too, so softly and you'll love it."

He shuddered at his own words; Sierra couldn't have moved if her life depended on it. The things he said were scandalous, and so exciting. The things he did were more so. Unfortunately, he couldn't do them to her. He seemed to have forgotten that this was a one-time deal.

Before she could figure out how to remind him, he said, "I love making a woman come that way."

Jealousy, surprisingly strong, struck her. He'd obviously been with dozens of women—and what he'd done to her had been perfected many times over. She turned her head on the pillow to glare at him, but he didn't give her a chance to protest.

"There are so many ways I can give you an orgasm." He looked very pleased with himself. "You liked this, didn't you?"

She wouldn't lie. A sweet lethargy kept her limp, kept her heart thumping in sluggish, heavy beats. Little throbs of pleasure remained just below her skin, in her thighs, her breasts, her belly. "Yes."

His smile widened, making him look very boyish. "And you said you weren't good at this."

"I'm not," she admitted, and then before she could measure her words, she added, "That was an astounding first."

Ben looked much struck. "No kidding? Your first orgasm?"

Good Lord, she didn't want to have a conversation about it.

He rubbed her bottom lip with his thumb, and then his look turned thoughtful. "You do mean with a man, right?"

Sierra drew a blank. What the heck was he asking her? "Uh . . ."

Ben frowned. "Surely you know how to—"

"That's enough on the subject."

He cupped her face, caressed her cheek. "Sierra? You're not telling me that was your first *ever?*"

Not liking the way he said that, as if she were odd or something, she bit her lip and refused to answer.

He looked . . . stunned. Disbelieving. Then soft with male condescension. "Ah, babe." Smiling, he pulled her into his body, forcing her head to his chest, rubbing his chin against her crown. "You couldn't come, even touching yourself?"

Sierra's face burned again for an entirely different reason. It was disgraceful, everything they'd done and the speed with which they'd done it. But still he could make her blush. She struggled against him, caught between wanting to slug him, and wanting to hide.

Typically, he tightened his hold. "It's all right. It's . . . well, hard to believe that you don't know your own body well enough to give yourself a climax. You said you're twenty-four, right?"

"None of your damn business." She felt humiliated beyond belief and blamed him. His unregulated speech was sometimes nice, sometimes a turn-on—but this wasn't one of those times.

She tried to get her cheek off his chest without much success. His scent was too wonderful, making her weak all over again. "Are we going to sleep sometime tonight?"

"Yeah, in a bit." He hugged her closer until her breasts flattened on his abdomen and her belly was pushed up against his fly. "Now quit shoving on me. I'm strung so tight that my body takes every little squirm from you as an invitation. I need to get control so I can hold you while you sleep."

She went still in shock. "You're going to sleep with me?"

He nuzzled her ear. "Why not?"

The thought wasn't at all repellent. She shrugged. Why not indeed? This was a very special night, one she'd remember for a long time, so she might as well finish it off right. Who knew when she'd ever do something this insane again?

"Don't worry, your innocence will remain intact." He kissed her forehead. "There'll be no sneak attacks during the night."

Sierra knew there wasn't anything truly innocent about her. Would her past disgust him? Somehow, she didn't think so. He wasn't brutal like her ex, judgmental and small-minded like her father had been. He wasn't like the people from her hometown. As far as Sierra could tell, Ben Badwin was unlike anyone she'd ever known.

He nudged her face up with his, while rubbing her back, her naked bottom. He was still smiling, and there was a hard edge of unfulfilled desire left on his face, a flame in his brown eyes that made him look more appealing than ever. But his hand was gentle when he tucked her hair behind her ear.

"You okay?"

"Yes." She doubted she'd ever be the same, but she was glad for all of it.

"You're awfully quiet."

Twisting two fingers in his chest hair, she gave a teasing tug. "You've worn me out, that's all."

His smile spread to a grin, then a laugh. "I also made you come." He kissed her hard and fast. "God, what a day it's been. I can tell you, when I got out of bed this morning, I sure didn't expect to meet someone like you."

Sierra yawned hugely before saying, "Someone like me?"

"Yeah, someone so sexy and sweet." He touched her breast, his look intent. "So hot."

"Ben . . ." Just that easily, he made her start shaking again.

He groaned. "Damn. Let's sleep before I forget my good intentions."

Guilt assailed her. She was now well sated, her body still buzzing in the aftermath of her first orgasm, while he remained rigid with need. His efforts at gallantry were ludicrous, and as far as she was concerned, unnecessary. What would it matter if they went a step further—not even that much of a step, all things considered—and had sex?

"You don't have to be noble, you know."

"Course I do. You keep making comments about men, grouping me in with some assholes from your past." He sounded more serious now. "I don't like it. So I'll keep my word."

"Just to prove a point?"

"You betcha." He swatted her on the butt. "The point being that I'm different, and when I promise something, I mean it."

"Won't that be hard on you?"

A dimple appeared in his cheek. "Yeah. Real hard." He nudged her belly, letting her know firsthand just where that hardness concentrated. His voice dropped. "I've never wanted to fuck anyone the way I do you."

Her breath caught in rising excitement. "Then we should take advantage of the circumstances—"

He laid a finger over her mouth. "But it's more than that. No, don't panic. I'm not going to invade your life."

"You've got that right!"

"But whatever reasons you had earlier tonight for swearing off sex, well, I assume they're still valid. If you've changed your mind now, it's because I've got you all softened up." He grinned hugely. "Wonder if I could control you with sex? Whatdya think? You're much more agreeable now than you were earlier."

"I think I might club you in your sleep if you're not careful."

He laughed, his good humor inexhaustible. "Let's sleep. I'll survive, I promise. Tomorrow, we'll discuss it again."

Tomorrow she'd be telling him good-bye, and that was that. No more fooling around, no more distractions. He could be a casual friend, nothing more. But she was too tired to argue further. "Suit yourself."

"Good attitude. Remember that later, when you're not naked in bed with me, okay?" He went to his back, pulled her atop him and arranged the sheet over her.

"What are you doing?"

"Suiting myself." He settled both hands on her bottom, kissed her shoulder, and sighed. "Sleep, Sierra. You've worn me out."

No way would she ever be able to sleep with his hard, hairy, very sexy body beneath her. She was too used to sleeping alone. But it was nice being held by him this way so she settled her cheek on his chest, curled her hand over his heart, and closed her eyes. She could feel his erection against her belly, feel the rhythmic thumping of his heartbeat, hear his deep breathing, smell him.

She couldn't resist pressing one small kiss to his sternum.

It was the last thing she remembered doing.

Throughout the long night, Ben lay awake, listening to the storm fade. The rumbling thunder and extravagant lightning moved into the distance until he could no longer see or hear it. It left behind a gentle, steady rain that gradually dwindled to little more than a sprinkle. Moonlight showed up in the wee hours of the morning, casting opalescent shadows over all the wet windowpanes. Then later, the first rays of the sun cut through the darkness, promising a beautiful, if muggy, day.

He was bone-tired, but somehow deeply satisfied. All night long, he'd held Sierra, touched her, petted her. She was there, and he knew it, and he didn't want to miss a single second of being with her.

He couldn't seem to quiet his awareness long enough to drift off to sleep.

Sierra suffered no such problem. She'd slept through his every touch, sometimes sighing softly, sometimes shifting position. But she hadn't awakened.

When bright morning sunbeams struggled to penetrate the curtained windows, Ben rolled her slight, soft form to his side. The electricity finally kicked back on, stirring the silence with a buzz of awakening power lines, circuits, and machinery. Sierra snuffled, moaned a little, then re-settled into a deep sleep.

Ben rose to one elbow and took the long survey of her body that he'd wanted to take earlier. He dragged the sheet all the way to her ankles. He'd slept in his jeans, both to guard against his own lack of control and to let her rest easy. Though they were glove-soft and well worn, they felt far from comfortable.

Sierra stretched one arm above her head, her slender legs moving on the mattress. A small sound escaped her, then a sigh.

Keeping his hands off her tested his resolve.

Her skin was flushed from sleep, dewy and damp; with the loss of electricity, the room had quickly become too warm during the night and they were both a bit sweaty.

Now, with the air-conditioning back on and running full force, cool air drifted across the room and over her body. Her nipples puckered tight. Ben hadn't been able to see her that well in the darkness, hadn't been able to de-termine the color, but now he could. To his delight and fascination, he found that her nipples were a soft brown, and he wanted to taste her all over again. Everywhere.

Her nose was small, a bit pointed, her cheekbones high. And that lovely, very kissable mouth . . .

Broad shoulders, strong thighs, and a very flat belly made her build a bit boyish. Her waist wasn't overly nar-row and her breasts, though round and firm, weren't overly large.

She was still the sexiest thing Ben had ever seen. His

desire didn't just stir at the sight of her, at being with her. No, it exploded with the force of dynamite. For whatever reason, she appealed to him on every level.

Other than the few freckles across her nose and cheeks, her skin was flawless. Her arched brows and lashes were brown, darker than the hair on her head, and without the reddish-gold cast. Ben looked at the tight reddish curls shielding her sex, and he smiled. He couldn't stop himself from touching her there, a light, easy touch that made him want so much more. He tangled his fingers in the soft curls, stroking her lightly, then cupped his hand over her. His eyes closed. She was just as hot as he'd remembered, and in her sleep, she parted her thighs for him.

Heart thumping hard, his fingers firmly pressed between her thighs, Ben sat up to look at her more closely. His gaze went from her face to her belly and back again, waiting for her to awaken, to maybe shriek or if he was lucky, moan in acceptance.

She slept on, her breaths even and deep, her lips slightly parted, her body relaxed and heavy.

He moved to the foot of the bed and tossed the sheet to the floor. Careful not to shake the mattress, he knelt between her thighs. Very slowly, he spread her legs wider, his blood churning at what he did, at the excruciating excitement of it.

Sierra accommodated him by bending one knee, opening herself even more to his hungry gaze and searching touch. She started to turn to her side but Ben quickly caught her hips and held her still until she settled back with a soft sigh.

He'd never known a woman to sleep so soundly. For one suspicious moment, Ben wondered if she wasn't asleep at all, if she was just playing possum. But no, her face and her body had that totally relaxed posture of deep slumber.

Poor baby. She'd worked herself to the bone yesterday, then been up half the night with the storm damage to her new place. And his lust.

Ben remembered how her body had tightened around his fingers, the small noises she'd made deep in her throat, the expression of wonder on her face . . .

He inhaled slowly and looked at her. Her inner thighs were very pale and so silky soft. She was small and vulnerable and she made him feel violent with need. Unable to stop himself, Ben put both hands on her upper thighs, caressing the smooth muscles, feeling the texture of her tender flesh. His heart pounded so hard, it threatened to break something.

He swallowed, and using only his fingertips, carefully opened her. Her vulva was soft, glistening pink, her clitoris small, delicate.

She was beautiful.

Overcome, shaking, Ben bent and lightly kissed her. He'd abstained all night, and now he couldn't wait. He hurt with the need to have her. With ultimate care, he rasped his tongue over her, up, licking gently . . .

All at once, her body stiffened. Ben lifted his head, Sierra did the same. Their eyes met.

"What are you doing?" she asked in a confused croak, her expression dazed.

Ben said, "Uh . . . molesting you in your sleep?" He still held her open, so there was no denying it. He fastened his gaze on her sex, so lusciously female, and his body went taut with raging need. *"Sierra."*

She didn't moan. She shrieked. Loudly.

He got kicked in the head as she scrambled away from

him and made a grab for the sheets. She hunkered against the headboard, her body now hidden from his view.

Seeing stars from the blow, Ben sat back on his heels, fighting his disappointment and his guilt at taking advantage of her. He rubbed his jaw, winced. "Judging by your look of horror, I take it you're not interested in a little morning nookie?"

Her eyes were so huge, her face so red, she looked comical. "You were . . . were . . . *looking* at me!"

"Yeah." Ben let his gaze rove over her small sheet-covered body and wished like hell she was still asleep. "I was considering having you for breakfast before you kicked me in the jaw."

Her mouth opened and closed twice. She frowned, looking very adorable to him with her puffy eyes and tousled hair. "Did I hurt you?"

Working his jaw, Ben nodded. "Yeah, a little."

"Good!"

He laughed. Even now, while he felt savage with lust, she amused him. "Witch." A knock sounded on his bedroom door, making Sierra jump and stare at it with renewed alarm. He patted her thigh. "Room service. Just sit tight."

She was still there, motionless against the headboard, the sheet clutched to her chin, when Ben returned with the tray of coffee, cream-filled doughnuts, and fresh fruit.

He sat beside her on the mattress. "Breakfast." She didn't move and he sighed. "Should I apologize?"

Her brows lowered. She looked charmingly disheveled and grumpy. "Depends on what you'd apologize for."

He did his best not to smile, but it wasn't easy. She delighted him in so many ways. "For taking advantage of you in your sleep, of course. Although, really, I'd only promised not to attack you during the night and it is morning." He winked. "You didn't think I'd be sorry for wanting you, did you? Or for tasting you, which I couldn't resist, by the way. Or for anything from last night, or—"

"All right!" She frowned even as she struggled with a laugh, giving him hope. Then she groaned. "God, I need coffee in the worst way if I'm expected to deal with you and . . . the stuff you do."

"Allow me. Cream or sugar?"

"A lot of both." She glanced at the clock, but it was electric and blinking from the blackout of the night before. After accepting the coffee he handed to her and indulging a long drink, she relaxed a bit. "Oh, that's good."

"The morning chef makes great coffee. Doughnuts too. Here." He handed her a Bavarian cream with chocolate frosting and watched as she juggled the coffee, her grip on the sheet, and the doughnut. One large bite and she rolled her eyes in bliss.

Enjoying himself despite the painful erection straining his jeans, Ben speared a fat strawberry with a fork and held it to her mouth. "Open."

She did, moaned again, and smiled. "Breakfast in bed. I can see why people like this."

Lowering his voice, Ben told her, "I like pampering you." Truth was, he liked pampering all women, but this was different. This was more than surface enjoyment. He wanted to take away the sheet and lay her down, part her thighs again then slide into her with one long thrust. He also wanted to talk to her more, and finish feeding her. And tease her and hold her.

He wanted . . . hell, pretty much everything.

"Uh-huh." She gobbled down the rest of the doughnut

in short order. There was nothing wrong with Sierra's appetite. "Is there a woman alive who you don't want to pamper?"

Ben eyed her sticky fingers, caught her wrist and brought her hand to his mouth. "Is this a trick question?"

"Just curious."

He drew her first finger into his mouth, curled his tongue around her, and sucked it clean of the sticky frosting. Sierra's expression became arrested, her eyes wide, her mouth parting in a small *oh*. Within a single heartbeat, she went soft and willing.

"Ben," she whispered shakily.

He had been joking about controlling her with sex, but the idea was appealing—and now, watching her this morning, he thought it might even be possible. Her eyes were dark and drowsy, her cheeks flushed. He'd done little enough to her and she was all warmed up and ready.

It was a unique role reversal, the guy using sex to call the shots. He liked it. He liked her.

"Ben," she said again. She tried to retrieve her hand without spilling her coffee. Ben held on and drew her middle finger into his mouth. He sucked gently until he heard her whimper. Gaze locked with hers, he licked down her finger, prodding the sensitive skin that joined her index and middle finger with the tip of his tongue. She drew a shuddering breath. "Oh, God."

Her eyes closed and the half-empty cup wobbled in her hand. Ben retrieved it from her, plunking it down on the nightstand and laying her flat so he could stretch out over her. She blinked up at him.

"Hi." Ben bent and kissed her, slow and deep while he rubbed his erection against her belly. It wouldn't take much for him to get off. He was so primed, she could have breathed on him and he'd come.

Her mouth was warm from the coffee, sweet from the doughnut. Delicious because this was Sierra and with no effort on her part, she'd turned him inside out. He nibbled on her bottom lip and admitted, "It was torture watching you sleep so late."

"Mmm . . ." She kissed him back, her mouth moving hungrily under his. All of a sudden, she went rigid. She pressed back into the mattress and twisted to see the window—where blazing sunshine burst through. She gasped. "What do you mean, I slept late? What time is it?"

A pulse fluttered in her throat, drawing his lips there. "Around eight-thirty or so."

She slid out from under him so fast Ben was left kissing air. "Sierra?"

She lost the sheet in her flight from the bed. "Eight-thirty! Damn it, I knew this would happen. I knew you'd be trouble." She glared at him, but it was so brief as to be ineffectual. Then she wailed, *"Where are my clothes?"*

I knew you'd be trouble. What the hell did she mean by that? "Sierra, just slow down . . ."

Beautifully naked, she ran around, hunting for her shorts and T-shirt while Ben took in the show. Seeing her naked in bed, flat on her back was vastly different from watching her move, seeing the flex of feminine muscles, her natural grace, and the delightful bounce of behind and breasts.

With any luck, he'd be able to talk her back into the bed.

"What's your hurry? It rained all night so it's not like you need to rush to the job. You can't possibly plant anything when the ground is this soggy, right?" She didn't reply, so he pointed out the obvious. "There are puddles everywhere."

Ignoring him, she bent at the waist, located her shorts half under a chair, and snatched them up. Ben's heart about stopped with the peek she'd given him, but she didn't give him time to enjoy it at all. Not bothering with underwear, she yanked the shorts on and tied the drawstring tightly with jerky movements.

"I was supposed to meet Kent this morning. He'll be frantic worrying about me."

Something dark and mean and sharp brought Ben slowly upright in the bed. "Kent?" He'd never in his life felt jealousy over a woman, but he had the sickening dread that this was it, gripping his guts with icy fingers, overshadowing the easy desire. "Who the fuck is Kent?"

She scowled at him and pulled her shirt over her head. Through the material she admonished, "You have a real gutter mouth, you know that?"

Ben watched her breasts disappear beneath soft wrinkled cotton. "Who is he, Sierra?"

"My friend. My assistant. My . . . Ben, I'm sorry but I gotta go. Thanks for . . ." She stalled, flushed, then gave a quick shake of her head. "Well, thanks." She rushed through to the other room, jerked the door open and headed off barefoot, her hair a tangled mess, her clothes twisted.

Ben stepped over the minuscule panties she hadn't put back on, and followed hot on her heels. She was bare-assed beneath her shorts, damn it, and racing off to meet another man. *No way in hell.*

Luckily the desk clerk was in the back doing something and didn't see them. Sierra went out the front door and Ben was right behind her, also barefoot, and bare-chested to boot. He'd meet Kent, and make up his own mind.

Before Sierra could step off the walk, Ben caught her by the arm. "Wait up a minute, damn it."

Across the street at her lot, a solidly built man dressed in a white muscle shirt and ragged, faded jeans looked up. Even from such a distance, Ben could see he was big and muscular. The jealousy boiled.

"Is that him?" His jaw hurt both from her kick, and the way he clenched it. But damn it, she was running from him to another guy.

"Yes." Sierra waved excitedly. "I'm here, Kent!"

Wearing a suspicious frown, the big bruiser started to-ward them, his gaze darting between Ben and Sierra. The closer he got, the faster he moved. Sierra tried to leave Ben to meet the other man halfway, and Ben tightened his grip. "Oh no, I don't think so."

She frowned up at him, her wide sexy mouth set in an-noyance. "You don't think so *what?*"

The man stopped in front of them. He was older, prob-ably in his late thirties, early forties, but he looked very fit. He had dark blond hair, piercing blue eyes, and he ap-peared as displeased as Ben felt.

Good. Ben was more than ready for a confrontation.

The man propped his hands on his hips and ignored Ben. "Sierra?"

She again tried to tug her arm free. When Ben retained his grasp on her, she frowned at him in question. "What do you think you're doing?"

The man raised both brows, taking in Sierra's sleep-rumpled appearance—and Ben's possessive hold. To Ben, he appeared to be struggling with a grin. "What's going on?"

Ben tensed. "You're Kent?"

"That's right." He dismissed Ben again, and instead gave Sierra a tender look. "What the hell have you been up to, young lady?"

She shifted and again tried to pull free of Ben. "Nothing."

"Yeah, right." His tone said clearly that he didn't believe her. "You look like you spent the night . . ." His words trailed off and very slowly, his grin won out. He even chuckled. "Well, I'll be damned."

At Kent's amusement, Ben relaxed a little. Sierra didn't. She jerked her arm fiercely, freeing herself, then shoved Ben hard in the shoulder, making him stagger. "What in the world is the matter with you?"

Kent leaned forward, eyes alight with humor, and said with relish, "Looks like jealousy to me."

Ben grunted.

"Don't be ridiculous." Sierra laughed a little too loudly. "I don't know him well enough for him to be jealous."

"Is that right?" Kent looked her over again, then glanced at Ben's shirtless chest. "By appearances, I'd say you know him plenty well."

"No." Sierra flushed with guilt and cast an admonishing look at Ben that warned him to stay silent. "You don't understand."

"He understands."

"Ben!" She elbowed him hard.

Kent laughed again, then reached out and tweaked a

tendril of Sierra's tangled hair. "Quit mauling the poor fellow or he's going to think you don't like him."

She threw up her hands in exasperation.

To Ben, they acted like siblings, not mere friends, not mere associates. Certainly not lovers. Kent in no way acted territorial. In fact, he seemed almost tickled that Sierra might have gotten laid.

Why would that be?

Curiosity replaced some of Ben's jealousy, but not all. He'd pleasured Sierra last night, he'd held her nude body close to his, watched her sleep, but all he really knew about her was that she had a quick temper, was independent, and turned him on in a big way. "You two are well acquainted?"

Kent said, "Mmm. You could say that. We . . ." His attention got caught by an approaching car. Ben followed his gaze and groaned.

From the moment he'd laid eyes on Sierra, he hadn't been able to think straight. Things had been moving way too fast—and at the same time, not fast enough to suit him. The last thing he wanted to do now was introduce her to his mother on the not-quite-proverbial morning after.

Yet, it was already too late. Brooke Badwin parked her sporty little black Celica a few yards from where they stood, and stepped out. Her soft brown hair was in a French braid, her eyes shaded by dark sunglasses. She wore a casual white sundress and sandals.

She looked as she always did, Ben thought, and started in surprise when Kent gave a low wolf whistle of appreciation. "Be still my heart."

Ben gaped at him, not quite sure how to react to that.

The man was ogling his mother—but then again, at least he wasn't ogling Sierra. What to do?

Brooke headed toward them and Kent murmured, "Damn, she's hot."

Ben choked, drawing Kent's brief notice. Kent took in his pained expression and scowled. "You know her?"

"Yeah." Ben rubbed the back of his neck, a little ill at ease on several levels. "You could say that."

His mother finally reached them. Without hesitating, she caught Ben in a warm familiar hug, leaving him no choice but to return her embrace. He looked over her shoulder at Kent, who had gone very still, and Sierra, who looked ready to spit.

Brooke pushed back, her hands on his bare shoulders. "Are you all right, honey? I was so worried last night but the phone lines were all down so I couldn't call and check on you."

Ben put his arm around her and turned her to face his guests. Sierra now looked furious while Kent looked equal parts fascinated and abashed. Ben grinned. Oh, this was going to be entertaining.

"Sierra, Kent, meet my *mother,* Brooke Badwin."

Kent blinked in surprise, looking her over again with slow deliberation. "Is that right?"

Sierra blushed. "Nice to meet you."

Ben enjoyed both their reactions. "Mom, this is Sierra and Kent. They work at the new landscaping business across the street."

"Oh?" Never one to miss a thing, Brooke briefly studied Sierra over her glasses. Her smile was very knowing, but then it was clear to one and all that Sierra had just gotten out of bed. Because his mother knew him well, she'd probably come to the correct conclusion that it was Ben's bed she'd left.

"It's nice to meet you, too, Sierra." Brooke transferred her gaze to Kent—and went mute.

It wasn't like her to stumble over an introduction, but then Kent had that intent look of a man on the make. Fighting a laugh, Ben nudged her. "You're supposed to say, hi, Mom."

"Hi."

Bemused by the situation, Ben reached around his stupefied mother and caught Sierra's hand. "I need a moment alone with Sierra. Why don't you two go grab some coffee? We'll be right back."

Eyes widening, Brooke said, "But . . ."

And Kent cut her off. "Hell of an idea."

When they were out of earshot, Sierra strained against Ben's hold. "Just what is so important that you have to be rude?"

"Your panties."

She tripped. "My what?"

Ben pulled her upright and kept walking. "They're still in my room, and I can see your sweet ass through those white shorts." He patted her butt, to emphasize his point. "My barbaric tendencies shock even me, but honey, you really need to finish dressing before you take off."

"Ohmigod."

"Yeah." It was all Ben could do to keep from laughing. "My mom is pretty cool, and she doesn't pry too much into my personal affairs, but I can guarantee she'll have a few questions about you. Best to address them fully clothed, don't you think?"

Sierra said again, "Ohmigod."

Ben laughed, leaned down and kissed her. She was so amusing and stubborn and proud and sexy. Being with her was exhilarating.

He had to keep nudging her along, she looked so dazed.

Ben eyed her askance. When she'd walked out of his room only moments ago, she'd thanked him as if what they'd done had been a one-time deal. Almost as if she truly expected things to end there. Silly woman. He wasn't even close to being done with her.

Not by a long shot.

So how could he change her mind? The only time she wasn't trying to push him away was when he touched her. Maybe he should just keep her aroused.

Ben smiled.

The idea of controlling Sierra with sex filled his mind with delectable possibilities. It'd take some iron control on his end, and he wasn't sure he was up to the task, not when he wanted her so much. But it would ensure him more time with her, and ingratiate him into her life when she'd claimed a preference to keep him out of it.

She'd claimed he was trouble.

Ben shook his head. Sooner or later, he'd break through her reserves. She'd admit she wanted him—and not just for one night. God, the things he wanted to do to her and with her would take at least a month, maybe longer.

As Ben tugged her into his motel room, he grinned with anticipation. He had several scenarios already in mind, and he was determined that she'd enjoy each and every one of them. He could hardly wait.

This was one challenge he fully intended to win.

He looked down at Sierra as she snatched up her underwear. Her face was bright red and taut with both bad humor and embarrassment. She looked around and Ben knew she was wondering where she should finish dressing.

"Sierra?"

Absently, on her way to the bathroom, she said, "What?"

"I have an offer for you."

She stopped in midstep, then slowly faced him with a groan. "I'm not at all sure I want to hear this."

Anticipation surged through his veins. "Oh, not only will you want to hear it, but you'll want to do it."

She shot him a wild, somewhat curious look, and fled into the bathroom. Ben smiled after her. He had her on the run. Things were looking good.

Chapter Five

Brooke had never felt so flustered in her life. But the man standing before her, eyeing her with open appreciation simply stole her breath away. He was big, blond, bold—and he was leering. Men didn't leer at her, ever. She lived in a quiet, older neighborhood. Worked as a legal secretary for a staid law firm. The men she associated with were . . . polite. Reserved.

When she got Ben alone, she'd smack him good for leaving her in this awkward situation.

"It's a lie, isn't it?"

Brooke blinked in surprise at the muscled Adonis. His sleeveless shirt was snowy white, a contrast to his bulky, tanned shoulders. She could see dark blond hair curling on his chest.

Worse than that, though, were his soft, faded jeans.

They hugged his thick thighs like a second skin. They also hugged his crotch, outlining his heavy sex and making Brooke feel far too warm. His jeans were positively scandalous in how they fit.

She realized he'd spoken to her and delicately cleared her throat. "I beg your pardon?"

Despite her dark concealing glasses, she was sure he'd been aware of her perusal; his very sensual mouth curled, making her heart turn over and filling her face with hot embarrassment. "There's no way you're the mother to a grown man. You're too young."

Out of long habit, Brooke's defense mechanisms were strong. As physically appealing as the man might be—if you liked big muscle-bound hulks—she wasn't interested. She raised her chin and gave him a truth that would obliterate his lame attempts at outrageous flattery. "I'm forty-five."

His piercing blue gaze went over her again, slower this time. His face was tanned, slightly weathered with smile-lines around his eyes and his mouth. His expression turned tender. "You became a mother at a very young age," he murmured.

Inside, Brooke trembled. She decided it was anger. "Yes, young and gullible. But I wouldn't have changed a thing. Ben has been the center of my life."

"Incredible." Disregarding her attempt to shift the topic, he leaned toward her, subtly crowding. "You don't look a second over thirty, you know."

The thin-strapped, tailored sundress, which had seemed appropriately chic that morning, now felt insubstantial. She knew her nipples had tightened and she was horrified at herself. Because she couldn't wear a bra with the dress, she also knew that he'd noticed. The fire in his eyes told her so, as did the way he continued to boldly look at her there.

Her face burned with shame but she kept her tone level, even condescending. "Is that your best line? Because it's really too absurd."

Smiling, he reached out and stole her sunglasses right off her nose.

Brooke gasped at his audacity and resisted the urge to grab for them, knowing she'd look ridiculous. With her mouth feeling stiff and her breath coming too fast, she stared at him. "Just what do you think you're doing?"

Holding the glasses loosely between his fingers, he propped his hands on his hips. "Come on, Brooke. There's no need to hide from me."

She almost gasped again. "I was not hiding." But she knew she had been. Meeting his gaze now was actually painful. It had been a long, long time since a man had stared at her with such intensity. It left her disconcerted.

He shrugged those broad bare shoulders. "And I don't have a practiced line. Truth is, I've never actually needed one."

Brooke could believe that. His grin personified wickedness, but she'd cured herself of attractions to wicked men a long time ago. She held out her hand. "My glasses, please?"

"Certainly." He didn't give them to her, choosing instead to glance at his watch. "Your son ran off with Sierra and I'm thinking we may have a few minutes to wait on them. Why don't we grab that cup of coffee, as he suggested? I haven't had any caffeine yet and I'm in need."

Brooke hesitated, and he tilted his head to say, his voice a rough purr, "It'll be painless. Scout's honor."

If the man had ever been a Scout, then the program was in serious danger. But Brooke didn't want him to think he scared her. That would never do. "All right. Fine. One cup of coffee until Ben returns. Then I need to . . . speak with him."

Her excuse sounded so lame, Brooke wanted to groan. Kent did chuckle, the sound low and rough and innately masculine. Disturbed, Brooke turned and headed for the bar. She was very aware of Kent behind her, his gaze a tactile touch on her back. Her sundress was modestly cut in front, hiding even a hint of cleavage, but low in back with criss-crossing straps. She now wished she'd worn a suit. Something sturdy and concealing, despite the weather.

They stepped through the doorway and the air-conditioning hit her full force, making her shiver. She used the excuse of the cold to wrap her arms around herself, hiding her breasts from his view.

One look at him and she knew he'd seen right through her ploy, but he said only, his mouth curling in amusement, "A hot cup of coffee will warm you up."

They sat at a small corner table and he returned her sunglasses—now that she was inside and had no reason to don them. His grand gesture also forced her to drop her arms. Brooke wanted to smack him, to wipe that smug confident grin off his handsome face, but she would *not* let him know how he bothered her.

The waitress poured their coffee, but otherwise they sat in silence. Tension vibrated between them, making her jumpier than she could ever remember.

Where had Ben rushed off to? She hoped he wouldn't be long. The last thing she wanted was to prolong her time in Kent's company.

But oh, it was so nice to see Ben taken with a woman. In less than two seconds, Brooke had realized that he felt differently about Sierra than most of the women who threw themselves at him. It was there in the way he looked at her and Brooke couldn't have been more pleased.

"You have a lovely smile, Brooke."

At Kent's comment, she glanced up and found him staring at her, or more precisely, at her mouth. Her coffee cup jangled in her hand. "Thank you."

Gently, his look knowing, Kent set down his cup, prompting her to do the same. Brooke cleared her throat, wishing she could think of something to say to break the tension.

As if he'd read her mind, he propped his elbows on the table and leaned toward her. "I'm sorry, but it just occurred to me." His brows pulled together, making the blue of his eyes icy hot. "Is Mr. Badwin around anywhere?"

Brooke nodded. "Yes, of course." Surely, Ben hadn't abandoned her altogether.

Kent muttered a curse and looked out the window at the broiling sun. "It figures." He slanted his gaze her way. "Where the hell is he?"

Confused, Brooke gestured. "He lives here in the motel. But I'm sure he won't be long. Did you and Sierra have an appointment this morning?" Brooke was thinking that if they did, she'd have a good excuse to seek Ben out and hurry him along.

The roguish grin slowly returned. "You're talking about your son."

"Yes, of course."

She paused, but it would be easier to simply converse

with him than sit in that edgy silence. "He said you're working at the new landscaping business?"

"Yeah. Sierra owns it, I work for her."

When she'd first met them, Brooke had assumed the opposite, based on their ages. "What is it you do?"

"Whatever needs to be done. Some of the labor, the heavier digging. Stocking. That sort of thing."

"I see." He had to be in his late thirties at least, but he worked a job often assigned to high school boys. Brooke didn't mean to judge him, but she couldn't help herself. She was well acquainted with men lacking personal pride and initiative.

His look said she didn't see anything, but that he didn't mind. "Any other misters around—like the type who can claim you for his wife?"

Brooke's back stiffened. When he'd first asked that, she hadn't realized . . . "No." And then, despite herself, she said, "Not that it's any of your business."

He looked at her mouth. "I want to make it my business."

Offended by his lack of propriety, she dropped back in her seat. "My God, are you always this forward? Because I must tell you, I don't like it."

He looked down at the table and toyed with his spoon. To Brooke, he seemed somewhat chagrined by his own behavior. "No, I'm usually more reserved."

She snorted at that bit of idiotic fabrication—and was appalled at herself. She *never* snorted, for heaven's sake. But really, there wasn't a reserved bone in his big body, far as she could tell.

With new determination, he faced her. "Have dinner with me, and I'll convince you."

He was very direct. "No, thank you." Brooke looked around, praying Ben would materialize. He didn't.

"Why not?" His work boots bumped into her sandals—and stayed there. "You involved with someone else?"

"No." Exasperated, alarmed, she slipped her feet back beneath her chair and out of his reach, then went on to say, "I like it that way."

"Safer?"

Her mouth fell open at his insight. She snapped it shut and gave him mulish silence for an answer.

"I'm forty," he offered. "Widowed, with a daughter who's finishing up college."

"A daughter?" Brooke had always wanted a daughter, but she hadn't wanted the marriage, the tie to a man, that would have made it feasible. She'd already done the out-of-wedlock parenting and knew it wasn't ideal. Thanks to her, Ben had always had a lot to deal with.

Pride shone in Kent's eyes, making him more appealing than ever. "Her name's Beth. She's a sweetheart, smart as hell, engaged to a young doctor." He sipped his coffee, thoughtful. His next words were very softly spoken. "Her mother died when she was sixteen."

Brooke's heart thumped in sympathy. "I'm so sorry."

With an arrested expression, Kent studied her face, then shook his head. "A woman as lovely and sexy as you should never be alone."

Brooke had begun to feel for him, her annoyance softening at his loss and the gentle way he discussed his daughter. And he'd ruined it with one line too many. She pushed back her chair and glared down at him.

One blond brow shot high as Kent looked up at her and took in her annoyed stance.

Brooke didn't mean to react so emotionally, to give so much away. Still, she couldn't stop herself from saying, "The last thing I want or need is a man in my life."

Kent whistled low at her vehemence, but he didn't stand up, didn't say anything. He just lounged there in his chair, judging her every reaction, dissecting her. His manners were inexcusable.

Brooke dug in her purse, retrieved two dollars and put them on the table. "Have a good day," she said, and turned to storm away. Just before she went through to the kitchen, she couldn't resist looking back over her shoulder. Kent was still watching her, his gaze so piercing she shivered.

She rushed through the door and let it swing shut behind her. The cook looked up, started to say hello, and Brooke let loose with a long, violent growl that startled him so badly he rushed off to the sink. *Men,* Brooke thought as she stomped to the break room.

That *particular* man.

But her pulse was racing, her stomach flip-flopped, and she felt flushed from head to toe.

No, no, no. Not again.

Kent was staring into his coffee, still grinning, when Sierra and Ben approached the table. Sierra, looking rather shell-shocked and red in the face, slid into the seat Brooke had vacated.

Somewhat curious, Kent looked up at Ben. The young man appeared very pleased with himself. "What's going on?"

Ben gestured toward the kitchen. "I was going to ask you that. What did you say to my mother to put her in such a huff? I saw her stomping off—and she never stomps."

Kent shrugged, and had to fight hard to keep from laughing. Her passionate outburst had reassured him that she'd felt some of the awareness, too. "I asked her out to dinner."

Ben stared in comical surprise, leading Kent into further thought. Was it so unheard of for his mother to get asked out? Or was Ben objecting to Kent on a personal level? Either way, he wouldn't accept any interference.

No sooner did he think it than Ben answered his question with a lighthearted statement.

"She doesn't date."

"She'll date me." Kent was sure he'd get around her prickly objections one way or another.

"Oh." Ben frowned, shrugged, then put both hands on the table and leaned over Kent. "I feel compelled here to offer the perfunctory warning about hurting her."

Kent eyed the young man with a new measure of respect and a good dose of humor. His mother was old enough to fight her own battles with men, but it was nice that her son cared enough to try. "That right?"

" 'Fraid so. You know how it goes. Make her cry, hurt her in any way, and I'll break your legs, and so on and so on."

Sierra straightened in alarm. "Ben!"

Waving her back to her seat, Kent laughed. "Warning noted."

"All right then. We understand each other." Ben nodded in satisfaction. "By the way, far as I know my mother is oblivious to men."

"Every son everywhere assumes his mother is oblivious to men." Kent took a quick sip of his coffee and then added, "Your mother is not."

Ben started to reply, then snapped his mouth shut and made a face. "Thanks. Like I needed to know that."

Kent laughed again. From the moment he'd seen Brooke, something had clicked between them. Something hot and thick and most definitely sexual. She'd done her best to hide that fact, which had only intrigued him more. "Why doesn't she date?"

"You'll have to ask her." Ben clapped him on the shoulder. "But a little advice, if you want to get on her good side, don't rush her. Give her time. She prides herself on her respectability, on always being proper. It's important to her."

Sierra choked and nearly spewed her coffee across the table. Ben just gave her a knowing look, making Kent wonder how improper the two of them had been.

At the same time, he disregarded Ben's suggestion. Brooke Badwin was in desperate need of a fast and furious, sizzling-hot love affair. Her son wouldn't know that about her, and that was as it should be. But Kent had recognized the flustered hunger in her in the same way men had through the centuries, with fine-honed animal instincts. She was a woman determined to hide from her sexual side. He was just as determined not to let her. Not with him.

He felt a thickening in his groin and had to focus on things other than getting the very respectable Ms. Badwin naked in his bed.

To aid him in that effort, he gave his attention to Sierra. "So what's on the agenda for today? With that downpour last night, I take it we won't be planting after all."

"The ground is soup." She propped her forehead on her hand and sighed. "With any luck and a favorable weather forecast, we'll plant tomorrow. I'll spend today getting my new place in order."

"I saw a window was out."

She glanced up at the young stud still hovering near their table. Almost grudgingly, she said, "Ben helped me last night. He put up the plastic."

Kent thought Ben might have done a bit more than hang plastic, but said only, "And you ended up here since it wasn't safe to stay at home?"

"That's about it."

Ben shifted his stance, not too thrilled at being ignored. "That's not even half of it, but it'll do for now."

A waitress approached with the coffeepot and a fresh cup. She bumped hips with Ben, grinned and winked. Ben winked back.

Kent watched Sierra silently stew.

As the waitress served Sierra and refilled Kent's cup, she said to Ben, "The phone's for you, Ben. It's Grace, and she said she has to talk to you about Aggie."

"Thanks." The waitress left and Ben bent to kiss Sierra. "I better take the call."

She leaned out of reach, her frown fiercer than Kent had seen since she'd moved away from her hometown. "Who," she demanded, "is Grace?"

Well, well, Kent thought, using his coffee cup to hide his smile. *Jealousy on both their parts.* He sat back, waiting to be entertained.

Ben touched Sierra's cheek. "Grace is my sister-in-law and a real sweetheart. You'll love her. Everyone does."

Slightly appeased, Sierra asked, "And Aggie?"

"Mrs. Agatha Harper, matriarch, society matron, and, at last check, my grandmother."

"At last check?"

"She goes back and forth on that one." He shrugged. "I call her Aggie just to piss her off, but now everyone is picking up the habit. She probably wants to raise hell with me about something."

"Why?"

"Because that's usually what she wants."

Sierra looked as stunned by his disclosure as Kent. It sounded like Agatha Harper was something of a wealthy woman, though Ben showed no signs of the privileged condescension familiar to people of affluence.

For one thing, he owned and ran a middle-class motel and bar. For another, he was too easy-going, too laid-back and casual to have been raised rich.

Regardless of that, Ben would have his work cut out for him. Thanks to some bad experiences, Sierra had a special aversion to wealthy families and the power they wielded.

But watching him, Kent decided Ben was up to the task.

Tired of her fending him off, Ben grabbed Sierra's shoulders and kissed her before she could dodge him. "I've got to go, but I'll see you later, okay?"

Sierra scowled and dithered. "I've got a lot of work to do."

"So I'll catch you when you're done."

She glanced at Ben, and away. "I'm going to be really busy for at least a week. Probably longer."

Kent looked up at the ceiling. Sierra's brush-off skills were sorely lacking. She could definitely use a few lessons on subtlety.

Ben leaned down nose to nose with her, causing Sierra to press back in her chair. He cupped her chin, brushed his thumb over her bottom lip. His tone was mild, a bit husky. "I will see you later." He gave her a brief, soft kiss.

Kent waited for Sierra to explode, to maybe even slug Ben for being so forward.

Instead she blinked her big eyes as if dazed.

Ben nodded at them both and walked away.

As soon as Ben was out of range, Sierra shook her head then glared after him. "He's impossible."

"What's this? Insults from a woman who looks like she had a night of wild debauchery?" Kent saw her face burn.

"I was not debauched."

"Really? Not at all?" He expected immediate confirmation. Sierra had been badly burned, and since then she'd turned every interested guy down flat—that is, when she even bothered to notice his interest. More often than not, she didn't.

The immediate confirmation didn't materialize.

"Well . . ." She hesitated, making Kent sit up a little straighter. She frowned in uncertainty, then shook her head. "No."

"Oh, now that just reeked of conviction." Kent tilted his head to study her. "So what the hell did happen last night?"

She shrugged and flushed at the same time. "Just what I said, the storm knocked out my window, as well as the electricity, and Ben came to my rescue. He let me stay at his motel."

"With him?"

She made a point of not meeting his gaze. "He lives

there. None of the key cards to empty rooms would work because of the blackout. His room was the only one he could get open because it has a regular key."

"Uh-huh. You slept in his room all night, but there was no hanky-panky?" Being male himself, Kent found that rather hard to believe.

Sierra held her head in dismay. "He promised we wouldn't have sex, and we didn't."

Kent stared. They'd known each other long enough to be closer than friends, without the baggage of relatives. Kent understood Sierra better than anyone. She said they hadn't gotten intimate, so he believed her. But her manner this morning suggested that something had certainly happened—and she didn't look completely happy about it.

After her marriage and her divorce, she was especially vulnerable. She considered herself a hard-ass, but Kent knew better. Her heart was more tender than most. It thrilled him that she was showing signs of interest in a man again, but at the same time, he couldn't bear the idea of her getting hurt. If she got involved with a guy like Ben, it had to be with her eyes wide-open.

As her friend, he felt bound to warn her. "He definitely wants in your pants, honey."

Sierra waved that away. "Yeah I know, he told me so."

Kent drew back in surprise. "He *told* you so?"

"Several times." She made a face. "He seems to think he can convince me to spend time with him."

Fascinating. "How's he going to do that?"

She dithered, stirring her coffee, chewing her lip. Finally she blurted, "He . . . did stuff to me." She stared at Kent hard, trying to see if he understood.

Oh, he understood only too well. "You don't say."

"But he didn't do anything for himself."

Kent sat back in his seat, a little discomfited by the ridiculous conversation. And strangely aroused. He knew he needed a woman bad when chatting with Sierra made him hot.

She confided in him as a sister might, and she deserved his undivided attention. Problem was, with Brooke still on his mind, he heard her as a man. He cleared his throat. "You're saying he concentrated just on you?"

She put her head in her hands and nodded. "And he's *really* good, Kent. Or else, I'm really easy, not sure which." She seemed bothered by that for a moment. "But I've never been easy before. Just the opposite."

"Maybe that's because you hadn't met the right guy."

Her head jerked up. "He's not the right guy, either."

"Why not?"

"You met him. He's a . . . a hound dog."

"A hound dog who knows what he's doing, evidently."

She grumbled under her breath, then said, "Yeah, with every woman he meets."

"You think?"

"You saw him with the waitress."

Kent shrugged. "He was just being friendly. Trust me, he didn't look at her the same way he was looking at you."

Her sigh was more of a huff. "Can I ask you something?"

He could hardly wait. "Shoot."

"Is what he did—with me—typical? I mean, I assumed guys were kind of selfish when it came to sex."

She looked so confused, Kent smiled, reached out and took her hand. "Your experience is sorely limited, honey."

"I know. But still, do other guys do that—go without so they can make a woman satisfied?"

Make a woman satisfied? What the hell had Ben done to her? Kent couldn't help himself—he laughed at the awkwardness of his own feelings.

"What's so funny?"

"You are a delight, Sierra. If you spoke like this with Ben, it's a wonder you didn't shock him to death."

She looked affronted. "Ha! There's not much that would shock *him,* I can tell you that!" But then she thought about it, and asked, "Why?"

"All this sex talk—men are susceptible to such things. And visual. I'm getting a real good mental picture here." She looked so appalled, he shrugged in apology. "Sorry."

Her face colored, then turned dark with a mortified frown. She leaned over the table to close the distance between them and poked him in the chest. "Well stop it, for crying out loud. I don't want you picturing . . . *that.*"

"Too late. I can't seem to help myself." Kent understood now that Ben had pleasured her. The various ways Ben might have done that had already flitted through Kent's mind in rapid order. No wonder Ben looked so territorial today.

Sierra groaned and dropped her head to the tabletop. "This is awful."

Kent had never seen her so forlorn, so he took pity on her. Smiling, he patted her shoulder and tried to speak as matter-of-factly as possible. "Okay, to answer your question: Men are men. Some are generous and considerate and some are pigs. Sounds like Ben is in the first category. Also, sounds like he's damned determined to get you in the sack, and to make sure you enjoy being there."

Relief that he'd answered her, and impatience to discuss it, got her attention and brought Sierra halfway back across the table. "I guess he is. Do you know what he told me?"

Kent wasn't sure he'd survive this. He'd only occasionally seen Sierra as a sexual person because he'd met her when her life had been upside down with strife. Since then, he'd been intent on helping her start over, and in the process they'd grown very close. He'd been mourning his wife and she wouldn't have allowed anything else. There'd been no room for sexual interest.

"Tell me."

"He wants to keep giving, *without getting*." She sat back, waiting for Kent's reaction to that. When he blinked at her, she nodded hard, as if to convince him it was true. "Do you believe that? Is that even normal?"

Again, Kent had to fight off a laugh. No, Ben didn't sound like a normal guy, he sounded better—and just what Sierra needed.

"It's not funny," Sierra grumbled. "I don't have time for this nonsense. But he seems so determined . . ."

Kent opened his mouth, not at all sure what he'd say, and Ben rumbled, "Are we interrupting?"

Kent turned, and found both Ben and Brooke standing beside the table. Suspicion and a touch of jealousy darkened Ben's eyes. It was clear that he didn't like the way they had their heads together, whispering. His body language, not to mention his gaze, challenged Kent.

Brooke, on the other hand, seemed determined not to look at him. Kent found that interesting, especially since from one breath to the next she lost the battle and her attention darted toward him, then caught. Kent refused to release her, and they stared at each other for a long moment. Her chest rose on a deep inhalation.

Damn, she was beautiful. And classy. And begging to be fucked. His voice dropped despite his best intentions. "Hello again."

Ben appeared irate until Kent realized he was holding Sierra's hand. He released her and sat back in his chair. "My mother has an offer for you."

"Yeah?" Kent felt his blood heat. "What kind of offer?"

Warily, Brooke dismissed Kent and turned to Sierra. "New landscaping."

Sierra said, "Excuse me?"

Brooke cleared her throat—and kept glancing at Kent. He shared an intimate smile with her that had her smooth cheeks turning rosy and her big brown eyes narrowing with annoyance.

Impatient, Ben picked up the explanations. "Mom bought a new house about two years ago and the landscaping is outdated. She wanted to see if you were available to give her a quote."

Kent knew Sierra would protest, that she'd see the ploy as a handout more than a legitimate offer. She was so stubborn, so damn independent she questioned any good fortune. Forestalling her, Kent pushed back his chair and stood. "That's my job, and I'd be glad to."

Brooke took a hasty step back. "But . . ."

Her son frowned, ready to intervene at this sign of his mother's distress, and Kent continued. "Sierra has to work on unpacking and setting up house. But I can run out and give you an idea of what'd it cost, and how soon we can do it."

"I, uh . . ."

Kent turned to Ben, offering him a new focus. "Maybe if you're not too busy, you could see about getting Sierra's window replaced?"

Both Sierra and Brooke objected to that. Sierra shot to her feet. "I can take care of it, Kent, and you know it."

Brooke glared daggers at Kent. "You think a woman is incapable of something as simple as ordering a window?"

"I'm glad to help," Ben interjected, but the women paid him little heed.

Lord save him from independent women. Kent laughed out loud and that just seemed to set everyone off again. He held up both hands. "Acquit me, ladies, please. I wasn't insulting the whole of womankind. Sierra is the most self-sufficient person I know, but she is new to the area and with Ben owning an established business, I assumed he'd know who's reputable, reliable, and reasonable."

"Absolutely," Ben insisted, taking the bait gratefully. "Let me make a few calls and I'll see if I can't get someone out here today."

Sierra wasn't ready to relent, but she quieted when Kent sent her a look. If Ben stayed busy with Sierra, he couldn't be playing watchdog over his mother.

"There, it's all decided." Taking a step closer to Brooke, Kent noticed that she was a slender woman, fragile in size and features, unlike her son, though the family resemblance was still strong. This time, just to get to her, he deliberately lowered his voice. "When do you want me?"

Heat rushed to her face and she gasped in affront. "I beg your pardon?"

Oh, she might deny it, but her mind was there in the gutter with his, centering on carnal thoughts. Kent did his best to sound innocent. "At your house? To discuss what you have in mind?" And then, with a grin, "For the land-scaping."

"Oh." She laced her fingers together over her belly. A softly rounded belly that Kent wanted very much to kiss. "I have errands to run, and a meeting. It's really a rather busy day, and I . . ." She stopped babbling to blurt, "Around two?"

He had her confused, and he liked it. "You want to give me directions?"

Ben stopped a waitress and tore a page off the back of her order pad. Using her pen, he jotted down the address and the simplest route to the house. "It'll take you about twenty minutes from here, give or take five depending on traffic. White two-story on a corner lot. You can't miss it."

Kent accepted the paper and tucked it into his back pocket. "I'll be there."

Brooke tore her gaze away from his. Her smile was shaky as she faced her son. "I suppose I better get going or I'll be late."

Ben enfolded her in his arms and lifted her off her feet for a bruising bear hug, making her laugh. Brooke clung to him, hugging him back and admonishing him at the same time.

They were so comfortable with the embrace, Kent assumed it was typical. He liked seeing her this way, at ease, happy, secure. Her laugh was low and throaty and to Kent's overwrought senses, very sexy.

Sierra, who'd never known a mother's love, watched their easy affection with a wistful kind of melancholy. Kent felt for her. The transition to her new place wasn't going quite as smoothly as she'd probably hoped.

She appeared mired in confusion and no wonder with

her background. How much of her past, if any, had she shared with Ben? Probably none, considering how private Sierra could be.

Kent would have reciprocated with the warning Ben gave him, except that he knew Sierra would have a fit. Her independence was hard won and she refused interference, even the well-meaning kind, with ferocity. One reason they'd remained close friends was that he never underestimated her strength, and he respected her pride— something her ex had failed to do.

Damn. There'd been times when he'd wanted to kill her ex, but he hadn't.

His morbid trip down memory lane jolted back into the present when Ben set Brooke on her feet. She patted Ben's shoulder, kissed his cheek. Her smile, the love she felt for her son, shone in her light brown eyes when she turned to Sierra and caught both her hands.

"Sierra, it was wonderful meeting you." Soft as butter, Brooke's voice stroked over Kent, and she wasn't even addressing him.

Pathetic, he thought. *I'm turning into a lovesick pup.* But he couldn't look away from her.

Sierra gave an awkward nod. "You, too."

"I'm sure we'll talk again later?"

"Uh, sure." Sierra glanced at Ben then tugged away from Brooke, uncomfortable with the show of affection.

Drawing a breath, Brooke faced Kent with discreet caution. "Mr. . . ?"

"Monroe, but Kent will do." He propped his hands on his hips and stared down at her meaningfully.

"Mr. Monroe." Her prim, aloof tone tickled him. "I'll see you at two." She strode out, her hips swaying gently, her head held high.

Kent watched the show with burning eyes until Ben shoved him. Drawn from his sensual perusal, he said, "Hmm?"

Ben frowned, but Kent could see he tried hard not to laugh. "Don't gawk at my mom, damn it. It's unsettling."

"That right?" Kent glanced out the window in time to see Brooke getting into her car. He straightened. "Well, you might as well get used to it, since I'll be seeing her a lot."

Ben shook his head. "Sorry, but I know she'll refuse."

"I'll convince her."

Startled by that proclamation, Ben barked a laugh. "God, she's going to kill you." He reached for Sierra, kissed her hard and fast, and with a negligent, "Later," he headed off.

Kent took in Sierra's chagrined expression and smiled. "We should get to work, too. The lot is a mess."

In something of a stupor, Sierra stepped outside with him. Already the day was so humid, the air seemed to sweat. The heat brought her around and she elbowed Kent in the side. "God, you were embarrassingly obvious. I've never seen you carry on like that before."

"Yeah?" That was like the pot calling the kettle black. "Well back atcha, honey."

Her lagging steps made Kent slow his pace. Normally she left him in her dust with her inexhaustible energy, but now she seemed very pensive. "You think it has something to do with the air here in Gillespe?"

The bright sun reflected off all the wet leaves and pavement, the remaining puddles. It was going to be a scorcher. "Maybe."

"I've gotten so used to being alone, I don't know if I like liking him."

Kent laughed and gave her a squeeze. "You like it. I can tell."

"It's not smart." She wore her most mulish expression. "I can't afford any interruptions."

"You don't have to decide anything right this minute." And Kent wasn't at all sure Ben intended to leave the decision up to her. "Why don't you give him a chance?"

For a brief moment, she considered it. Then she shook her head, resolute. "No. For a million reasons, it'd be a dumb thing to do, and I'm not dumb. Ben is a complication I do not need."

Kent smiled. "Whatever you say."

She gave him a sharp look, but Kent kept his expression impassive. "I say one night with him was enough. Any more than that, and I'm just asking for trouble."

She stomped on past Kent, and since she couldn't see him, he gave into a grin. He had the feeling Sierra was in for the surprise of her life.

Chapter Six

Kent and Sierra stopped in the lot. They both looked around, Sierra with determination to get her mind back on track, Kent with consideration for what needed to be done. "It's going to take all day to get this mess cleaned up."

Kicking at a fat limb in the drive, Kent said, "He's not Griffin, hon."

"He could be." She squinted, shading her eyes with a hand. "I barely know him."

She watched as Kent picked up the heavy limb, braced it on his shoulder, and toted it toward her truck. She picked up several smaller twigs and followed him.

"You've got good instincts, Sierra. No, don't say it." He dumped the limb, then leaned on the back of the truck bed and studied her. "You were little more than a child when you married Griff, so he doesn't count. And you know well enough that most men aren't like him anyway. He was a major asshole, and I should have beat the hell out of him at least once."

For a single moment, alarm skittered up her spine. But Griffin was far away, and both she and Kent were safe from his petty revenge. "You'd have ended up in jail and we both know it."

"Would've been worth it."

Damn, she was lucky to have him for a friend. "You're a nut, Kent, and I love you." Then, as she'd done so many times, she put the past behind her.

With a disgusted look at her wrinkled clothes, she said, "I'm going to go in and change, then I'll be right out. With any luck, we can get the biggest part of this mess cleaned up before you head to Mrs. Badwin's. The rest of the stuff I can do on my own."

"Take your time."

Sierra spent a good ten minutes washing her face, brushing her hair and containing it in a braid, cleaning her teeth. Mostly she used the time to regroup, to regain some of her self. She hadn't felt this muddled since the night her father had kicked her out and she'd had no place to go.

Except to Griff.

She shook her head. No this was different, even a little exciting, but still wrong. From the moment Ben had said he wanted her, she hadn't been able to not think of him. He was just so . . . different.

He'd introduced her to his *mother*.

She still couldn't get over that, over him and what he'd done, to her and with her. His casual attitude about it all. He perplexed her with the various sides to his personality, generous and humorous and so damn open.

He kept nothing hidden, when she hid so much.

His mother had appeared to like her; that was odd, too. Sierra wasn't a woman to primp, but Mrs. Badwin had seen her at her absolute worst, with her hair a mess and her clothes rumpled from a night on the floor. Not only that, but Sierra was sure Mrs. Badwin knew that she'd just left her son's bed. Sierra closed her eyes as embarrassment washed over her again.

She'd never had a mother herself, at least not that she could remember. Her father had raised her, and he'd never been a very affectionate person. Her father's concerns had been of the soul, of staying pure, not of showing or sharing love. Watching Ben hug his mother with so much exuberance, so much caring had wrenched something deep inside her. How must it feel to be loved so unconditionally?

Uneasiness held her for another reason, too. She now understood that Ben's forthright manner had been just that—his manner. He was comfortable with himself to the point he had no secrets, no regrets. He loved his mother and showed it. He wanted Sierra and said so.

Sierra had matched his honesty out of a deeply rooted, self-imposed principle. After her divorce, she'd sworn never again to defer to a man for any reason. She'd been playing one-upmanship, and it had backfired in a big way because, as Ben said, he felt challenged.

Resisting him was not going to be easy.

Kent stuck his head in the door and yelled down the short hall. "Hey, you okay in there?"

"Fine." Sierra leaned out of the bathroom so she could see him over the packing boxes and crates. "I'll be right there."

Kent was silent a moment, looking her over, then he shook his head. "No rush."

But there was a rush. She had a lot to do to get organized if she wanted her business to be a success. She absolutely did not have time to waste on Ben Badwin—no matter how sexy, funny, and unaccountably generous he might be.

She'd just have to force herself to remember that.

At one-thirty, Ben found Sierra at the back of her lot, on her hands and knees, digging at weeds around a colorful, freshly planted flowerbed. The red highlights in her hair shown brightly in the afternoon sun. She'd contained it in a thick braid, and it was now damp at her temples and the nape of her neck. Her gray shirt, smudged with dirt, was two sizes too large, hanging limp on her small frame. Her frayed cutoffs rode just high enough on her pert behind to stir his already teeming hunger.

For several minutes, Ben indulged his need to watch her. Every so often she muttered to herself, her words indistinct but the tone clearly one of encouragement in the face of her weariness.

In the short time he'd known her, he'd already realized they had a lot in common. For one thing, Sierra had the driving urge to be her own boss, and she relished the hard work that took her one step closer to that goal. Ben understood that because he'd already gone through it. It wasn't an easy road to take, but he had the gut feeling she was more than up to the task.

He'd known a lot of women, but none who seemed to enjoy good old-fashioned labor the way she did.

For another thing, he liked challenges, and whether

Sierra admitted it or not, she liked issuing them. Her exotic eyes lit up with defiance every time she felt a loss of control. She had a way of getting pugnacious real quick whenever she thought someone had stepped on her independent little toes. It was a rather endearing trait, especially since he was used to women catering to him, going out of their way to encourage him.

Sierra tried to push him away by word and deed every chance she got.

Except when he touched her. Then she thawed so fast she took his breath away.

Finally she sat back on her heels, wiped the back of her wrist across her brow, and surveyed the rest of the area in front of her. The rows of bushes, which had been displaced by the storm, now sat neat and orderly again. Small balled trees were arranged by type, and landscaping stones were stacked in rounded piles here and there.

He'd like to think Kent had done most of the heavier lifting, but he knew better.

Though she'd planted several bright flower borders and beds, more weeds grew in smattered clusters from the hard ground. She put her hand to her back and groaned as she came to her feet. Looking up at the sun, she stretched.

Watching her further stirred Ben's blood. She was such an earthy little pagan. "You had lunch yet?"

She jerked around to face him and to Ben's alert eyes, she looked a little sunburned. "What are you doing here?"

In the glare, her eyes were impossibly green and accusing. Ben took one measured step toward her, and she backed up. "Hey, don't look so panicked. I just want to feed you."

"Oh." Sullen indignation drew her brows down. "I'm not panicked, and I already told you I have work to do."

Every time he got near her, he had to fight a grin. "What did you think I wanted, Sierra?"

She searched his face, chewed her bottom lip. She looked beyond him, then back. "What you said earlier."

The break in her voice, the slight tremor, gave her away. "About pleasuring you?"

She frowned, a little cautious. "Yes."

Earlier, while she'd donned her underwear, he'd offered to show her all the ways she could reach her release—without actually having sex. She'd made her reservations on intercourse clear, so Ben had decided to work around them by offering her a compromise.

She'd flat-out refused him, but now Ben could see she'd considered it in more detail, and had aroused herself in the bargain.

Damn.

Ben took a leisurely review of her body. Even wilted in the heat, she stood straight and proud, her shoulders squared, her gaze direct. Her breasts rose and fell with deep breaths—either from exertion or excitement, he wasn't sure which.

In select places, her shirt stuck to her with perspiration—at her chest, below her breasts and belly. The leg creases of her shorts were damp, and though he'd planned to give her some time, once Ben noticed that he had to touch her.

The ways they affected each other were unbelievable.

He strode forward. "I'll feed you lunch after."

Startled by his approach, she again backed up a step. "After?"

"Yeah." He touched her cheek. "Look at you. You're trembling."

He heard her swallow, saw the way her eyes darkened. "I'm tired."

"And turned on."

"It doesn't mean anything. It's just that I'm not used to this. To guys like you." He continued to touch her, trailing his fingertips over her cheek to her ear, the side of her throat. It was only a light touch, but she shook her head as if to clear it. When she spoke again, her voice was lower, less strident. "You're making me loopy."

Her skin was soft, dewy. He saw her eyes close, heard her draw an uneven breath. Jesus, she was so hot and so quick to react.

Ben trailed his fingertips along her jaw, down her throat to her breast. Watching her, he circled one firm nipple. "Loopy?"

Her breath caught. "I've never thought about sex much, at least not since my marriage."

Not since my marriage. Ben thought that an odd way to put it. Surely she meant since her divorce. A lot of women were bitter after going through such an ordeal, and they temporarily swore off men.

Or had her husband been a lousy lover, leaving her to believe all men were the same?

He raised his free hand and treated the other breast to the same treatment, touching lightly, cupping her. "Kent is gone?"

She nodded, swallowed hard. "He's got it bad."

Ben's hands stilled. "Got what bad?"

Without him tormenting her, she got her eyes to open. "For your mother. Long as I've known him, he's never acted this way."

Ben scowled. "Let's save that discussion for later, okay? Some things just don't mix well. Let's concentrate on this instead." To emphasize *this,* he rubbed his thumbs over her nipples. They thrust against the damp cotton of her shirt, making it very hard for him to concentrate.

Her gloved hands curled into fists, her low moan sounding hoarse and raw.

Ben smiled knowingly. "You're almost ready now."

"No . . ."

"Yeah, you are. Why do you want to fight this? It'd be so good, Sierra."

"No." Even as she said it, she leaned forward, into his touch, and she bit her lip.

"We're both adults, both single." He kissed her sun-warmed nose, her cheekbone. "There's something special going on here, Sierra. Why deny it?"

She shook her head.

"All right. You can keep your secrets." He didn't want to interrupt the carnality of the moment. He kissed her full on the lips, breathed in her intensified scent. "For now."

Continuing to hold her breasts, he said, "Tell me what you've been doing today."

Two deep breaths later, she mumbled, "Cleaning up the lot. Rearranging things. Putting up—*Ah, Ben.*"

He brushed her nipples, plucked, lightly pinched. "Talk to me, Sierra."

"I can't." Her hands closed over his wrists, holding him tightly. "Not while you're doing that."

The lot was deserted and only someone watching closely would even notice them. Still, Ben backed her up beside a shed, into the shade and out of sight of passersby. He pressed into her, bending his knees a little so his cock rested against her plump mound.

She moaned and her open mouth found his, hungry, anxious. Ben released one breast to cup her bottom, to lift her into the gentle rhythm he set, stroking her and himself through their layers of clothing.

Her gloved hands caught at the back of his neck. She began to shiver, to tighten, and Ben was amazed at how fast she got there, how little effort it had taken on his part. She was a sexual powder keg, and he was one lucky man.

Sierra tried to pull away as the sensations swiftly built, tried to gasp for air, but Ben didn't let her. He kept her close, taking her small cries into his mouth, stroking harder and faster, determined to take everything. Suddenly she stiffened. She wrenched her mouth free and groaned harshly, gulping air, trembling all over. Ben watched the sensual agony on her face and felt the bite of her hands on his shoulders.

He felt so much a part of her that he almost came, too.

Sierra seemed bewildered as her climax faded and she went limp, only to realize Ben was rigid, his teeth clenched, his fingers digging into her hips. He pressed his face to her throat and concentrated on breathing, on holding back the tide of sensations. He didn't want to shock her by coming in his pants.

At the last moment before he regained control, he felt her kiss his temple with infinite tenderness.

As his sluggish brain started to function again, Ben managed a chuckle but the sound was rusty and weak. "Damn. That was too close for comfort." He still didn't trust himself to move too fast. Things were getting out of hand. He'd have to have her—and soon.

She removed her gloves, dropped them to the ground, and her slender fingers stroked through his hair. "Your hair is so soft," she murmured with what sounded like wonder, and Ben had no idea what to say to that.

She tipped her head in an effort to see his face. "Are you all right?"

"Yeah." He raised his head, took in her perplexed, fascinated expression, and felt his heart twist. "Seeing you come makes me want to come. Bad." Trying not to smile, he said, "Don't think less of me, okay? I'm only a man, and you're irresistible."

Her brows beetled as she considered that, taking his teasing words seriously. "No, I won't think less of you. It's exciting that you get so . . . turned on."

She'd been married, and Ben wondered if her husband hadn't been just as turned on. It seemed impossible to him that any man could be with Sierra and not lose himself in her natural sensuality. None of it added up. In some ways, she was so sure of herself, so brazen. But in others, in sexual matters, she was far too inexperienced to have been a wife.

Questions crowded his brain, but for now, Ben kept them to himself. He'd pushed her enough for one day.

She groaned, this time in annoyance, and shoved against his shoulders. "Look at all the time I've wasted now."

A weaker man would have no ego left. "Take it easy on me, honey. I'm working on a hair-trigger here."

"And whose fault is that?"

Their combined scents mingled with the musky aroma of sexual excitement. Ben smoothed Sierra's warm cheek with his thumb. "What can I say? I like being sweaty with you."

She shook her head. "I don't understand you." Her exasperation, her confusion, were plain in her tone of voice. "Why do you keep doing this if it's so difficult for you?"

Because he knew he'd eventually tempt her into his bed. But he wasn't fool enough to tell her that. "Why don't you take a quick shower, then come over for lunch and we'll discuss it?"

"Ben . . ."

Still holding her shoulders, Ben took a step away from her so they could both gather their wits. "The special today is a killer chicken salad on croissants, with fresh fruit." Maybe he could entice her with food, since his sexual techniques hadn't gotten her yet. At least, not beyond the moment.

But even before he'd finished the offer, she was shaking her head. "Can't." She bent to pick up her gloves, then pulled them back on. "I've got too much work to do yet."

"You've been working all morning."

"Yeah, and I haven't even started inside. I told you it'd take me at least a week to get everything unpacked and organized, but I want to at least get the kitchen done before bed."

So she wouldn't have to come to him for coffee in the morning? Ben frowned, annoyed and beyond sexual frustration.

Oblivious to his turmoil, Sierra swiped at her forehead, pushing her damp bangs out of her face. "I should have taken care of that first, but I wanted to be outside for a while. It makes it easier for me to think."

"You were thinking about me."

She didn't confirm or deny that. She gave him a level

look and said, "The sun feels good, and with the ground softened from the rain, pulling weeds is easier."

"You have to eat," Ben reasoned, disgruntled with her continued rejection. Every time he thought he'd made headway, she found a new reason to refuse him. "I'll help you after lunch. With two of us it won't take as long."

"No."

Ben gave her a long look. "I prefer your moans to your refusals, you know."

Hands on her hips, she stared down at the ground for a few seconds before replying. "Look, I don't want you to feel obligated to help me just because we were . . . well"—she glanced at him and gestured helplessly—"fooling around."

"Who's fooling?" Ben bent to brush a soft kiss over her mouth. In a low whisper, he said, "I'm very serious about making you moan."

It took her a few seconds after his kiss to get her eyes opened again. She sighed. "You're very good at it, too."

"Thanks."

"But that's just it." She turned and walked away, heading toward the front of the lot. "With you around, I doubt I'd get any real work done."

Annoyed, Ben followed her. She wanted to put distance between them, both physical and emotional. He was doubly determined not to let her.

Just as she reached the front of the building, he caught her shoulder and brought her around fast and hard into his chest. She grunted with the impact, started to object, and Ben caught the back of her neck, then bent to kiss her again before she could pull away.

His last kiss had been gentle. This one was hungry, meant to gain her cooperation.

Sierra held herself rigid, her mouth tightly closed, for about three seconds before she made a small sound of surprise, and her lips softened. Ben took instant advantage, thrusting his tongue inside, tasting her deeply. But kissing her affected him, too, and the kiss slowly became deep and hot and devouring.

He didn't want to stop, but knew he had to.

Against her lips, he whispered, "Indulge me on this, Sierra. Have lunch with me; let me help you unpack."

She dropped her forehead to his chest. Ben could feel her warm breath on his flesh, through the open collar of his shirt.

He shuddered.

Retrenching rather than pushing her, he released her and stepped back.

She looked warm, confused. Beautiful.

"I'll give you fifteen minutes. Be neighborly, honey. Don't disappoint me, okay?" He left before he said anything more. It wasn't his plan to beg her or even cajole her. He wanted her to want what he offered enough that she'd give in to him. On everything.

When he stepped into the motel, he turned and glanced back through the window. He could just barely see Sierra, still standing where he'd left her in her yard. She hadn't moved an inch. He smiled in satisfaction.

Until he heard his grandmother's strident, outraged voice behind him. "Ben Badwin, you get more disreputable by the day. Have you no sense of decorum at all?"

Ben cringed but quickly wiped all expression from his face. He turned, fashioned a mocking grin, and said, "Hey Aggie. What the hell are you doing here?"

Chapter Seven

Sierra's work gloves had left dirt on his shirt and in his hair. He'd taken time to change and clean up, but his temper hadn't cooled at all. The very last thing he wanted to do was visit with his cantankerous grandmother. He'd intended to sweet-talk Sierra, to do a little more verbal foreplay while they shared an intimate lunch.

Now he had to contend with Agatha Harper.

Hoping to end her visit before Sierra arrived, Ben hurried through the motel and into the diner by way of the kitchen. He was dismayed, and satisfied, to see Sierra standing in the front doorway. At once, she made eye contact with him. Looking resigned, she started in his direction. Shit.

He'd finally gotten her to come to him, but he couldn't give her his full attention.

Agatha sat at a booth, her back rigid, her gray head

held erect, her aristocratic face twisted in distaste as if she expected to find a cockroach in her seat. Like he would have bugs in his place.

Ben ground his teeth together and walked past Aggie to greet Sierra. She was halfway through the diner when she caught his frown, and faltered.

The second Ben reached her, she asked, "What's wrong?"

She'd showered and changed into work-worn jeans that sported holes in the knees, a sleeveless white blouse and ratty sneakers. Her damp hair hung loose to her shoulders and sure enough, she'd gotten too much sun. Her nose, forehead, and cheekbones were pink.

She was the most irresistible female he'd ever known. "My grandmother showed up."

"Oh." Her smile was forced. "I'm sure you want to chat with her. We can do lunch another time. You know I need to work anyway."

He'd been anticipating that reply, even counting on it. But now, being perverse, he said, "No. My visit with her won't take long. You can wait for me in the break room. Okay?"

She started to reply, then her gaze drifted from his face to look over his shoulder. He could tell by her expression just exactly what—or rather whom—she saw. Annoyance swamped him, and he turned.

"Aggie." Wearing his most enigmatic expression, Ben brought Sierra forward. He and his grandmother had called a tacit truce of late. They still twitted each other, but there was no real bite to their antagonism, and in fact, Ben often thought she enjoyed bantering with him. Given the bloom in her wrinkled cheeks, she enjoyed cursing, too, a new vice for Aggie, which she blamed on him.

With their easier camaraderie, he hoped to get through this meeting without any bloodshed. Not always a possibility; sometimes it seemed Agatha deliberately sent his temper through the roof. "This is Sierra Murphy. She works across the street."

Agatha's sharp speculation landed on Sierra, making Ben stiffen. "Yes, well, your definition of *work* needs help, young man."

Sierra puckered up in umbrage. She looked between him and his grandmother. "Just what does that mean?"

"Aggie . . ." Ben put as much warning in his tone as he dared, considering they stood in the middle of the diner. Agatha could be unpredictable, and already they were drawing attention. Sierra had opened a new business. He wouldn't let his grandmother say or do anything to damage her reputation. He took his grandmother's arm and started her toward the kitchen. "Let's go, Sierra. We can talk back here."

In military fashion, her pique plain to see, Sierra marched behind them. Agatha just sniffed and allowed herself to be led like a queen.

The break room was empty, and Sierra immediately dropped into a chair. Ben kept one eye on his grandmother as he instructed the cook to bring them each a Coke and three plates of the day's special.

As soon as the cook was gone, Sierra leaned forward, her arms on the long table, her pride in evidence. "I know that my business doesn't look polished yet, but I only just opened yesterday and then the storm hit. I can tell you, no one works harder than I do."

Realizing that Sierra had totally misunderstood his grandmother's innuendo, Ben choked.

Agatha corrected that posthaste. "I saw you both through

the motel window. Quite shameful behavior. You were cavorting there for everyone to see."

Sierra shot upright. "Cavorting?" Her wide eyes slanted toward Ben, then narrowed dangerously. "People could see us?"

Pleased with her results, Agatha motioned Sierra back into her seat. "No one noticed but me, however the fact is that anyone might have."

Twin spots of heated color pulsed on Sierra's face. Ben growled. "All we did was kiss." He prayed that was all Agatha had seen.

"Kissing should be done in private." She looked at Sierra. "You would be well advised not to let my grandson corrupt you. I've noticed that where the females are concerned, he knows no moderation. And of course they don't help matters any by throwing themselves at him."

She was trying to warn Sierra off. Ben lost his temper and slammed a fist down on the table. Sierra jumped, but Agatha seemed unmoved. "Don't go there, Aggie." If she wanted to talk about corrupted men, he could bring Pierce's name up real quick.

She gave him a cool look. "Noah would be appalled."

"Baloney. Noah would understand, believe me." His half brother had thoroughly debauched Grace before marrying her. Grace had enjoyed every second of it.

Sierra looked between them. "Understand what?"

"Noah," Agatha said, still addressing Ben, "was in love. Do you have the same excuse?"

Ben drew back, no appropriate reply coming to mind—and the cook appeared, presenting their food with a ludicrous flourish considering where he worked and the casual atmosphere of the diner. "Here we are. Eat up, and enjoy."

Sierra ventured cautiously toward conversation. "Thank you. It looks delicious."

Horace, Ben's cook since he'd opened, grinned widely. "And tastes delicious, you'll see. Ben here knows you need good food to make a diner work. He's a sharp one." With that, Horace went back through the door to the kitchen, wiping his hands on his apron.

Agatha inspected her food, forked one tiny piece of chicken salad, chewed thoughtfully, and then tipped her head in approval. "Very tasty."

It amazed Ben how much her approval pleased him. "You expected gruel?"

She forked another bite. "Did Grace tell you to call me?"

"Yeah."

"Then why didn't you?"

Ben flopped into his seat and picked up a ripe melon ball with his fingertips. He popped it into his mouth. "The phone line goes both ways. Besides, I was busy."

Full of righteous disdain, Agatha said, "There's this wonderfully civilized invention, Benjamin. It's called a fork."

Sierra choked on a laugh. When Ben glared at her, she blurted, "Who's Noah?"

"He's my brother." And with a look, Ben dared Agatha to say any more on the subject. She pinched her mouth shut.

"Do you have big family get-togethers?"

Ben laughed. "Hardly."

To Ben's discomfort, Agatha looked wounded, and he regretted the gibe. Since Noah and Grace had married, she'd been trying to be less spiteful—and she'd openly accepted him. The thing was, he didn't think he was ready to let it go. Not when she still didn't accept his mother; not when they'd never really discussed the past.

"We aren't a large group," Agatha explained. "My son, Pierce, died some time ago."

Full of sympathy, Sierra said quietly, "Oh, I'm so sorry." She turned to Ben. "Your mother is a widow?"

"No." He shook his head, wondered how to explain, then gave up. "She was never married to my father."

Agatha gasped. "Ben! Must you air our dirty laundry?"

"*Your* dirty laundry." As usual, the subject filled him with churning resentment. "My mother has nothing to be ashamed of."

Their gazes clashed for a suspended moment before Agatha faced Sierra. She gathered her aplomb with an effort. "There are only my two grandsons, my granddaughter-in-law, Grace, and myself."

Sierra looked both sympathetic and unsure, and no wonder. She'd inadvertently gotten caught in the ongoing family squabble—not that Ben really considered himself part of Agatha's family. Well, sometimes he did, but more often than not . . .

Sierra's foot touched his beneath the table.

Ben's turbulent gaze shot up, locked on hers, and her smile soothed him like a soft stroke. She didn't say anything, and their silent exchange hadn't been obvious, but Ben felt comforted by her presence. He couldn't recall any other lover who'd affected him that way.

Drawing a calming breath, he stared at Agatha. "I was going to call you later on today. Did you need something?"

She glanced pointedly at Sierra. "I have private business to discuss."

"Oh, of course."

Sierra started to push back her chair, but Ben caught her hand before she could dismiss herself. "Go ahead. I'm listening."

"Ben, really," Sierra said in a rush. "I don't mind . . ."

"My grandmother and I have no private business. Isn't that right, Aggie?"

Agatha wasn't a woman to be intimidated. "Fine." She pushed her plate away and folded her hands on the table-top. "I need you to attend a meeting with my lawyers."

Ben stiffened, inadvertently crushing Sierra's hand in his. "Why?"

A sort of wary caution crept across her features, though she tried to hide it behind bravado. "I've changed my will and I need you to look things over before we finalize it."

"Forget it." He realized he gripped Sierra's hand too hard and released her. Feeling turbulent, he stood to pace.

"I will not forget it." Agatha too, came to her feet. "You're only being stubborn. If you'd just look things over . . ."

He flashed her an irascible glare. "Not interested, Aggie."

They squared off over the table, both of them stiff, both of them too damn proud. Ben couldn't bring himself to relent, so finally Agatha had to. "You are the most stubborn, hot-tempered, prideful person I know."

"Damn, think anyone will notice we're related?"

She huffed and her tone became imperious. "All right, know this you scamp."

"Scamp?" Ben did a double take. "What the hell kind of insult is that?" He laughed in genuine amusement. "Scamp, huh? You're slipping, old girl."

Agatha frowned so hard, Ben thought she might have given herself new wrinkles. "I'm making my will out as I see fit, and you can't do a thing about it." Her chin rose, regal even in her anger. "If you choose not to take part, that's your business."

"I'll throw it away," he promised, his humor dulled by her insistence. Agatha had only recently claimed him as her grandson, and she had yet to speak civilly to his mother. What Ben wanted from her, respect and a full acknowledgement of what her son had done to his mother, she wasn't willing to give. So he'd take nothing.

"You can't throw it away." Such a sentiment obviously stunned her. "Don't be absurd."

"Whatever it is, whatever you leave to me, I swear to you, Aggie, I'll toss it."

"Fine." Her voice lowered, her anger smoldering. "It'll be yours to do with as you please. If it pleases you to be so wasteful, then that's what you'll do. But you *will* get your share of my wealth." In a regal huff, Agatha turned and swept out of the room.

Ben watched her go, annoyed, offended, perplexed, then he slammed a chair into the table. *"Goddammit."*

Sierra sat in stunned silence. He struggled to get himself together.

"Jesus, I don't believe this." Trying to blow off his anger, but unable to manage it, Ben ran a hand through his hair. He glanced at Sierra, saw she watched him closely, and wanted to groan. "I'm sorry, Sierra. It's just that she takes every opportunity to rile me."

Sierra tipped up her Coke, ice cubes clinking, and finished it off. She was the only one who'd eaten all of her lunch. Sitting back, her hands laced over her full stomach, she said, "Looked to me like you both excel at annoying each other."

Ben grimaced. He hadn't exactly shown her his better side. "Yeah, you can say that again." Briefly, he wondered if anything interfered with Sierra's appetite. But then, she worked damn hard and probably burned off a lot of calories that had to be replaced. "I seem to be the only one who won't go out of my way to placate her."

"Maybe that's why you're special to her."

Ben almost laughed. "Special? Hell, most times she acts like she wants to box my ears."

Sierra smiled with the faintest hint of amusement. "I noticed. But at the same time, she's set on taking care of you. If she didn't love you, you wouldn't be able to rile her."

Ben didn't let himself dwell on that possibility. He and Agatha would never see eye to eye, and he'd be damned if he'd let the differences bother him. "Did you enjoy the meal, if not the company?"

"Actually the food was delicious, and the company was . . . fascinating." She scrutinized him. "I'd already assumed your grandmother was rich, but seeing her confirms it."

"Rich? Yeah, extravagantly. So is my brother, Noah."

"But not you?"

He pulled up a chair next to her, wishing he could change the subject. "Does it matter to you?"

Her jaw locked and her eyes narrowed. "Yes, it matters. I'm not real partial to wealthy people who think they own the world."

Ben whistled. Now what did that mean? "You've known a few, have you?"

Her mouth set, and he knew she wouldn't answer him. More secrets. Sierra had a way of keeping his curiosity keen and his determination throbbing. Sooner or later, he'd get her figured out.

He held out his arms. "Well, you can rest easy on that score, sweetheart. I'm as poor as they come."

She grunted. "Yeah right. You own your own motel."

"Right now, the motel still owns me." He smiled at her. "And as for rich people, you're right about my grandmother. She expects her money to get her just about anything she wants—including me. But she does have the occasional moment that proves she's human with a touch of sensitivity. Plus she loves Noah to distraction. And despite being rich, Noah is as real as they get. He's a good man."

Sierra frowned again, but not for the reasons Ben suspected. "Well, so are you. Doesn't your grandmother know that?"

Ben grinned. Damn, but she was defending him. Now that definitely felt like progress. "It's a long story, and I'd rather seduce you than discuss my family foibles."

She caught his hand before it could land on her knee. With a chastising shake of her head, she placed it on the table. "I've got work to do, remember?"

Like she'd let him forget. Ben gave her a mocking grin and asked, "Did you think I'd lay you out on my break room table? People eat in here."

She flushed, but grumbled, "With you, I never know."

Ben eyed the table. "Then again . . ."

She surprised him by laughing, and even that made him hot. Ben decided she didn't laugh often enough. He'd have to see what he could do about that.

"Your mother is very different from your grandmother."

She'd made that comment as a statement, but Ben heard all her unasked questions. "I suppose you're wondering about that little exchange concerning her?"

She gave her attention to her empty glass. "I don't want to pry."

Despite her averted gaze, her curiosity was plain to see. She was so transparent, so unique, she lightened his mood just by being herself. "Not a nosy bone in your sweet little body, huh?"

She poked him in the ribs.

"Okay. Here's the short version: Pierce Harper, my father, Agatha's son, got my mom pregnant when she was barely sixteen; then he walked. Wanted nothing to do with her or me." He tried to make the telling as simplified as possible, with no emotional inflection. "It wasn't the first time he'd abandoned one of his children, either. At least when I was born, I had my mom looking out for me."

"You're really close to her, aren't you?"

"Yeah." Ben smiled, thinking how obvious that was to everyone. His mother freely showered him with affection, and she loved to hug and compliment and praise. "Though I never met Pierce, and didn't meet Agatha until I was fourteen, not once did I ever feel neglected or want for anything important." He looked up at Sierra. "Noah wasn't so lucky. He didn't have anyone. Sometimes it rips me apart to think about what he went through as a kid."

Sierra leaned off her seat and curled into Ben. Surprised at such a show of comfort from her, especially when she usually chose to push him away, Ben said, "Hey," and tried to tip her back.

She wouldn't let him—and Ben suddenly wondered if she was offering comfort, or taking it. "What happened to Noah?"

Ben enjoyed holding her, so why fight it? He spread his hands over her narrow back and rubbed his chin against the top of her head. Her hair was very soft and smelled like flowers. "It's amazing that Noah's such a good man, considering he grew up in a string of foster homes, sometimes even on the streets." Remembering made Ben agitated all over again. It literally sickened him to think of what his brother had gone through, how basic his survival had been. All because their father had been a selfish, irresponsible son of a bitch.

"I'm sorry."

Ben heard her sincerity and returned her hug. "He was alone his whole life until Pierce died and Agatha decided she needed an heir."

Horrified, Sierra leaned back to stare at him. "She knew about him all along, but didn't do anything about him?"

Ben shrugged. "She'd always suspected Pierce of less than honorable behavior, so she hired a detective to check around." Ben rubbed her back, nestled her closer to his heart. "She only wanted one heir, Sierra. She didn't even mean to find me, but she didn't call off the private detective fast enough and before she knew it, she was saddled with one grandson too many."

Sierra again pushed back to see his face. "She refused you?" She looked as though she found that prospect impossible to believe.

"Pretty much, yeah. I'll admit I had a huge chip on my shoulder. I didn't even want to meet her, but my mother had encouraged me to give her a chance because she said you can't have too much family."

"Sometimes it's better to have no family at all."

Ben wondered at how she said that, at what her own family situation might be. She sounded far too grave, too . . . hurt. Was she an only child? Estranged from her parents?

She fascinated him, and he wanted to know everything about her, what made her smile and what made her sad. Why a woman so sensual seemed determined to deny herself? But every time he tried to know her better, she closed down on him. Ben decided he'd have to earn her trust before she'd share herself, and he supposed the best way to do that was to share parts of himself first.

"I think Mom worried that if anything ever happened to her, I'd be alone, just as Noah had always been. So I met Agatha—and my only brother." Ben smiled, remembering his adolescent fascination with Noah. "We hit it right off. I had a bad case of hero worship and Noah fell right into the role of big brother. And when I say big, I mean big. He was seventeen then, but every bit a man. Quiet, strong, and . . . I dunno. It's hard to explain but Noah's always been a little like a wild animal. Not reckless, just dangerous. And powerful, with or without our grandmother's money and influence. He intimidates everyone. Well, except Grace, but no one intimidates Gracie, and besides, she loves him."

Sierra idly traced a circular pattern on Ben's chest, distracting him from his explanations. She seemed very pensive. "You've been close with Noah ever since?"

"Real close. We may differ on Agatha, but I respect him more than any other man I know."

"I can certainly understand why." She continued to caress him, but it was negligent, as if she were unaware of it, while Ben was very, very aware. "I take it Noah gets along well with your grandmother?"

Ben laughed. "More like he humors her out of a sense of obligation to family—something he takes very seriously. But he has an undeniable fondness for her, too. She gave him a home, stability, and that means a lot to Noah. And since his marriage, she's softened a lot, with Grace's help."

Sierra's fingers slipped inside the collar of his shirt, touching his throat. "Maybe you can help her to soften even more."

Ben closed his eyes and concentrated on their conversation. She was practically in his lap, freely stroking him, and his body wanted more. Much more. "We started out antagonistic, and haven't gotten beyond that yet. Not entirely. I can't even say it's all her fault." Ben caught her teasing fingers and held them in his own. "At fourteen, I had a monumental chip on my shoulder. I deliberately provoked her every chance I had."

"No way!" Her facetious teasing made Ben smile. "I just can't imagine you provoking anyone, Ben. You're always so proper and polite."

Ben squeezed her for her impertinence, and she laughed.

"So you both antagonized each other and you're letting it affect your relationship still?"

"It's a little more complicated than that. You see, Agatha tried to insist I have a blood test done, to see if I really was her grandson. She refused to take my mother's word for it."

Sierra curled her fingers in his. "I can understand why that would anger you. But she accepts you now. She made that clear."

"True. But she's still stiff-necked about my mother. Much as Mom says it doesn't matter, it matters to me."

"And it should."

Ben drew a deep breath, relieved that she understood. "I won't take anything from her. She's trying to mend fences, I know. As I said, Noah getting married softened her a lot, and she's feeling her age, dealing with some health issues. There are times when we get along just fine." He ran his free hand through his hair. "Hell, I don't know. I feel like a real bastard for not cutting her more slack, but she just pushes my buttons on some issues, you know?"

"Maybe you should try sitting down and telling her how you feel? I can't say I know you real well. And what I do know—well, it's hardly applicable to family relationships, is it?"

Ben grinned. "Speaking of the ways you know me . . ."

She interrupted him, set on her course. "But you're a nice guy, Ben, and you have the ability to charm any female, young or old."

"Is that right?"

"Being that I'm sitting here with you, instead of working as I should be, I'd say so."

"Have I charmed you, sweetheart?"

Sierra pushed him away when he tried to kiss her, but Ben could see she wanted to laugh. More progress.

"You're capable of being generous. And she's not exactly young. If you know she's proud and set in her ways, maybe you could be the one to initiate things." She stopped, then shook her head. "Once someone's gone, so is your chance to make amends. I'd hate to see you have regrets."

It seemed every damn thing she said had some grave, deep meaning to it. She was the most complex, restrained woman he'd ever met, and, rather than annoying him, it tugged at his heart.

Ben put his hand on her knee again, inside a frayed tear so he could touch her silky skin. "Have dinner with me tonight and we can discuss it."

"We just finished lunch."

"And you enjoyed yourself, didn't you?"

She saw right through his ploy. "You're incorrigible."

"And charming?"

She rolled her eyes, aggrieved. "Yes, I enjoyed myself. But that's not the point. You run your own business, Ben. You know the job requires my attention twenty-four/seven, at least until I get established."

Stubborn to the core. Ben shook his head, but he wouldn't let her reticence bother him. She'd relent once she got to know him better. He'd see to it. "I do understand, which is why you should let me help."

"Help me how?"

"In any way I can. Unpacking, cleaning. Maybe I can even give you a few business tips. What do you think of that?"

She didn't budge. "I think you're used to having your own way and don't know how to take no for an answer."

"Guilty." Ben cupped her cheek. "And I think you've

gotten so independent, you don't know how to accept freely offered help."

She stared at him, her expression tense.

Ben softened. "Come on, honey. Use me."

She rolled her eyes and gave up with a growled laugh. "All right. *For work.*"

"Exactly." Ben followed her as she strolled out of the room. He watched her hips, her lengthy stride, and whispered to himself, so low that she couldn't hear, "For now."

Chapter Eight

Filled with churning frustration, Agatha paced around her library. Damn, this was like déjà vu. Noah had once driven her to pacing, too, and she hated to pace. She hated to fret. Before getting involved with her grandsons—handsome devils, both of them—she'd always known her own mind, always known what she wanted to do, what was right, what was proper.

Now they had her second-guessing herself all the time.

It was invigorating when it didn't annoy her so much.

Her grandsons . . . Well, they were something else, with the Harper pride and initiative but some other less-sterling qualities as well. Like stubbornness and independence and a tendency to disagree just for the fun of it.

Many of her friends were wary of her older grandson, Noah, because of his unfortunate background. There was an edge of darkness about him, a barely leashed power gained from an early life of poverty and abuse. Remembering that, knowing how he'd suffered because of her neglect, made Agatha hurt down deep in her old bones.

She paced a little more vigorously, trying to outrun her own personal demons. Noah was with her now and that was all that mattered. Except that she needed Ben to be with her one hundred percent as well.

She thought of Ben and found herself with an unwilling smile. Immediately her mood lightened. Ben was the polar opposite of Noah. Though they were both hard workers, dedicated to their livelihoods, Ben was carefree where Noah was intense, playful while Noah was forever planning. Though they were half brothers, they were now as close as if they'd been raised side by side.

Outrageous, impudent, full of teasing charm, Ben was such a handful. The ladies loved him, of course, and he was rascal enough that he loved them right back. He was a complete and utter hedonist when it came to his leisure time, but unlike his father, he was always discreet. Except for today. Except with that young woman she'd met.

She'd seen Ben kissing her with a total disregard for their location.

Still, Agatha knew that no matter how carried away Ben might get, no matter how passionate he might feel toward a woman, he would always behave responsibly. Never would Benjamin disregard a woman's feelings, and never would he abandon one of his children—as her son had done. Twice.

The shame of it nearly suffocated Agatha. No, if Ben got a woman pregnant, he'd insist on marrying her, or at the very least fulfill his financial obligations. Beyond his mocking facade of endless good humor, he had an honor that came straight from his heart.

He'd gotten that from his mother, Agatha knew, because he sure as hell hadn't inherited it from Pierce. Her son had been a disappointment, but still she'd loved him. So much.

Agatha sighed. There was no changing the past, but she did her best to make the future right. If only Ben wouldn't keep refusing her financial goodwill. She had enough wealth to make his life easier, safer, more comfortable.

But he seemed to take berserk pleasure in refusing her.

He also underestimated her far too often. Did he think she was blind? Did he think she was so damn old she couldn't see what was right before her face anymore?

She said, "Ha!" all to herself.

Nothing got by her. *Nothing.*

Oh, Ben didn't know it, but she'd been aware of them playing footsies under the table, of the intimate looks that had passed between them.

Noah had reacted the same way to Grace—and that had enabled Agatha to mend fences. She freely admitted to herself that she'd used Grace as a cushion to soften the backlash of their disagreements.

Perhaps, given Ben's over-the-top behavior, it'd be the same with . . . What was her name? Something different. Yes, Sierra. An interesting name for the tattered little red-haired female. Agatha smiled. What the girl lacked in proper attire, she made up for with spunk. Nothing seemed to really shock her. She'd sat through their argument without once involving herself.

Ben needed a woman with backbone, because God knew he wasn't always that easy to get along with. And though he'd been raised without the luxuries she could give him, he had more than his fair share of arrogance and determination. She liked that about him. Even his irreverence amused her and made her proud.

Damn it, he would be in her will. He would accept her benevolence because no matter what he said, no matter how he felt, it was rightfully his. She didn't want her money, her holdings, going to strangers, and there was no reason for Noah to take it all.

She smiled. Noah didn't really need it, either. He'd done so well for himself. But her grandsons would take what she had to give, even if she had to use underhanded methods to force it on them.

Agatha made a sudden decision. She'd give it a little time, make certain of Ben's feelings, and if he stayed infatuated with the young ragamuffin, she'd pay a call on her. Sierra could be her ally, just as Grace had been. It'd all work out.

It had to. She wasn't getting any younger, damn it.

Sierra looked around her small home with undeniable pride. For the past seven days she'd started at dawn and worked well into the night, but today she could finally take a break.

Her home wasn't impressive by anyone's standards. It bordered on sparse with only a few pieces of furniture, along with the necessary desk and computer equipment she used for the business. But it was enough for her. The living area was so small, it wouldn't have held much anyway, and besides, she'd never been one to enjoy clutter.

Now, thanks to all her efforts—and Ben's constant assistance—everything was clean and neatly organized and functional. Best of all, it all belonged to her.

She'd never had her own house. She'd gone from being her father's daughter, living under his dominant will, to marriage, under her husband's twisted control. Since then she'd lived so frugally, even the smallest apartment was a stretch. Finally, she would be her own boss, with no one to order her around, and no one dictating to her. *No one.*

Ben stepped up behind her. "What are you thinking?"

Startled, Sierra twisted to see him. Well, there was Ben. No way could she discount him and his overwhelming presence. But she knew what Ben wanted—and it had nothing to do with bullying her.

It seemed every time she turned around, he was there, smiling at her, teasing, trying to feed her, kiss her, give her a helping hand. He made her nuts, and he made her hot. He most definitely distracted her. But he didn't get in her way. In fact, she had to be honest and admit that he'd been an enormous help.

Since moving in, her spare time had been slim to nonexistent, yet Ben managed to show up every time she stopped to rest, and more often than not, he had food with him.

Maybe the way to her heart was through her stomach, because she had started feeling very softhearted around him.

That was a surprise, but an even bigger surprise was that Ben hadn't tried to talk her into bed again. He touched her and kissed her and left her with no doubts that he wanted her, to the point that she wasn't certain she could take it anymore. But he didn't push beyond that. He seemed to understand that she needed time to get used to him and the effect he had on her.

The only problem was that she'd begun to realize she'd never get used to Ben. He left her so unsettled she could barely think, unless she was thinking of him.

Today, he'd come over while she was struggling with her software program, inputting the latest bids on jobs, and the money she'd already been paid. Indoor office work was her least favorite, so she wasn't in the most pleasant of moods. With a total lack of regard for her privacy, Ben had looked over her shoulder, promptly proclaimed her software garbage, and then shown her the accounting software he preferred.

Because she liked it and found it to be much simpler than the one she'd been using, he loaded it into her computer. He even went to the trouble to transfer all the data for her. It had taken him half the time she would have needed to do the same thing. His computer skills far surpassed hers.

It seemed that every day she learned something new about him, and everything she learned added to his allure.

One side of Ben's mouth kicked up. "Why are you looking at me like that?"

Bemused by her own introspection, Sierra shook her head. "No reason."

"I asked you what you were thinking."

"You did?"

He slowly nodded, his gaze on her mouth, and Sierra knew he was going to kiss her. After the path her thoughts had just taken, that might prove unwise. So she blurted a reply. "My freedom."

"What?"

"I was thinking of my . . . freedom."

He rubbed his thumb on her jaw. He was forever touching her—and she liked it.

"Just what the hell does that mean?"

Wanting to kick herself for saying too much, Sierra lifted her shoulders. "Nothing. I'm just happy to be in my own place."

Too shrewd for his own good, Ben turned thoughtful. "Did you and your husband live with your father?"

"No." She shook her head a bit too adamantly, but the idea of living with her father during her marriage—oh, no. She shuddered. "Griffin's father gave him a down payment for a small house."

While he'd worked on the computer, she'd cleaned her floors and baseboards and under her sink. Ben pushed aside a pile of her cleaning rags and leaned back on a countertop, then pulled her between his legs. He loosely draped his arms over her shoulders in a casual and now familiar embrace.

He'd gradually taken more liberties with her, and she'd gradually allowed him that privilege. "Griffin? That's your ex?"

"Yes."

"You've never talked about him much."

They had discussed her plans for the future, especially where the landscaping business was concerned. Ben had shared his own plans for some day buying a house so he could live separate from the motel. But she'd steered clear of anything that touched on her past, and he hadn't pried. Until now.

"There's no reason to talk about Griff. He's old news."

"He kept the house when you divorced him?"

"Yes."

Sierra tried to edge away from him, but he clasped the back of her neck, massaging the tense muscles there.

His touch never failed to affect her and she had to struggle to keep her wits. "Why all the questions now?"

"Just curious."

She frowned, determined to avoid certain topics. "Don't be."

Ben let her pull away. She walked to the opposite side of the minuscule kitchen and opened the fridge. She'd bought food as she needed it, but now that things were in order she really needed to stock up. "I suppose I should make a list of stuff to get from the grocery, huh?"

Her attempt to change the subject brought on a heavy silence. Sierra glanced back at Ben. He watched her so closely, his gaze probing, unsettling. He wanted to read her mind, to know her every secret. No way would she let him do that. He couldn't get that close.

She gave him her back.

"Come here, Sierra."

Drawn by the sound of that compelling voice, she froze. Still not looking at him, she squeaked, "Why?"

"I want to kiss you."

Her heart gave a heavy thump in anticipation. Ben's kisses were addictive and the more she got, the more she wanted. She closed the refrigerator and gave him a suspicious look. "Just a kiss?"

His smile enticed, his eyes darkened. "No, of course not. One kiss with you is never enough. You already know that."

True enough. Whenever he kissed her once, she wanted more until finally he would call a halt, because she never could.

Knees turning into noodles, her heart soaring, Sierra succumbed. Just that easy, just by the tone of his voice and the look in his eyes, he aroused her. She'd had no idea she was such a sexual person. Her indrawn breath was shaky, giving her away. It should have embarrassed her, the way she reacted so strongly whenever Ben got near.

She walked to him.

Satisfaction curved his hard mouth. That damn irresistible dimple appeared, accompanying the dark flame in his eyes with devastating effect.

He pulled her close and nuzzled below her ear. "Kent's gone for the night?"

"Yes." Kent spent his spare time working at Brooke Badwin's. To Sierra, it seemed he took inordinate pleasure in spending time at her place.

Ben smiled. "He's driving my mom crazy."

"And vice versa."

He laughed. "I think she likes him; she just doesn't want to like him."

Sierra knew how she felt, because she had the same quandary with Ben. "Kent is a good man."

"I'm not arguing with you." He smoothed her hair back from her face, grinning wickedly. "If I thought otherwise, I wouldn't find this so entertaining. I've never seen my mom so befuddled. It's good for her."

Sierra could only stare at Ben. He stunned her. No man should be so damn sexy, so adept at lovemaking, and be able to handle any chore with ease. He ran his own business, loved his mother to distraction, and was generous to a fault. He was far too perfect to be taken seriously.

Sierra wasn't at all sure it was fair to pack so much emotional wallop into one exquisite body. How was any woman supposed to resist him?

With melting intent, his breath soft and warm, he licked her ear, and Sierra realized she wasn't supposed to resist. A man like Ben came along once in a lifetime. Only a complete fool would waste such an opportunity.

The trick would be to enjoy him, without getting emotionally trapped.

The sun had already started its descent into the horizon. Sierra didn't have air-conditioning, so her home was warm despite the fan in the window stirring the less humid evening air. Ben's richly scented body heat encompassed her, turned her bones liquid, her mind into mush.

"Let's call it a day, sweetheart." His voice dropped to a low rumble. "I'm dying to lie down with you."

Sierra, already lost, went over the edge with the husky way he said that. She was about to groan out her agreement when her phone gave a loud jingle. Since it seldom rang after business hours, she nearly jumped out of her skin.

Ben sighed in resignation as she stepped away to answer it. "Hello?" She listened, frowned, then said, "Sure. Um, just a sec."

Shrugging, she handed the phone to Ben. "It's for you."

"Me?" Wearing a frown, he took the receiver from her. "Ben Badwin here." The frown lifted, replaced with a warm smile. "Hey, Gracie. What's up?"

Grace? Sierra remembered the name. She was Ben's sister-in-law, married to the awesome Noah. Ben's family wasn't big, but they did all sound impressive in one way or another. Perhaps it was the love Ben felt, and the way he spoke of them, that made them seem so.

Since her father's passing a year ago, she'd had no family at all.

Ben listened, made a face, and cursed. "Well, hell. Have you tried . . . Well, what about . . . I see." He groaned in disappointment, which Sierra assumed meant she'd be disappointed as well. "Yeah, all right. I'll be right there. Thanks, babe."

Sierra stiffened. "Babe?"

He gave her a quick look and replaced the receiver in the cradle. "My sister-in-law." Laughing, he chucked her under the chin. "Grace is a babe and an employee. Much to Noah's annoyance, she works as a waitress for me."

That sent her thoughts in a new direction. "I thought you said Noah was rich."

"He is."

The suspicion in her voice proved unavoidable. "But he makes his wife work as a waitress?"

"*Make* Grace work?" Ben gave her a piercing glance. "Hell, no. He can't make her do anything. If you'd ever met Grace, you'd already know how silly that is." Ben tipped his head, scrutinizing her. "He wouldn't even want to try to force Grace to do something she doesn't want to do. Believe me. But he loves her, so when she insists on working for me—and she is the one insisting, Sierra—well, he tries not to grumble too much about it."

Knowing she'd given herself away again, Sierra flushed. All she could think to say was "Oh."

Ben looped his arms around her waist with his hands resting on her bottom. She started to object to that, but then he arched her pelvis into his in a casual, yet secure embrace, and she forgot her objections. "You want to tell me why you made such an asinine assumption?"

She might have been insulted if she hadn't been more concerned with evading his questions. "No."

Ben looked far too serious for her peace of mind.

"Sierra." He gently rocked her. "Why would you assume any man would try to force a woman to—"

"Let's go to bed." The blurted words hung heavy in the air between them. Sierra winced. She'd wanted to distract him—and she definitely wanted to have sex with him—but she was stunned by her own audacity.

Surprise, hot desire, and finally regret passed over Ben's features. Pressing his forehead to hers, Ben groaned. "Damn. That is by far the nicest offer I've ever had, and there's nothing I want more than to stay here with you and taste you from your ears down to your toes."

Taste her?

"But two people called in sick and Grace is swamped. She tried calling in two other people but struck out." He rubbed her back. "I'm so sorry, sweetheart, but I have to leave."

Common sense told Sierra that she'd just escaped by the skin of her teeth. It was better that he leave now before her unruly mouth gave away any more secrets. She hadn't even known him that long and already she'd let slip things that were better left buried.

Knowing it was best didn't stop the disappointment, though. She'd only just decided that it was safe to let him a little further into her life. "It's all right." How could she not respect Ben's sense of responsibility to his business, when he'd respected hers?

Keeping her pressed to his body, he asked, "What are you doing tomorrow?"

Excitement of a different kind filled her. "If the weather forecast is right, I'll be working all day. I should be able to get the finishing touches on Parker's Point, then I have another estimate to give at a doctor's office." So far, the jobs had been steady, with another planned for when she finished with the good doctor. On a professional level, she couldn't have been happier.

She touched a button on Ben's polo shirt. "I won't be home till really late."

"And you'll no doubt be worn-out."

She pushed so hard that she stayed tired, but she hated to admit it so she just shrugged.

Ben smiled. "Can I bring you over something to eat when you get in?"

"Ben." Her automatic objection mingled with a laugh at his persistence. The man was just too outrageous, and damned if she wasn't starting to like it. "This is starting to become a habit."

"You don't hear me complaining. But for tomorrow, I have ulterior motives." The soft promise teased her lips.

Breathless, she said, "You do?"

"Hell yeah." He brushed her mouth with his. "I thought I'd let you eat"—his lips touched her ear, his tongue tickled, stroked and his voice dropped to a exciting rumble—"then I'd eat you."

Excitement exploded. Breathing became an impossibility. He said the most shocking, stimulating things and constantly kept her off balance.

His lips moved against her jaw, her chin, the corner of her mouth. "You'll come, Sierra, at least once. Maybe twice. Have you missed it? Because I have."

A groan bubbled up inside her. "Ben, I'm really not sure . . ."

His kiss turned hard. His hands slid to her bottom, caressing, grinding her into his pelvis so she could feel his semierection.

When he let her up for air, she was dizzy with need.

Sierra felt sure that once she gave in to Ben, the challenge would be gone and he wouldn't want her anymore. That thought made her chest feel tight, but at the same time she knew it'd be for the best.

They could still be friends, because Ben was friendly to everyone, especially the women he knew. But once she got him out of her system, then she could concentrate more on her future plans. They'd settle into being friendly neighbors, and that would suit her just fine.

All plausible reasons, Sierra thought, and said, "All right. Yes." She gulped air past the restriction in her throat. "That'd be wonderful."

Ben's eyes flared, his hands tightened. "Damn right." He stepped back, giving them both the chance to recover from that killer kiss. Half a minute passed before he'd regained his control. In that time, he watched her face with an intensity bordering on satisfaction. "I'm glad you're finally going to trust me a little. You won't regret it."

Her mouth fell open. "Trust you?"

He gave a sharp nod.

Sierra threw up her hands. "I didn't say anything about trusting you, Ben. I said I'd sleep with you."

"It's the same thing."

"It isn't!"

Exemplifying patience, he touched her cheek and explained. "If you didn't trust me, you wouldn't get involved with me."

Sierra trotted after him, determined to make her point. "We're not involved . . ."

He slanted her a look. "Yeah, we are."

"No!" They'd only fooled around a little. Or rather, a lot. Almost daily in fact. And he'd already claimed he wasn't fooling, but still . . . Surely, that didn't indicate any real involvement. Sierra squared her shoulders. "I never agreed to that, Ben. I agreed to . . . to . . ." *What the heck had she just agreed to?*

Ben pulled her to her tiptoes and kissed her. "Don't panic. I'm not asking you to elope with me."

Now why should that make her blush?

"But common courtesy dictates that while we're exploring all this intense sexual chemistry between us, we shouldn't be making time with anyone else. Right?"

Like she was supposed to believe he'd give up other women? Ridiculous. The man lived to flirt. Feeling cornered, she said, "I wouldn't ask you to do that."

"You don't have to ask. I don't want anyone else, and I'm assuming you don't either."

Ben waited, but when she just stared at him, unwilling to admit there was no one else, he continued. "That makes it exclusive and makes us involved. Which has to mean you trust me."

Sierra wasn't ready to agree to anything. "I'm going to have to think about this."

Ben smiled slowly. "You do that. And while you're at it, think about this." His mouth took hers, both tender and ravenous, his tongue moving against hers, his hands everywhere, stroking her, inciting her, until Sierra forgot what she'd objected to.

By slow degrees, he ended the kiss and Sierra struggled to open her heavy eyelids. When she did, she saw that Ben was just as affected.

"Damn. It's not going to go away, Sierra. At least admit that much." He touched her swollen bottom lip with apology. "I better go before Grace gets too overwhelmed." Their gazes locked. "I'll miss you tonight."

It took an effort, but Sierra rallied enough to snort at

that. She doubted Ben would miss any woman, and she wouldn't let herself start thinking impossible things.

"You little cynic," he teased with a laugh.

She was cynical, but with good reason. Any involvement carried risks that Ben would never understand. "Good-bye, Ben."

He stepped outside. "Think of me tonight, okay?"

Refusing to answer, Sierra watched him until the lengthening shadows swallowed him up. "As if I'll have any choice," she whispered to herself once he was out of sight.

She closed the door, dropped back against it, and wished like hell she could figure him out. Or figure herself out. She knew what she wanted, what she needed, and Ben didn't figure into that. He *couldn't* figure into it beyond a brief fling.

So, why was she already missing him?

She groaned, then jumped when her phone rang yet again. Thinking it had to be Grace intent on hurrying Ben along, Sierra answered with a smile. "Hello."

"Hey, baby. You been missin' me?"

Brittle, painful memories threatened to crash down on her. Her smile froze in place, the hand holding the phone trembled. Griff had found her.

Her first thought was, *Thank God, Ben has already left.* She didn't need his probing questions now.

Her second was to wonder how close Griff might be. Was he in Gillespe? Had he followed her? She glanced toward her darkened windows and visions of him just outside, perhaps looking in, sent a chill down her spine.

"You're so happy to hear from me that you're speechless, huh?"

It wasn't easy, but Sierra dredged up her strength and

her pride and her confidence. "You always were pathetic, Griff." She hung up the phone on his mean curse, not slamming it down, but settling it gently in the cradle.

Arms around herself, she dropped against the wall, her eyes wide, her thoughts whirling. He'd found her already when she had hoped he wouldn't bother.

Why had he? What did it matter to him? It didn't make sense.

She'd thought that moving out of state would satisfy him, put her far enough out of reach. But he'd called, and that had to mean . . . what?

He claimed she'd stolen his life by forcing him into marriage, then humiliated him by leaving. But what alternative had he given her? None.

She jerked around and took the phone off the hook. Oh no, he wouldn't call her again tonight. She wouldn't let him throw her off, wouldn't let him make a shambles of her life. Again.

Filled with renewed purpose, Sierra checked to make certain all the floodlights were on outside. She gazed through the darkness, but her yard looked as empty as ever. She checked the locks on her doors and windows and knew that was an expense she'd have to take care of immediately. But until then . . . she hesitated, her independent nature warring with common sense.

Common sense won out.

She set the telephone receiver in the cradle long enough to get a dial tone, then called Kent. By the sound of his voice, he'd been sound asleep. "H'lo?"

"Kent, I'm sorry to wake you."

He responded with a new alertness. "What's wrong?"

Sierra hated herself, hated Griff for his petty persistence. He'd chased off every friend she'd ever had, not that she'd had many. Only Kent had refused to budge. "He called."

"Griffin?"

"Yes. I guess he knows where I'm at."

"Fuck."

"He didn't threaten me or anything. Just asked me if I'd missed him, but . . ."

"I'll be right there. Don't answer the damn door until I show up, all right?"

Tears filled her eyes when she hadn't cried for so, so long. "Kent, I am sorry."

"Don't make me turn you over my knee, young lady." Sierra could tell he was dressing as he talked.

She smiled and wiped at her eyes, knowing that at least this threat was empty, a term of affection but no more. "All right. Thanks."

"Hang tight. I'm on my way out the door now."

He hung up and Sierra left the phone dangling off the hook. She turned out all the lights inside her small sanctuary and stood in front of the window, watching the yard. It didn't take Kent long to arrive. His truck, a much newer, fully loaded black Ford that cost more than she expected to make in a year, pulled into the lot with undue haste. Sierra opened the door to greet him.

His look was grim, his attitude more so. He stepped into the house and shut the door behind him. "I'll kill the son of a bitch this time."

"No." A new fear took hold of Sierra. "Kent, you know what he can do, the connections he has."

"Fuck his connections."

"Your diction has deteriorated horribly."

"My mood is way beyond my diction, hon. I've had it with that sniveling coward."

Sierra closed her eyes, remorse filling her. Griffin was capable of so much, which he'd already proved. She and her father had never been close, but she hated what Griffin had done to him, how miserable his last year of life had been. He'd known true humiliation, true shame—and he'd blamed Sierra.

Because of her, people had lost jobs, lost loans, even lost their homes. She would not let Griffin hurt Kent in the same way.

She knew that somehow she had to protect him, even while she relied on him to protect her. At least for tonight.

"Promise me you won't do anything stupid, or I swear I'll never call you again for help."

Impotent frustration darkened Kent's handsome face, made the muscles in his neck and shoulders stand out sharply. He had his balled fists on his hips, his head down as he paced angrily around her small living room.

"Kent? Please."

He scrubbed at his jaw, his gaze locked on hers, flinty and bright. Finally, he nodded. "I'll promise to try, but that's all I can promise."

Sierra let out a breath. "Thank you."

Kent started through the house, flipping lights back on, making himself at home by stealing one of the pillows off her bed and finding himself a top sheet in her closet. "You know," he said to Sierra as she trailed him, "I'm the least of your worries right now."

She hated fretting but couldn't help herself. "You think Griff is going to do something so soon?"

He stopped by her tiny couch and tossed the pillow and sheet down, then faced her with his arms crossed over his chest. "Actually, I was talking about Ben."

Stumped, Sierra shook her head. "What about him?"

Kent gave her a wry look. "He's staked a claim, Sierra, and that's one young man who isn't going to take kindly to any exes sniffing around, hostile or friendly or otherwise."

Tension made her tone sharp. "These are modern times, for crying out loud. He has no rights over me."

"I bet he'll see it differently."

Indignation, and a good dose of worry, rose sharply. "My life is none of his business."

"He's spent a week hanging around, helping out, making it his business."

"We're . . . friends." But she knew it was more than that, because she'd wanted more. She'd wanted everything Ben offered.

"Yeah, tell him that."

Left with no choices, Sierra scowled. "I will."

"Uh-huh. Just don't expect him to be as easy to sway as I am." He flicked the end of her nose. "He wants you, and I have the feeling he's not going to let anyone get in his way."

With her heartbeat jumping into double time, Sierra stared at Kent—and knew he was right.

God, she'd have to cut all ties with Ben or put him at risk. He was so easy going, so open and accepting and nice, he wouldn't have a clue how to deal with someone like Griffin Ross.

Sierra made her decision and immediately felt the wrenching loss to the point her stomach ached and her heart felt hollow. She just hadn't realized how much she wanted Ben, until she made the decision to give him up.

Chapter Nine

Ben stretched as he stepped out of the shower. He'd been up half the night working and when he had made it to bed, he hadn't been able to sleep because he'd wanted Sierra. Bad.

Damn, but she managed to dredge very unfamiliar feelings out of him. He'd never had a woman occupy his every thought, but he liked thinking about her. It made him smile.

Hell, he was smiling now.

Ben laughed, toweled off briskly, and reached for a pair of khaki slacks. He should have been exhausted, but he wasn't. He felt filled with purpose, energy. Lust.

Sierra trusted him. She didn't want to, but little by little he was winning her over.

He finger-combed his hair on the way to the phone to ring the diner.

He wanted to know if Sierra had shown up for coffee. God knew he should have been sleeping. And his own experience told him he should stop looking so eager to be with her. He'd all but run her to ground, occupying every available free second she had. At this rate, she'd figure out that she had him wrapped around her little finger and the fun would end.

Course, that went both ways. Though she never seemed as eager to be with him, last night had been a milestone. If Grace hadn't called, he might have awakened with Sierra in his arms.

Getting the responses he wanted—both verbal and physical—were easy when he touched her just right. The woman wanted him, and soon she'd have him.

One of his waitresses, harried by the sound of it, answered his call on the fourth ring. "Yeah?"

Ben would reprimand her later about her phone manners. "This is Ben Badwin."

"Oh. Morning, Ben."

Ben could hear the contrition in her tone and smiled. This particular waitress was fairly new, still learning, and not as aggressive in her flirting since she had a young fiancé to contend with. And because she was saving up for a down payment on a house, she worked whatever hours Ben wanted to give her. She'd been in since five that morning. He'd keep her for sure.

"Do me a favor, Cathy, and check to see if Sierra's in the diner." After a weeklong routine of sharing coffee, conversation, and a lot of smiles, all his employees knew Sierra—and they knew the boss was smitten.

"She just came in, Ben. She asked for you, but I told her you were still in bed."

She'd asked for him? Ben hated the idea that he might

have missed her and was disgusted at himself for caring one way or the other. But this would have been the first time that she'd sought him out. Normally he was up and waiting for her when she walked in. "Did she leave?"

"Not yet. She's got some big bruiser with her insisting she needs coffee."

Ben stiffened for one alarming moment before realizing it had to be Kent. More often than not, Kent met her on a job rather than picking her up. He was probably here today with the hope of running into Brooke.

Ben carried the phone to his closet to pick out a shirt. "Ask her to wait. I'll be right there." And then, because he couldn't seem to help clarifying things, he added, "And Cathy, the guy with her is an employee."

Cathy said, "Right."

Her tone held some underlying meaning that grated Ben the wrong way. His hand froze on the sleeve of a dark green shirt. "What does that mean?"

He must have sounded peeved, because Cathy stammered, "Look, Mr. Badwin, I gotta go. You know mornings are busy."

With an effort, Ben moderated his tone. "That's right. Just tell me what you meant so you can get back to work."

Ben could almost see her fidgeting. Finally, she blurted, "He spent the night. I heard her grumbling about it being his fault she hadn't slept and was grumpy. He laughed at her, and she said he snored like a freight train."

A red haze closed in around Ben. His hand gripped the phone too hard. They had to be sharing mighty close quarters for Sierra to know that Kent snored. Through his teeth, Ben said, "Thanks. I'll be right there." He hung up without hearing if Cathy replied or not.

Kent had spent the night with Sierra.

Ben headed for the door, and realized he didn't have a shirt or shoes on. Cursing, he grabbed a shirt and yanked it on, fumbled with his belt and shoved his feet into socks and shoes. Within one minute, he was out the door.

Damn it, from the start he'd thought their relationship a little too secure, too intimate. He should have known something more was going on. Men and women as friends? It didn't happen, not that way, not that close. Especially not when the woman was so damn sexy and God knew, with the way Sierra affected him, she had to be sexier than most.

Of course, Kent had made a play for his mother as well, and in front of them all. Sierra hadn't acted jealous.

Ben's stomping stride slowed as he considered that and tried to sort it all out in his mind. But he couldn't get beyond the fact that they'd spent the night together. What reason could there be, except the same one for why he wanted to spend the night with her?

He stormed into the diner—only to see that his mother was also in evidence, with Kent fawning all over her. Sierra stood next to them, looking tired and antsy, but not in any way resentful toward the other two. They were near a table, but not yet sitting.

"Shit." Ben hated being at loose ends, and he absolutely detested this sense of jealousy. He'd never felt it before and he didn't like feeling it now. Ungluing his feet and attempting an air of negligence, he sauntered up to the small group and was met with a variety of moods.

Sierra's disgruntled gaze slanted his way. She did indeed look as though she needed some caffeine. Had she been up all night? Doing *what?*

His mother blushed, leaving Ben to wonder what Kent

had just been saying to her. Or what she might have been thinking. He'd never before seen her with a lack of poise and if it weren't for his suspicions over Sierra, he would have found the situation hilarious.

Kent, who was obviously on the make, ignored Ben. He had eyes only for Brooke.

Just what the hell was going on? "Good morning, everyone."

Ben knew his smile appeared more of a snarl when Sierra glared at him and Brooke blinked.

Kent gave him the once-over, reminding Ben that he hadn't really combed his hair and had forgotten to shave. "Get up on the wrong side of bed this morning?"

Ben narrowed his eyes. "Got out of the wrong bed, actually."

Shocked, Brooke said, "Ben!"

Sierra locked her jaw, appearing contentious and riled enough to spit. "Well, that'll make things easier then."

Ben didn't trust the way she said that. "What will?"

"Knowing you were out carousing last night."

"Carousing?" Ben shook his head, thrown off by her misassumption. "No, I meant I'd have rather gotten out of your bed, instead of my own."

Brooke took him by surprise with a hard pinch.

"Ow, damn." Ben jumped and rubbed his side. "That hurt."

"I meant for it to. You're behaving abominably." She sent a furtive glance around the diner as if she thought all present were privy to his comments. "You're embarrassing all of us."

Far from being embarrassed, Kent looked on the verge of laughing.

Sierra just looked put out. She rubbed her forehead

and mumbled under her breath. Today she had her silky hair in a ponytail and her jeans seemed relatively new.

She drew a breath and announced to no one in particular, "I need to get to work."

Ben pulled out her chair. "One cup of coffee first." No way in hell was he letting her out of his sight until he knew what had gone on last night.

"No, I . . ."

With a type of sibling irreverence, Kent took her shoulder and pushed her into her seat. "Coffee, Sierra." He held her down when she would have bolted back up. "I need it even if you don't."

"I could have made some this morning," she grumbled, casting a sour glance at Ben. But she did give up and slump into the chair.

"I'd like to keep the lining of my stomach, thank you very much." And as he seated Brooke, Kent explained, "She makes horrid coffee."

Ben stared at Kent hard. "Since you spent the night, why didn't you just make it?"

Sierra's head shot up, her eyes narrowed in astonishment. Brooke went pale, then flushed.

Kent held up both hands. "Hey now, before anyone starts jumping the gun, I can explain that. You see—" In the next instant, he jerked hard, yelped, and bent to rub his shin while glowering at Sierra. She gave a short, quick shake of her head.

Ben decided to get right to the point. "Did you sleep with him?" This time his mother didn't seem to mind his bad manners at all. She looked glacial with her own curiosity.

Sierra turned a falsely sweet smile on Ben. "It's really none of your business."

Ben started to speak, and Kent said, "The hell it isn't. Don't make it sound like something it isn't, Sierra, just to irk the young bull here, because you're crucifying me in the bargain." He caught Brooke's hand and held on when she frantically tried to pull free. "Sierra and I are friends. Period. End of the road. Never anything more than friends. Okay?"

Ben wanted to believe him. "So why'd you spend the night?"

There'd been no coffee served yet, and still Sierra shoved her chair away. "You're overstepping yourself, Ben. I made it clear from the start that I didn't want you intruding into my private life. Just because I've agreed to . . . to other stuff, doesn't give you the right to question me."

Her vehemence, her trembling reaction, threw Ben. It hit him on a gut level that something must be very wrong this morning. He'd known her a little over a week and not once had she sounded so devastated.

Jealousy and curiosity faded beneath his concern. He slowly stood with her. "What is it, sweetheart?"

She blinked hard at the endearment and his tender tone, as if fighting off tears, then predictably enough, straightened her small proud shoulders.

Sounding strangled, unable to meet his gaze, she said, "That's it. I'm sorry Ben, but . . . I don't want to see you anymore." She turned to Kent, who still held Brooke's hand, his face set, his mood heavy. "Stay and enjoy your coffee. I'll see you at the site."

"Damn it, Sierra," Kent called after her, "this isn't what I meant . . ."

"It's for the best." She walked out, head held high, spine erect.

For the moment, Ben let her go.

"Ben." His mother's voice softened with concern. Again she tried to free her hand and again Kent held on. She gave up and addressed Ben. "Maybe you should . . ."

Kent cleared his throat and spoke over her. "She needs a little time to think things through, that's all. Trust me on this, Ben."

Ben didn't say anything. He didn't know what the hell to say. Never in his life had a woman dumped him. If he hadn't liked the jealousy, it was a damn sure bet he *hated* this.

He made a disgusted sound to himself. Hell, she'd made it clear from the start that she didn't want to be bothered with him. She'd suffered him all week only because he'd been so determined. So why did he want to go after her and shake some sense into her? Why did he want to drag her off to his room and keep her there until . . .

He tightened his fists. Time? He'd give her all the damn time she needed.

Kent lifted Brooke's hand to his mouth and kissed her knuckles. "I'm sorry, but I need to go with her. She's . . . upset."

Brooke nodded, realized what she was doing, and snatched her hand away only to flap it at him. "Yes, of course. Go. You certainly don't need my permission."

Kent turned to Ben, did a double take, then rolled his eyes. "Oh for pity's sake, man. You look like a damn thundercloud and it's not even necessary. You'd probably already know that if you stopped to think, instead of wallowing in your male ego."

Insults were the very last thing Ben intended to put up with this morning. "What the hell am I supposed to think?"

"Let's see. You might consider the fact that Sierra's protective of everyone she cares about."

Because Sierra kept herself closed off from him, Ben didn't know her well enough to know that, which only added to his ire. "She's protecting you?"

Kent shook his head. "Me, you, everyone but herself." He pointed an accusing finger at Ben. "If you're half as smart as I think you are, you'll realize she isn't a woman you should give up on."

Anger and frustration rippled through Ben, making him shake, setting him on edge. "You wanna explain all these cryptic comments?"

Kent dropped his head forward and pinched the bridge of his nose. Ben heard him curse softly. "Can't. Sierra would kill me if I did." He looked up at Ben. "She's protective, but she's also damn private."

"Not with you."

"Yeah, well, our relationship is special."

"Special enough that you sleep with her?"

"Jesus, not the way you mean." He turned to Brooke. "I'm going to call you later. We'll talk."

Brooke, who'd been silently listening to the exchange, shook her head. "No. I . . ."

Kent touched her chin. "Yes." And he left.

Though Ben's mother was unsettled by Kent's pursuit, she turned to Ben with concern. "I feel like something's wrong here."

Ben kept his gaze on the door where both Sierra and Kent had walked out. "Yeah, me too." It seemed every day with her uncovered a new challenge. "You believe what Kent says?"

"That they're just friends? Yes."

"But?"

"Ben." She touched his forearm. "Honey, I know Sierra is special—"

"You do?"

"I'm your mother. It's pretty obvious to me."

Ben scowled over that. Damn it, nothing seemed obvious to him.

"The thing is, do you think it's smart to get overly involved with someone who might have some very real problems?"

What kind of very real problems could an intelligent, independent twenty-four-year-old woman possibly have? And why would she need to be so protective of everyone, and why so many secrets? Ben just didn't know, but Kent was right. He couldn't give up on her.

"Smart? Probably not." He patted Brooke's hand. "But I don't seem to have any choice."

"Nonsense. I didn't raise a fool. You always have control."

Slowly, Ben's dark mood cleared. Control. Yeah, he could control Sierra—with sex—and that was a fantasy destined to make him into a tyrant. He'd given her a week without testing that control, because strangely enough, he wanted more than just her sexual surrender.

He'd made a lot of headway, too. She'd gotten easier with him, less rigid. She returned his kisses, freely touched him, and finally, she'd admitted to wanting him.

But something had happened last night to change her mind.

So many times since first meeting her, he'd glimpsed the deep mysteries in her eyes, the defensiveness in her prickly pride. He wanted Sierra to trust him enough to confide in him.

He wanted her to trust him enough to give him . . . *everything*.

Ben hugged his mother and kissed her cheek. "You're right about that. I am in control. And I intend to take complete charge tonight."

His statement brought a troubled frown to Brooke's brow. "Now, Ben, I didn't mean for you to overreact."

"I won't." He tipped his head, studying her. "I have to get to work, so tell me, were you visiting for a reason, or did you just stop in with the hope you'd get to see Kent?"

He'd only been half-serious, but the second he saw his mother's face, he knew he'd caught her. With mocking shock, he said, "Why, Mom, you flirt."

She jammed her purse strap over her shoulder, gave him an austere frown, and started grousing. "It's a sad day when a mother can't visit her only son without being harassed."

With that parting shot, she turned and flounced out.

Ben chuckled as he watched her go, feeling reassured on many levels.

No, whatever Sierra and Kent had between them, it wasn't sexual. But it was special and Ben couldn't help but be envious. Sierra shared herself with Kent, but she wouldn't share with him.

Throughout the rest of the day, he found himself watching for Sierra to return. He could hardly wait to start his newest campaign. One way or another, he'd get her figured out. He hadn't met a woman yet who could completely stump him, though Sierra was by far the most complex female he'd ever known.

Sexually, he wanted her more with every second. She was so intrinsically female, so . . . earthy. There wasn't an ounce of artifice to her, not makeup, not perfume. Her physical appeal came through in womanly pride and confidence mixed with soft skin and hair, and the most luscious, kissable mouth he'd ever seen. Just thinking about her mouth sent his temperature up a notch.

He enjoyed her company, too. She was responsible, independent, and she vied with his grandmother for having the shortest temper. She was cute, candid, often too serious but also sympathetic. And she kept some mysterious secrets.

All those things made her a most unique and, as his mother had pointed out, special person.

Ben had assumed it would be late when she got home, but at five o'clock, Gary, who'd been manning the front desk, jogged into the restaurant to tell him she was back. Ben might have felt stupid putting his staff on the lookout for her, but determination overrode such mundane considerations.

He didn't wait to see if Sierra would come to him; he knew she wouldn't. Empty-handed, not a single peace offering to his name, not even a sandwich, Ben strolled across the street.

Sierra hefted a large hardware bag from the back of the truck.

She saw him but didn't say anything.

Ignoring her silent rejection, Ben caught up to her, kept pace at her side, and peered into the top of the bag. She'd bought locks. Lots of them. "Planning to lock me out?"

"No." She made a face, shook her head. "I mean, yes, you are locked out. But no, they're not for you."

More secrets. Ben lifted the top package, an extra

sturdy deadbolt lock, from the bag. "Getting nervous at night, are you?"

Her jaw clenched, and again she said, "No," but Ben knew she lied. He didn't know how he knew, he just did. She was a woman alone, so she should be cautious. But why now? Had someone or something spooked her?

At the front door she juggled the big bag in one arm and shook her key ring around until she got her door key in position. Ben didn't offer to help her. He hoped to eventually confuse her as much as she always confused him.

Once she got the door open, she stepped inside and turned to face him, blocking his way so he couldn't follow. Given her expression, Ben assumed she felt safer inside, while he remained outside.

"What do you want, Ben?"

"You."

Her mouth opened, and then closed with a snap. She frowned.

He eyed her militant stance. "I gather this means I'm not invited in?"

Being rude didn't come easy to Sierra. Ben saw her guilty flush before she firmed her resolve. "I'm sorry, but I've got a lot to do."

"Installing locks?"

Her chin lifted. "That's right."

Ben had no problem being rude, not when there was something—or in this case, someone—he wanted. He stepped forward, forcing Sierra to move out of his way. She did so automatically, then realized what she'd done and squawked at him.

Ben wrested the bag from her arms and set it aside. In

the process he noticed a sheet and pillow on her couch and looked at her with raised brows. "This is where Kent slept?"

Her eyes glittered dangerously. *"It-is-none-of-your-business."*

Ben whistled. The careful way she enunciated each word should have made him back off. He wouldn't. "Sensitive today, aren't you?"

Disbelief, quickly followed by outrage, darkened her color. She crossed her arms tight over her chest. "Damn it, Ben. I told you at the restaurant that I didn't want to see you anymore."

"I know." His soft tone served a direct contrast to her near shout. "I was thoroughly humiliated in my own workplace."

Sierra flushed with a wave of guilt. "I . . . I didn't mean to do that." Then with a renewed scowl: "It's just that . . . I've changed my mind about things."

"That's what I want to talk to you about. And I'm not leaving till I do, so how about just listening?"

Her gaze filled with disgust. "It's so like a man to leave a woman with no choices."

Such bitter words, Ben thought. Suspicions edged their way into his consciousness, and none of them were pleasant. Who the hell had taken away her choices? He discounted himself and his present actions because he knew he'd never hurt her.

There were a hundred questions he wanted to ask, but he decided it might be better to put his queries to Kent. "Listen, sweetheart, I don't mean—"

The ringing of her phone interrupted him.

Like a deer caught in the headlights, Sierra froze, but only for a second. She jerked around and rushed into the kitchen. Ben followed her. She sounded very tentative when she said, "Hello?"

Ben took in every nuance of her features, and saw the dread that she quickly masked. Without a word, she dropped the phone back in the cradle.

"Wrong number?"

"Yeah." A pulse raced in her throat. She took two slow, deep breaths. "Now, what do you want?"

Despite her work clothes and firm determination, she looked so vulnerable, so small and delicate that Ben wanted to fold her into his arms and make all sorts of promises. He swallowed down that absurd inclination. "We should be friends."

She managed a credible smirk. "Yeah, like that's even possible now."

"Why?" Ben hoped he looked more innocent than he felt. "You think there's too much sexual tension between us?"

She crossed her arms around herself defensively and refused to answer.

He'd convince her somehow. "I can control myself, and I'm assuming you can, too."

She didn't look overly positive, but she nodded.

Ben held out his hands in surrender and shrugged. "You're off-limits from now on. I won't touch. I sure as hell won't kiss. But we can talk." He bent his knees, lowering himself so he could look her in the eyes, to read her myriad expressions. "Come on, Sierra. I enjoy your company. I really do. And we're neighbors. That's not going to change, right?"

"You're damn right." She turned combative, jutting her small jaw at him as if he personified everything evil in her life. "I'm here and I'm not going anywhere."

Ben drew back in surprise. "I want you to stay." He tried a laugh that sounded flat. "No reason to attack me, I swear."

Her small body trembled with upset. In a rush that mirrored desperation, she said, "Ben, I really do have a lot to do."

"Throwing me out already? Okay, but have we made a truce?"

"All right, sure."

This time his laugh was genuine. "You agreed so fast, I'm not sure I believe you."

Her phone rang again. Sierra started, then set her jaw, stared Ben in the eyes, and ignored the phone.

Ben gazed at her quizzically. "You don't want to answer that?"

"Whoever it is will call back."

"Right. I guess I'm so engrossing, you can't pull yourself away?"

A low growl erupted from deep in her throat. She whirled away from him and snatched the phone up. "Hello."

This time the fear was buried beneath rage. "No, and no." And in a near shout: *"And no."*

Floored by her display, Ben watched as she slammed the phone down, slammed it twice more. She kept her back to him, her body held rigid, her labored breaths sonorous in the otherwise quiet room.

Kent's words came back to him, loud and clear. She wanted to protect everyone. *Was she trying to protect him now?*

Gently, his heart breaking with the need to hold her, comfort her, Ben asked, "Another wrong number?"

She'd been pushed beyond her limits. Her voice broke as she said, "Please leave."

"Not on your life." He couldn't leave her like this. The mere thought of leaving went against every fiber of his masculine being. Not only was she female, smaller, and more fragile than he, but he cared about her. A lot.

She'd allowed Kent to get close. Sooner or later, she'd grant him the same rights.

Ben touched her shoulders and when she didn't jerk away, he smoothed his hands over the small bones, cupped the ball joints in each palm. She was so stiff, so tense.

"Ben . . ."

"No, shhh. I'm not coming on to you, I swear."

She laughed brokenly and dropped her head to the wall behind her with a solid thunk.

Wincing in sympathy, Ben eased her back away from the wall so she couldn't inflict more damage on her poor skull. "Regardless of how you might prefer it, Sierra, we're friends now. I meant what I said. I'll go on wanting you, just as I suspect you'll go on wanting me. But I won't go away."

"You don't even know what you're doing."

"Sexually?" he asked, because being this close to her, feeling so protective, so defensive of her, made him more aware of his basic nature than ever before.

Laughing again, Sierra turned. She was breathing hard and her eyes were bright. "You want to have sex? That's what it'll take to get rid of you?"

She sounded so desperate, his insides twisted. He kept his tone calm and sure. "I just told you, babe, you can't get rid of me."

"You said I was a challenge for you. But if the challenge is gone . . ."

"Sierra." He touched her sun-kissed cheek and tried to

make her understand. "How can it ever be gone when you provoke me with your determination to keep me away? Oh, no." Ben shook his head, very sure. "You're a bundle of contradictions, a constant dare to my manhood, and I like meeting each and every challenge."

"That's ridiculous." She softened and tried a new tack. "Ben, you haven't known me that long, so there's no reason for you to get drawn into my problems."

What she said was true, in the normal course of things. But his relationship with her hadn't been normal from the start. He'd gotten one look at her and wanted her so badly he hurt. Ben wondered if she really had no idea how deeply involved he'd gotten.

He gave her one truth she couldn't refute. "I know you better than any other man knows you." His voice dropped, reassuring and reaffirming. "I'm the one who gave you your first orgasm. Right?"

Her eyes rounded, her breath caught. "That was a mistake."

"No way, sweetheart. I knew exactly what I was doing."

A comical look crossed her features, sort of a mix of chagrin and disbelief, then she exploded. "Fine. Great. You don't want to leave, that's just dandy."

She stormed away from him, slammed open a kitchen drawer, ripped out a hammer and tossed it to him. At least, Ben chose to see it as a toss, rather than an attempt at bodily harm. He was quick on the draw and caught the thing before it hit him in the abdomen.

"Stay if you insist. But you can help me get my locks in. I don't have time to stand around arguing with you." And just to be nasty, she added, "Unlike *some* people, I'm busy trying to run a business."

She located another hammer and a screwdriver set.

Her slurs had no effect on Ben. She'd invited him to stay, to help, so he could forgive her anything else. Besides, he knew she'd spoken in anger. And she'd looked so cute in her pique.

Smiling to himself, Ben followed with the hammer while she carried her tools to the tiny living room. "Are we doing all the windows?" Luckily, there weren't many.

"That's right." She watched him, just waiting for him to complain. When he didn't, she frowned. "Are you handy?"

"Very."

She thrust a few screwdrivers at him. "So you know what you're doing?"

"Absolutely."

She glared at him in suspicion, her face hot. "I'm not talking sexually, you know."

Ah, but she obviously had sex on her mind. Ben gave her a sunny smile. "You think I can afford a full-time handyman for the motel?"

He could tell he'd taken her aback with that disclosure. She gave a hard nod. "Fair enough. You start in here, and I'll start in the kitchen."

Working side by side with her would have been nice, but he supposed that was out of the question. And in her present mood, it was probably safer. An irate woman with a hammer was never a good thing.

Ben heard her rip a package open with unnecessary force. Since she was on the other side of a wall, he couldn't see her, but they could still converse with ease. "I don't suppose you'd care to tell me what troubles you have."

"No."

He'd expected that reply. "If I knew, I could keep an eye on things."

"No."

Three layers of paint covered the rickety lock on her living room window. Ben frowned at it. "I'm going to keep a lookout anyway, you know."

Silence.

He wedged the screwdriver into place against the lock and struck the end of it three times carefully with the hammer. The lock cracked into two pieces, leaving only one embedded screw. "Piece of crap," he muttered to himself, glad now that she'd had enough initiative to change the locks.

Because everything was warped and rusty, the job took longer than it should have. Each room possessed one window only. While Sierra finished up in the bathroom, Ben took care of the one in her bedroom.

Since he was alone, he looked around in undiluted curiosity. He'd been inside her tiny home many times, but never in this particular room.

She'd decorated in a bare-bones fashion. Her twin size bed consisted of a mattress and box springs on a frame. Period. No headboard or footboard, no colorful spreads or dust ruffles. White sheets, a plain brown and blue quilt, ragged in places, and a standard pillow were tossed atop the mattress. Ben remembered the other pillow and sheet on the couch and knew she slept with two pillows, though he'd hardly consider that extravagant.

A cheap window shade provided privacy. There were no colorful throw rugs to soften the cracked linoleum floor. A windup clock rather than a radio alarm sat atop a wooden nightstand that didn't match the cumbersome dresser. There was nothing on the walls, not even a mirror. The dresser top held a set of keys, a little change, a few plain rubber bands and nothing more. No makeup, no perfume, no bright hair clips.

Sandals peeked out from beneath the bed, and in her closet hung a few shirts, a jacket.

Her bedroom looked much as he envisioned a prison might.

Her existence was meager beyond what most people could tolerate. Emotionally numb, Ben dropped to the edge of her mattress and just sat there. A strange, nearly painful emotion swelled within his chest, like his heart had just broken.

Sierra stuck her head in the door, frowned when she saw him sitting on her bed, and said, "What are you doing?"

Her tone dripped of suspicion. Ben pushed himself upright from the bed. "Nothing."

She didn't look as if she believed him and glanced around her room as if expecting to find evidence of some nefarious deed. When she found nothing, she grudgingly asked, "You want something cold to drink? I've got iced tea."

Ben looked at her with new eyes, and the feeling in his chest changed, became dangerous and unsettling. He watched her so intently, she squirmed.

"It was a simple enough question, Ben. Why are you staring at me like that?"

Ben shrugged. What the hell could he tell her?

Hands on her hips, she said, "Well, just stop it, all right?"

He felt tense with the need to coddle her but still found a small smile. She was in such a bristly mood today. "Iced tea would be great. Thank you."

Slowly, as if she had to tear her gaze away from him, she glanced toward the window. "You through?"

"Just taking a breather." His voice was soft, his heart softer. Damn it, he didn't mean to give himself away, but so many emotions churned inside him he could barely rationalize them all.

Wearing a deliberate expression of indifference, Sierra shrugged. "Why don't you just head off, then? I can finish this up."

Ben turned back to the window. "Nope. I'll be done in a minute." And then what? He'd have to find an excuse to come back tomorrow, and the next day, and the day after that. For some reason, despite their sexual compatibility, Sierra wanted rid of him. But the sexual attraction was strong, and he'd build on it, slow but sure, until he'd won her over.

Grumbling low, she muttered, "Fine. Suit yourself."

Ben waited until her footsteps faded away toward the kitchen before allowing his grim smile to appear. "Oh I will, babe." He attacked the old lock with a vengeance. The lock broke and he tossed it aside. "You can bet on it." He'd suit himself, and he'd win her over in the bargain.

Chapter Ten

The moon was so bright, it left long shadows on the ground as Sierra loaded her truck. She'd been home about an hour, had already showered and changed into loose shorts and a big comfortable tee. Because she couldn't settle down, and she knew she wouldn't sleep, she decided to prepare the truck for the morning.

Unable to stop herself, she glanced across the street at the lights coming from Ben's lobby and the diner, which by this time of night was only serving drinks. She could hear the low thrum of conversation and laughter carried on the night breeze, mingling with music from the juke-box. He had a crowd there every night, not just the guests, but locals as well, truck drivers . . . women.

Sierra forced herself to look away.

For a man who kept such long hours, Ben never seemed overly tired. He worked every aspect of the motel and diner and never complained. In fact, he seemed to love it all.

Especially the flirting.

Sierra had watched the days tick by, three, four, a week, a week and a half—ten days of being "friends" with Ben. Ten days since they'd installed the locks.

Ten days since he'd kissed her.

True to his word, he'd put his sexual interest on hold, or else he was appeasing himself elsewhere. Damn it, if he hadn't already shown her how nice it was to be more than friends, she'd be happy with the situation.

But she did know, and regardless of what she knew to be wise, even necessary, she wanted more.

It had become a familiar routine for Sierra, returning from a long day of work, preparing for another, and seeing Ben. He'd so thoroughly invaded her life that she now *expected* to see him, when she didn't have that right.

She'd set the boundaries of friendship, while other women threw themselves at him. It made her crazy to think about it.

It made her really hate Griff for forcing her to it.

She'd been working full steam, hoping to stay so busy she wouldn't have time to think, not about Ben and not about Griff. She was so thoroughly spent that even her bones ached, but she still tossed and turned all night. At least she'd gotten ahead on her jobs and had new jobs scheduled, and the success of her business looked promising.

If only her worries ended there.

Amazingly enough, other than a few more calls, Griffin had left her alone. All of the threats that she'd imagined, both physical and to her business, had never materialized. She was nearly weak with relief, but unwilling to let down her guard for a single moment. She'd learned the hard way that you could never second-guess Griff, and that he was vengeful beyond her wildest imagination.

Why he felt so vengeful, she didn't know. It certainly wasn't from a broken heart. The man had no heart, and he sure hadn't held any affection for her when they'd been together. But with a father as mayor, and powerful relatives with money to burn, her ex had the means to win whatever campaigns he started.

She only hoped his newest campaign wasn't against her.

Again.

In the past, Griffin had hurt her by hurting those she cared about. She could never forget that.

Because damn it, she cared about Ben.

Nights were the worst, when she was in her lonely bed with only the silence of her small home to comfort her. She'd driven herself into the ground trying to avoid thoughts of Ben, but it hadn't worked. She was so fractious, so overwrought and short-tempered and jumpy, she could barely stand herself.

All because of a sexual frustration she hadn't even known existed a month ago. It grew every day, despite their lack of intimacy, but that was likely because Ben was so wonderful—as a neighbor, as a lover, and now as a friend.

He was often watching for her when she got home at night, sharing a friendly ear and that dimpled smile. In the mornings, she saw him when she went for coffee. He kept his conversations generic, his touches avuncular, and she was slowly becoming demented with desire.

If Griffin had truly given up on harassing her, then what did it matter if she got involved with Ben?

She heard someone behind her, thought it might be Ben conjured from her thoughts, and she grinned with a measure of happiness that shook her sensible foundation.

Trying to wipe away her smile, she turned—and came face to face with Griffin Ross.

His appearance threw her, especially since she'd been half expecting Ben. Panic slammed into her full force, momentarily stealing her breath. Griffin noted her reaction. His grin wasn't nice and wasn't encouraging.

"Hey, baby. You look real happy to see me."

Sierra pulled herself together. "Get off my property." The words, meant to be shouted, came out as a whisper of sound.

His grin widened. "Now what kind of greeting is that for your husband?"

Sierra forced her muscles to loosen. Kent had taught her things, self-defense methods, and she knew she had to stay relaxed, had to stay ready. She rolled her shoulders, flexed her hands. Griff just watched, smirking at her efforts.

She would need emotional strength, more than physical strength, to defy him and his effect on her.

Her voice grew stronger, her repugnance plain. "Oh no. You aren't my husband, Griff. I gave up everything to be rid of you—and believe me, it was well worth it."

"You gave up nothing because you had nothing, isn't that right?" Pale blue eyes narrowed on her face. "And you know deep down you'll never be rid of me. You fucked up my life, and that pisses me off."

"I—"

He moved so fast, a startled screech escaped her. One second he was several feet away, the next he was right in front of her, gripping her upper arms with deliberate, bruising force. Griffin loved to see her recoil in pain. She'd found that out right after the wedding.

He pulled her up on her tiptoes until she felt his hot breath in her face, could smell the beer he'd drunk and the sour odor of his hatred. "You always were a stupid little bitch, Sierra." He gave her one hard shake, his voice humming with excitement and triumph at her small sound of discomfort. He looked at her mouth. "If you had any smarts, you'd be nicer to me."

The familiar insults had always precluded an attack, and she'd learned to brace herself. But this time they had a peculiar effect on her. By small degrees, her fear receded. Her racing heartbeat slowed to a solid, steady thud. Her breathing calmed and finally evened out. She hung limp in his hold, knowing a battle, regardless of what Kent had taught her, would be useless.

In the past, she'd cowered from him, unable to meet his gaze. Now she stared him in the eyes and dared to smile. "Only a pathetic worm would need to hurt a woman to make himself feel more like a man."

And she spit in his face.

Outrage washed over Griff in trembling force. His blue eyes bulged, going icy pale against the dark color pulsing in his face. He released her left arm and drew back to slap her—and Sierra moved. She twisted, ducking away and wrenching her other arm painfully in the process but still freeing herself, which had been her objective. Feeling far too slow and clumsy, she snatched up the sharp edged shovel she'd just put in her truck.

A sense of power and adrenaline coursed through her, making her audacious in her anger. She taunted him, almost wanting him to lunge, to try something. "C'mon,

Griff. C'mon, you bastard." Her hands felt sweaty on the wooden handle, and she gripped it harder, moving it like a ballplayer ready at bat. "Touch me again and I swear I'll take your head off."

Incredulous, Griff stood stock still, her saliva slipping down his cheek until he slowly reached up and swiped it away. His teeth clenched and his lips pulled back so that his words slurred with rage. "You little bitch."

"That's right, Griff. I'm a bitch. A maniacal bitch, and believe me, I'll gladly do you harm."

"You wouldn't dare." He drew one breath, then another. "Do you know what would happen to you if you even tried it?"

"What? You'd go crying to Daddy? Haven't you grown up yet?" She curled her lip. "I live in Gillespe now, Griff. Out of your reach."

He smiled slowly. "If you believe that, you're dumber than I thought. You already know that my family has a lot of influence with bank owners." He gestured at her surrounding land, now lit by outdoor lights. "I can't believe you got a loan for this dump, but you better believe I know people who can call in the debt."

He meant it. She'd hoped that moving so far away would put her out of his reach, that his influence would be contained by distance. Remorse made Sierra queasy; rage made her want to weep. She wouldn't give him the satisfaction of seeing either. "You make me want to puke, you're such a coward."

"Sierra?"

Griff and Sierra both jerked, Griff with a curse, Sierra with new alarm.

Shielding his eyes from the glaring streetlights, Ben rapidly approached from across the street. Sierra knew she stood more in the shadows than not and she prayed Ben didn't comprehend the situation.

Griff turned back to her. "Now who could this be?"

"Just a neighbor." She'd answered too quickly, showing her urgency, and Griff gave her a speculative stare.

Trying to offset her reaction, she lowered the shovel and leaned on it, hoping to look nonchalant. "Why don't you get out of here now before someone calls the police?"

"But I want to meet your neighbors, baby. I want to know everything there is to know about this new life of yours."

So he could destroy it. "Griff . . ." She was too late. Ben marched toward them, somehow looking twice his size, and twice as threatening despite his normally pleasant manner. Sierra set the shovel aside and tried for a casual pose. She even stepped out into the lighting, so Ben could better see her.

But he wasn't looking at her. He stared at Griff.

Stationing himself in front of Sierra, Ben totally blocked her view of Griff. All she could see was his broad back, taut with anger.

"Just what the hell is going on?"

Sierra groaned. Even though she felt certain Ben hadn't seen their physical conflict, there was still no mistaking the hostility in the air. She felt ready to choke on it. "Ben . . ."

He reached back, putting his left hand on her waist and keeping her from stepping around him. By attitude and deed, he let Griffin know that they were more than mere acquaintances and Sierra wanted to smack him.

Unwilling to test Ben at the moment, she stayed behind him, but strained to see past his wide shoulders.

Griff smiled. "A little family reunion, that's all." And because he knew she hated to involve other people in her problems, he looked at Sierra for verification. "Right, baby?"

Sierra had never seen Ben angry until that moment. Oh, she'd seen him annoyed and peeved and put out. But not true anger, not this volatile rage that radiated off him in waves.

He took an aggressive step toward Griffin. The two men were of a similar height, but while Griffin looked trim and slim, Ben suddenly bulged with muscles and menace. "Who the fuck are you?"

Oh no. Sierra touched his arm from behind him. Trying to hide her anger and her worry, she said evenly, "Ben, please don't do this."

Griff laughed when Ben shook her off. "I'm her husband, actually. Has she told you all about me?"

"She hasn't had to. Get off her property."

Sierra couldn't decide if she wanted to hug Ben or hit him with the shovel. "Ben, I can handle this myself. And Griffin, please, use what little brain you have to remember that we are *divorced*."

He took his attention off Ben to give her a warning. "You've gotten a smart mouth since last I saw you." His pale eyes glittered, his tone dropped. "We'll have to do something about that."

A rumbling growl erupted from Ben and he moved to strike.

"Ben, no, damn it." Sierra wrapped both hands into the back of his shirt and jerked. He kept going, which caused her to slip across the loose gravel, stumble into him and nearly fall. He paused to right her with a curse and she used the opportunity to move around in front of him, clinging to him.

"Sierra, stop it." Ben tried to pry her loose, but unlike Griff, he wasn't willing to hurt her.

She held on until he stopped, then thumped on his chest with both fists. "No, *you* stop."

He looked at her in startled surprise.

For good measure, she thumped him one more time. She was near tears, her control fractured, her emotions battered. And for the first time since seeing Griff again, she was very much afraid. "How dare you do this? How dare you—"

He softened immediately. "Hey, shush. It's all right, sweetheart."

She heard a car door slam and turned to see Griffin had crossed the street and gotten into a sporty Camaro. Relief nearly dropped her to the ground. Thank God, he'd left before Ben could hit him. He didn't know Ben's name, didn't know where he worked. Ben was safe—for now.

As she slumped into him, Ben caught her upper arms where Griff had held her moments ago, inadvertently making her wince. Luckily, he didn't notice. "He threatened you, Sierra."

Leaning into Ben, not yet ready to face him, she asked, "And you thought I needed you to save me?"

Sounding confused, Ben nodded. "Yeah."

"He's nobody. Nothing. Forget about him."

"Like hell."

It wasn't over yet. She knew Griffin would be back, and then what? She swallowed hard and did her best to straighten, and to push Ben away.

He surprised her by scooping her up.

"Ben!"

His arms held her close to his chest and his face pressed into her throat. "Shhh. Just let me hold you a second."

She couldn't. If he kept this up, she'd be bawling in no time. The aftershocks of seeing Griff, of Ben almost being drawn into her nightmare, took its toll. "Put me down."

"Okay, okay." He set her back on her feet, but his hands touched her everywhere, smoothing her hair, her face, her jaw. "Are you okay?"

How could he possibly care so much for her? Yet . . . he looked as though he cared. He looked devastated that she might have been in danger.

Emotions choked her. "I'm fine."

A stern frown replaced his concern. "We have to talk."

She needed him to go just in case Griff came back around. More than anything she wanted to keep Ben from getting involved. She could deal with Griffin; she always had. But she couldn't handle seeing Ben hurt. "We've talked all week." She pushed her hair away from her face and saw that her hands were shaking. She put them behind her back. "Really, Ben, I just want to go to bed. I'm tired."

He paced away from her, rubbed his face, stared at the moon. Sierra half expected him to start baying at any moment. He stuck his hands in his back pockets. "You won't give an inch, will you?"

Sadness, a sense of loss, tightened her throat, but she couldn't give in. Especially not now. Griffin used every weakness against her, and Ben had definitely become a weakness.

Mustering up her spirit, she tossed back, "What does

that mean? That I won't let you take over my life? That I won't play the poor little female who needs the big male to run interference for her?"

Too late Sierra saw that the rage hadn't left Ben yet, it had only been banked. He pinned her with a hostile look. "I'm finally starting to figure a few things out."

She tossed her head, trying to brazen it out. "Yeah, like what?"

"Like what a coward you are."

She reeled back.

Ben advanced. "Whatever that bastard did to you, you're letting it still affect you. It's easier, *safer*, to let him win, isn't it, Sierra?"

"I am not a coward."

"Right. Well, I know you're not stupid, which means you have to realize all men aren't the same. So what else am I supposed to think but that you're afraid to give me a chance? God knows you want me."

Sierra bit her lip, wondering how he could know.

His gaze tracked over her body with insulting familiarity. "I know women, Sierra, not that you're hard to read. Hell, I get near you and you tremble. I barely touch you and you start moaning." His smile was nasty and mean. "Most women make me work a little for it. But not you."

Her teeth clicked together so hard, it hurt. In dangerous undertones, she asked, "Are you calling me easy?"

His eyes nearly black, his cheekbones slashed with color, Ben leaned toward her. Their noses almost touched, and she could feel his breath on her mouth. "Where I'm concerned, *yeah!*"

A hot reply boiled up inside her, expanding, choking her, ready to burst free—and a snicker sounded from the darkness.

As one, Sierra and Ben whirled toward the sound. Sierra didn't recognize the plump woman with long brown hair or the giant behemoth beside her. But Ben apparently did.

He snarled in vexation. "Damn it, Noah, what the hell are you doing skulking around in the dark?"

"Just watching the show." Noah smiled at Sierra, and she was struck by how much that smile reminded her of Ben's. "And feeling sorry for my dumb-ass brother who's burying himself pretty deep."

The woman elbowed him hard, then reached out a hand toward Sierra. "Hi. I'm Grace, Ben's sister-in-law and despite his current behavior, I swear Ben is *not* a dumb ass. He's really very, very sweet."

Because she didn't know what else to do, Sierra took Grace's hand. She was taken totally off guard, her mind a void, her thoughts blank. "Uh . . ."

"I'm sorry if we're interrupting. It was such a passionate argument, too." Grace smiled and released Sierra. "But Ben, people leaving your motel can hear you both. That's how we knew where to find you."

Sierra looked at Ben for help, but he was still rigid with anger and just shrugged.

Noah turned to his wife. "Why don't you grab her and I'll corral Ben and we'll head inside where we can talk privately?" He stared pointedly at Sierra, his look as commanding as a general's. "That is, assuming you'll let us all in?"

He'd said it as a question, but Sierra could tell he expected her agreement.

She quite honestly didn't know what to do. This was Noah, the man who'd been raised on the streets, the man who hadn't had anyone. She'd felt so much sympathy for him, that even now her heart softened just looking at him.

Ben had described him as dangerous. Well, other than his impressive size, he looked harmless enough now, but there was a distinct wildness shining in his electric blue eyes that was missing in Ben.

Though, come to think of it, Ben was looking pretty savage himself at the moment.

Her long delay in replying made Ben explode anew. "Are you going to let us in or not?"

She glared at him. "*They're* more than welcome." And she shoved past him to the front door.

From behind her, Sierra heard Ben groan, heard Noah burst out laughing, and then Grace whispered, "I'm sure she didn't mean it, Ben. Come on, you can help us all get acquainted."

She'd meant it all right, but ten minutes later they were all settled in her tiny living room. She and Ben were on the couch, and because it was so short, they practically touched though Sierra did her best to keep space between them, without being too obvious about it.

Grace was in a kitchen chair, which she proclaimed more than comfortable, and Noah had propped his big body up against the wall. For just a moment, Sierra was embarrassed that she didn't have more furniture. Of course, she'd never expected to have guests, either.

That worry was forgotten, however, when Noah said, "We'd like to hire you for some landscaping."

"Lots and lots of landscaping," Grace added with a happy smile.

Sierra knew they were only trying to help her, offering her work because they thought she needed it. Had Ben put them up to it? Did she look that desperate? Didn't anyone trust in her capabilities? She'd been through too much that day to take a handout.

Despite his size and dark countenance, she scowled at Noah. She could always use the work, but not out of pity. And the fact that these people were related to Ben would only tie her more tightly to him, when now, more than ever, she needed distance from him.

She met Noah's icy-blue gaze and straightened her shoulders. "Now why would you want to hire me?"

And Ben, who evidently took exception to her tone, muttered, "Well, it sure as hell isn't for your sweet disposition."

When Sierra looked ready to clout him, Ben regretted his words. There was a fragile look about her tonight, and it pulled at him, making him want to lift her into his lap and kiss away her worries. But she was being so surly, her mood toward his family so distrustful, that he wouldn't take them back.

Noah didn't seem to think anything of her grumping. But then Noah hid his thoughts well whenever it suited him to do so. "I saw the work you did at Parker's Point, and I saw how fast you got it done."

Grace nodded. "We own condos here and in Florida. We like to keep them looking nice. But we just bought a place that's in horrible shape. No grass, scraggly shrubs, not a single flower or spot of color anywhere. We can't very well keep the units rented when it looks so ugly. We were hoping you'd have time to give us an estimate on a custom design. I can tell you what I'd like, but I don't know enough about sunlight and soil to know what'll grow well there."

Bless sweet Grace, Ben thought, when she finally wound down to take a breath. Now there was a woman with a lovable personality. Unlike Sierra—Ben gave her a dark look—Grace was always happy to see him, always smiling at him. He looked at Sierra's profile, watching her swallow her annoyance long enough to talk business with his brother. For the first time, he noticed the dark shadows beneath her eyes.

Hadn't she been sleeping enough? How long had her ex been bothering her?

With sudden clarity, Ben remembered the phone calls. She hadn't wanted to answer, but he'd goaded her into it. "It was him on the damn phone, wasn't it?"

Everyone went silent, until finally Noah asked, "Him who?"

Sierra glowered. "Not now, Ben."

Grace stared in fascination.

Ben withdrew, but only for the moment. He continued to think, to ponder different things that were starting to make sense to him now. Perhaps Sierra wasn't comparing him to her ex. Perhaps she feared what her ex might do to her if she got involved with another man. Ex-husbands could still be very jealous, even territorial. Had Sierra left him, or vice versa? Did the man still care about her?

No one bothered Ben in his sullen ruminations because they were all too busy ignoring him. That suited him just fine. He felt like he was finally getting some things figured out and he didn't want to be interrupted.

Kent had said that Sierra tried to protect everyone but herself. Uneasiness prickled along Ben's spine. Did that mean her husband might hurt her? Or that he'd already hurt her? *Or both?*

Sierra had made statements about men taking away choices, making women do things, and now those comments took on new meaning.

His hands curled into fists. He should have beat the shit out of the guy when he'd had the chance.

His only excuse was that Sierra had bordered on hysteria, and that had knocked his knees right out from under him. She was usually so confident, so strong, that seeing her shaken had shaken him. He'd been frantic to reassure her, to make certain she wasn't hurt. She hadn't wanted them to fight, that was certain. But why?

Did Sierra think her ex could hurt him? Ben snorted, drawing startled glances from everyone. He waved them and their unwanted attention away and went back to pondering the puzzle of Sierra's behavior.

Usually she was so tough . . . No. Ben shook his head, disregarding that thought and drawing more curious stares. Sierra was small and sweet, she just pretended to be tough.

Because she'd had to be in order to survive?

Well, that was over. He gave a sharp nod and again had his brother and Grace glancing at him. He wouldn't let anyone hurt her ever again. He'd take care of her.

But Kent had claimed her independence and privacy to be very important to her, and from what he'd learned of her, it was true. She wouldn't take kindly to him interfering in her troubles, even if he acted in her best interest. So what should he do?

Grace touched his knee. "Ben? You're sitting there muttering to yourself and gesturing like a deranged man. Are you okay?"

He was so lost in thought that for a moment, he had no idea what Grace had asked him. He stared at her, totally blank, then he gathered himself and slapped his knees. "Yeah, I'm fine. Is your discussion over?"

Grace settled back in her seat, bemused by him. "Yes. Sierra will give us an estimate tomorrow."

"Great." He pushed to his feet, eager to be alone with her. "Then if you two will excuse us?"

Grace coughed away her smile, but Noah didn't bother. "A little tact wouldn't kill you, you know."

Sierra stared at him, her look mean, her tone more so. "No, but I might."

Ben *tsked-tsked* her, grinning all the while and filled with purpose. He herded his brother to the door. "Thanks for stopping by Noah, Grace."

Grace hugged him, and whispered in his ear. "You're coming on awfully strong, Ben."

He smacked her on her ample behind. "Trust me, she loves it."

Noah scooped Grace away from him. "Yeah. She looks real smitten the way she's grinding her teeth." Then he punched Ben in the shoulder. "Keep your hands off my wife's ass."

Rubbing his shoulder, Ben repeated, "She loves it," and had to duck when Grace swatted at him.

He was still chuckling when he turned the deadbolt on the front door and walked back to Sierra. One look at her tense, sullen expression and his humor died.

He'd known her less than a month. Except for that first night, he hadn't had her naked, hadn't been able to touch her as he wanted to. But he'd gotten closer to her in other ways than any other woman he'd known.

Most times she was so easy to read, so open to him.

Other times she shut him out completely. Always, she tugged at his heartstrings.

Looking at her now, he smiled. "Uh-oh. Am I in trouble here?"

She opened her mouth to blast him and he blurted, "I am so damn sorry, sweetheart." Sorry for the assumptions he'd made, sorry for not understanding. Sorry for trying to manipulate her.

While she sputtered, Ben sat next to her, caught both her hands in his, and kissed her. It had been far too long since he'd had her mouth and his senses rioted. He meant the kiss to be brief, a show of tenderness.

Her mouth was already open and she didn't pull away, so he took advantage, licking along her bottom lip, slowly, gently, then slipping inside. Sierra made a soft sound and tipped her head back a little, inadvertently giving him better access. She always tasted so good to him, so . . . perfect.

She didn't slap him, so Ben continued, dipping, retreating, dipping again. When she still didn't object, he settled in for a long, slow, tongue-thrusting, mating-of-the-mouth kiss.

Like a snowball in July, Sierra melted.

Ben heard her gruff moan, felt the way she shifted marginally toward him. God, it had been an eternity since he'd tasted her like this. A week had felt like a year when he'd wanted her mouth his every waking second.

Her hands first touched his chest, tentative and shy, then moved to his shoulders before looping around his neck so her fingers could twine in his hair.

He was lost.

"I've missed you so goddamned much." Ben groaned

that sentiment against her lips, unable to stop himself. Before the words were fully said, Sierra pulled him back, fusing their mouths together again, catching his tongue and sucking on it.

It seemed every bit of anger she'd felt, all his frustration and worry, had exploded into blinding passion. In a near frenzy, he searched out her breast and cuddled it in his palm, found her nipple with his fingertips, teased and rolled and plucked. She arched into him with a soft, hungry cry.

"Jesus, you are so hot." She took his breath away with her quick acceptance. When Ben lowered her to the couch cushions, she didn't complain. In fact, she opened her legs to make room for him, allowing him to settle into the cradle of her body. It felt like she'd been made for him, the alignment perfect enough to drive him wild.

He struggled with her shirt, shoving it up until it tucked beneath her chin leaving her nearly naked from her chest to the waistband of her shorts. She looked so pretty with her pale breasts rising and falling, her abdomen expanding, her belly pulled tight.

Using his teeth, Ben caught her nipple through her bra. Her fingers clenched painfully in his hair and she groaned. He nipped at her, tugged insistently, and when she cried out, he tugged again.

"Ben."

"Swear to me, Sierra." He raised up to see her and caught her face in his hands so she had no choice but to look at him. "I'll trust you to know what's best for you. But you have to trust me a little, too."

She twisted against him. "No, I don't know how."

There was so much sadness in her tone, it scared Ben.

He took her mouth again, long and hard and thorough, just to erase that awful desolation from her eyes. "Swear to me that if you need me, you'll call."

"Ben." Green eyes smoldering, she ran her hands over his chest, down his sides to his hips, making him shudder. "I haven't been able to sleep for wanting to touch you again."

"You'll sleep tonight, sweetheart." He traced her cheekbones, seeing the signs of fatigue that proved her words. God, he'd been a fool with his stupid plans of a bogus friendship. He'd been playing cat and mouse games, with Sierra as the mouse. She deserved better. He should have told her all along that he needed everything. "Now swear to me."

"There's so much you don't understand."

And so much she didn't want to explain. It shook him, this great reserve of hers. No one should be so alone. "We'll figure everything out later. But for now I just want your word that you'll let me know if you need me."

"All right." She drew in a deep, uncertain breath. "But otherwise, Ben, please don't interfere."

It was a start. Ben nodded his agreement and saw the smile in her eyes, the softening of her worry.

And the burning of desire.

"You care about me, Sierra."

Her mouth trembled, and she swallowed hard. "Maybe."

That small admission made his heart thunder, made him shake with urgency. He had to brace himself to keep from moving too quickly. She'd been through a lot tonight and he didn't want to rush her.

"Ben?"

He drew a calming breath and summoned a smile. "Yeah, sweetheart?"

"I . . . I can't take it anymore."

Ben's first thought was that she meant her situation with her ex. Fury stirred within him, warring with his need to comfort her. His muscles hurt from clenching so hard. "Tell me what I can do, Sierra. Anything."

Her gaze dropped to his mouth, and with one fingertip, she touched his bottom lip. "What you've done to me, the ways that you've touched me . . . it's all been so wonderful."

Ben held his breath. "But?"

Her gaze locked on his. "But I want more than that now."

Damn. The husky way she said that proved his undoing. Already he burned, and his words emerged as a growl. "How much more?"

"Enough to get you out of my system."

"Sierra . . ." She'd never be rid of him, but she didn't give him the chance to explain that.

Opening her thighs wider, she arched up, pressing her soft belly against his erection, and Ben was lost.

He tried to tell himself to slow down, but he couldn't. He felt primitive, and he felt protective. The two combined were potent enough to blur his vision and steal what little common sense he possessed. Getting her naked, getting inside her, seemed more important than anything else possibly could. His muscles throbbed and his guts cramped.

Ben tugged her shirt off over her head and heard a seam rip. Sierra didn't care. She struggled with her bra, trying to help him get it open so her breasts would be naked to his hands and his mouth. The small plastic front catch finally gave way to her frustration, and Ben shoved the cups aside.

Already her nipples were puckered tight, flushed dark. He lowered his head, closed his hot mouth around her and sucked.

With a long moan, Sierra shivered under him, trying to wiggle away from him, instinctively fighting such an onslaught of pleasure even as her hips rolled against his, stroking the length of his cock, further inciting him. He was voracious in his hunger, deaf to her small cries.

Locking his arm beneath her, Ben curved her back, keeping her breasts raised up while he feasted on her nipples. He drew on her, nipping, licking, sucking hard until both nipples were ripe and swollen and tender. Her legs wrapped tight around him, her ankles locked at the small of his back. He couldn't get enough of her. They moved together in a parody of intercourse, both fevered, both anxious. The thin cotton of her shorts and panties weren't much of a barrier. The material of his slacks was rough, rasping against her.

Ben felt her tighten, heard her breath catch sharply.

He was swirling his tongue around her left nipple one last time when suddenly she came. Her neck arched, her eyes squeezed shut and she clasped him tightly with her thighs. A little stunned, Ben continued to move on her, keeping the hard ridge of his cock in just the right spot, pleasuring her and relishing the bite of her nails on his shoulders.

He stared down at her in awe, watching her face as it crumbled in her pleasure, seeing her glossy hair tangle on the couch cushion, enjoying the sight of her heaving breasts. He struggled for breath and knew in that moment he'd fallen in love with her.

She went pliant beneath him. Overcome with tenderness, Ben smoothed her hair away from her face. "You needed that," he whispered.

She was panting hard, her eyes closed, her lashes resting in damp spikes, her cheeks flushed. He felt good, very good. He felt like a man who'd found that one special woman.

"You okay, sweetheart?"

She swallowed, drew a shuddering breath, and nodded. Two seconds later, she chuckled roughly, but the humor faded into a groan. "God, I am easy."

"You," Ben said, punctuating his words with a kiss, "are incredible."

You, he added to himself, *are mine.*

Her lashes lifted. Her eyes were dark and stormy. "What you do to me is incredible. And wonderful. But I want—I *need*—to know what it feels like to have you inside me." As she said it, she caught the hem of his shirt and pulled it up.

Hell, yes. Ben helped, reaching back and catching the shirt in his fist, ripping it off over his head. Sierra's eyelids went heavy as she touched him.

"I've been obsessed." Her hot little hands coasted over him, making his muscles ripple in pleasure. She thumbed his nipples, tangled her fingers in his chest hair, looked up at him with wonder. "I can't seem to get through the day without thinking about you and this, and how you make me feel. I've had more fantasies since meeting you than ever before in my whole life."

Ben barely heard her words. Watching Sierra explore his chest was a distinct pleasure, and he couldn't take it for long. He trembled like a virgin at an orgy. "There are more interesting places for you to check out."

"Yeah?"

"Oh yeah." She didn't say anything more, so Ben prompted her with a quick peck on her smiling, teasing mouth. "Want me to take my jeans off?"

Her smile turned impish, sweet. "Sure."

Ben rolled to the side of her. The damn couch was fat, but short, and if he had any sense, he'd drag them both to the bedroom.

Lust ruled the day, not sense.

His shoes got kicked off and fell to the floor. He struggled with his belt, cautiously slid down his zipper over his engorged erection. Sierra rose up to her elbows to watch. Her gaze was so direct, so unflinching, he would have smiled if he hadn't been so close to losing it.

She still wore her shorts.

Ben nodded at them. "Take 'em off."

She kept her gaze glued to him while she did as he asked. They bumped elbows and shoulders, tangled their legs, and it took a little acrobatic work but finally they were both naked. Breathing hard, Ben moved on top of her and growled with the sheer pleasure of feeling her small, silky body beneath him. He closed his eyes and absorbed the feel of her, where she belonged. *Heaven.*

"No fair, Ben."

Her grumbling tone barely penetrated his fog of need. "How's that?"

"I want to look at you, too."

God, he hurt. "How about showing a little mercy, here, sweetheart? I promise when we're done, you can look at me all you want."

"All right, but I'll hold you to that."

How the hell could she string so many words together?

She touched his nipple, and Ben inhaled sharply. "What about birth control?"

Ben's sluggish brain refused to work. He had to concentrate hard. "Yeah. Rubbers. Got 'em in my wallet." He ruthlessly brought himself under control. Never in his life had he forgotten birth control. More than most men, he understood his responsibilities. He would never compromise a woman that way, and Sierra wasn't just any woman. He stopped and drew several deep breaths.

"Ben," she complained, her hands busy on his chest, his shoulders. "Why are you waiting?"

"I don't want to rush things." He wanted to blow her mind with pleasure, to overwhelm her with his finesse, to hook her for good.

When he finished with her, she wouldn't have him out of her system at all. Hell no. She'd be addicted.

He heard her long sigh, then: *"Ben."*

Eyes closed, nostrils flaring, he said, "What?"

"Rush things."

He blinked at her insistent tone, smiled despite himself, and smoothed his hand over her rounded hip. "So demanding."

Snagging up his jeans, he located his wallet, but his muscles were so tight he felt awkward and accidentally dumped it. Jesus, where had his finesse gone?

He ignored the scattered bills and credit cards and grabbed for a condom. He got it on in record time and settled over Sierra again. She moved against him, making his breath catch.

"Damn, I'm on the ragged edge here, Sierra. I want to be careful with you, I really do. But I've waited too long, wanted you too much, and more than anything I'm dying to get inside you."

Her arms looped around his neck. "It's where I want you to be."

Damn. "You don't understand. One fast tumble isn't even going to take the edge off."

Sierra stroked her hands down his back to his bare buttocks. She lightly stroked him with her nails. "I've got all night."

Ben's flagging control shattered. Seeing her through a haze of need, he reached between their bodies and slid his fingers between her thighs until her swollen sex was slick and open. Sierra moaned and squirmed. She was so wet, both from her recent climax and from renewed desire, that Ben knew sinking into her would be damn sweet.

He watched her face and slowly pushed two fingers into her, opening her more, preparing her.

She twisted beneath him, sexy little sounds coming from deep in her throat. *"Ben, please."*

He withdrew his fingers to touch her swollen clitoris and she bowed so hard, she nearly dislodged him. Her breath came fast and hard and she held him so tight, he knew she was ready. He directed the head of his cock inside, felt her open around him, felt the wet heat closing on him, her clenching muscles pulling at him.

Sierra's eyes closed on a gasp; his jaw locked in acute pleasure.

Steadily pushing forward, Ben sank into her until they were fully joined, his whole length buried deep. Sierra caught her breath and held it; he growled.

Their heartbeats galloped together.

"Ah . . . God." Her fingers tangled in his hair, and she whimpered.

Ben couldn't take it. "Damn it." He levered up on stiffened arms, withdrew and drove hard into her again. She raised her arms above her head, wanton, vulnerable, and she sobbed, a sound of mind-numbing excitement. She was slick, her muscles grabbing hold of him, squeezing. He pulled almost all the way out, felt her try to follow, and drove back in.

She wrapped her legs high around his waist and that opened her even more, sent him deeper inside her. He hammered into her, his gaze fierce on her face, his jaw locked, his muscles sweating and clenching and quivering.

Her plump breasts shivered from his thrusts, her nipples puckered and flushed dark, still wet from his mouth. He could smell her, the combined scent that was uniquely Sierra and the spicy aroma of her arousal. He felt cocooned in sensuality and heat and something more, something he'd never experienced with any other woman. This was Sierra, and goddammit, it was different.

Her eyes went blank as she stared up at him and Ben knew she was ready to come. Keeping his thrusts steady, all his concentration now on her pleasure, he watched her lips part in a silent cry, her body straining. "Come on, sweetheart," he urged, thrusting, withdrawing, thrusting again. "Come for me."

She called out his name, caught on the waves of sensation—pleasure that *he'd* given her.

It was enough. It was too much.

Ben closed his eyes and groaned out his own release. It seemed she wrung him out, the tension going on and on until he didn't think he could move again, until he was too drained to hold himself up. He dropped down onto Sierra and heard her small huff as she took his weight. He knew he needed to say something good, something endearing. But the only words that came to his mind were too profound.

I love you.

Don't ever leave me.

Damn. His brain throbbed in the aftermath. She wasn't ready to hear that. She still thought in temporary terms.

Ben squeezed his eyes shut and forced himself to think logically. What did he usually say to women afterward? Something about it being nice, about it being special. Something sincere but noncommittal. He joked or teased, lightening the mood.

But that didn't feel right, to use catch phrases for Sierra. She *was* special, and she went a far sight beyond nice. He couldn't make light of it. Making love to her was . . . well, mind blowing.

God, he'd blown his own mind, not hers. Pathetic.

Ben argued with himself for several more minutes before the silence stretched out to an uncomfortable degree. He didn't want to hurt her, ever, so he'd just have to think of something.

"Sierra." He lifted his head and saw her eyes were closed, her body utterly still, her breathing deep and calm. He had to kiss her open mouth, had to touch her small ear. "Sweetheart?"

Her reply was a snuffling snore as she settled more comfortably into the sofa cushions.

Eyes widening in surprise, Ben said again, "Sierra?"

She stirred but didn't awaken. Ben chuckled to himself, grateful for the reprieve so he could figure himself out before he had to make any declarations to her.

Carefully, not wanting to awaken her, he separated

their bodies. She'd wanted to make love all night, but she obviously wasn't up for that. Hell, Ben thought, she wasn't even conscious. He pressed a soft kiss to her temple.

How much of an emotional burden had she been carrying all alone? Why the hell hadn't Kent run her ex off for her? It seemed that for every advancement he made with Sierra, more questions arose.

She stirred against him, making Ben's heart pound. He considered his options and came to a quick decision. He hadn't liked the idea of leaving her alone to begin with, and now, if he could keep her asleep, he wouldn't have to.

When he stood, one of her slim legs slid off the side of the couch to put her in an inelegant but visually stimulating sprawl. He glanced at her nude length, but his eyes were drawn again and again to the damp auburn curls between her thighs, to her tender, swollen pink sex. So tempting.

Oh man, he wanted to touch her. He wanted to taste her.

Better not. At least not yet. She'd hoped to get him out of her system, so it was up to Ben to prove to her that she couldn't. If he took advantage of her now . . . no, she wouldn't like that.

She was so stubborn, so set on her course, he'd have to work hard to show her that he wasn't a temporary craze, that he wasn't a man she "could get out of her system."

Ben scooped her slight, dead weight into his arms and carried her to the twin bed. She must have been some time without sleep, given she didn't move from where he laid her. He literally had to put the pillow beneath her head.

He went into the bathroom to dispose of the condom.

He shook his head at himself; if it hadn't been for Sierra's reminder, would he have taken her without protection? What if she'd gotten pregnant?

He paused, hands braced on the edge of the sink, staring blindly into the basin. He adored women, and God knew he enjoyed sex, but he didn't let either rule his common sense. He *never* took chances, never forgot himself. He hated his father for what he'd done, how his mother and Noah had both paid for his irresponsibility. At a very young age, he'd vowed that he'd be different, that there'd be no similarities between himself and the bastard who'd fathered him.

Yet with Sierra, he'd nearly forgotten himself. If she hadn't stopped him, he'd have slid into her with no barriers, just flesh on flesh—and God, it would have been good. Ben shuddered just thinking about it. He'd never had sex without a rubber, but he'd love to feel Sierra and only Sierra.

Would it really be so bad if she got pregnant?

Appalled at his own thoughts, Ben jerked upright. He was rushing things again, damn it, when Sierra didn't even want him around. Yet.

He shook his head, anxious to get beside her again. He washed up, even borrowing Sierra's toothbrush without remorse. He loved her, he fully intended to sway her into loving him back, so sharing a toothbrush was no big deal.

When he finished cleaning up, he went through the living room and kitchen, checking to make sure the new window locks were secure and bolting her front door. He slept light, so he left her bedroom window wide open and positioned the box fan to bring in some of the cooler night air. Without air-conditioning, the small building was stuffy and far too warm—but he'd be sleeping with

Sierra, so he considered that discomfort only a small price to pay.

After turning out the light, Ben slid into bed naked beside her. It was a close fit so he spooned her, hugging her into his arms, loving the feel of her round bottom against his groin. He cupped a breast possessively, kissed her ear with absent-minded affection, and stared into the darkness.

He had a lot to think about—her ex-husband, her safety, his own incredible reaction to her and the fact that he'd fallen in love with a woman who fought him every chance she got—a woman who claimed she wanted to get him out of her system. Ben snorted at her silliness. He wasn't going anywhere and she'd just have to accept it.

But all that aside, he was here with her now—he gave her a squeeze to prove it to himself—and so he'd sleep, and hold her, and most of all, he'd love her.

Tomorrow he'd begin to work things out.

Somehow.

Chapter Eleven

S ierra stretched with a groan, and stilled when she felt the hard, hot, hairy body against her back. Her eyes rounded with shock and she went on one elbow to look behind her, and found Ben smiling at her in the dim morning light.

"Hey, sleepyhead." His arms tightened, toppling her off her elbow and landing her across his chest.

Utterly dumbfounded, she reared up to stare at him some more. He looked . . . wonderful. His sinfully dark eyes were heavy lidded, his jaw dark with beard shadow, his black hair rumpled. One side of his mouth kicked up and he stroked a hand down her back to her bottom. His palm covered her and he squeezed.

"Ben!"

His smile widened, sleepy and suggestive and oh so sexy. "Do you always look like this in the morning?"

Sierra blinked, trying to absorb the memories that came crashing back to her sleep-fogged brain. It wasn't easy, considering Ben was in her bed. And evidently, he'd . . . *slept* with her.

Damn, had she gotten him out of her system or not? As she wondered about that, his large rough hand lazily stroked her bottom cheek, making her shiver and giving her an answer. *Not.*

"It was a simple question, Sierra."

Her eyes nearly crossed. "What question?"

His fingers pressed between her cheeks, touching her sex from behind. "Do you always look like this in the morning?"

She could barely catch her breath. Her body automatically tightened, her back arched. "Probably," she squeaked. Then, feeling self-conscious, she shook her head. "How bad do I look?"

He fondled her upper thigh, squeezed. In a throaty rumble, he said, "You look entirely edible."

Oh God. "I have to pee."

In self-preservation, Sierra slid off the bed, realized what she'd said, and looked back at Ben in absolute horror. Sex had fried her brain!

He smiled in male indulgence. "Go on. I'll wait here."

Sierra fled. The bathroom was right around the wall, and she darted inside, then accidentally slammed the door behind her. Dropping against it, she stared blankly at the far wall. Gray predawn light filtered in through the small window. She was naked and had slept with Ben. All night.

All night.

And he wanted to get sexual again this morning. Her heart began racing and already a funny stirring made her belly tingle and her breasts feel full and sensitive. *Damn, damn, damn.*

Vaguely, she remembered thinking she'd get her fill of him, sate herself on his body, and then be done with him. It was the safe thing to do.

Logically, she'd expected him to be ready to walk. Regardless of anything he'd said, she knew her biggest lure for Ben had to be that she didn't fall at his feet as most women probably did. That thought made her scowl because she had seen his effect on women. They all wanted him—hell, they'd probably all had him.

She still wouldn't fall at his feet, but she'd intended to make last night one that would last her a lifetime and would appease his need for conquest.

Instead, he'd had sex with her only once and then slept with her. Sierra closed her eyes on a moan. Ben had been naked next to her all night long. The thought was enough to boggle her already fractured mind.

Well, there was no going back now, so she'd just have to make sure that no one knew they'd spent the night together. If Griff found out, she didn't know what he might do. But Ben had worked too hard on his business and had been far too nice to her to be forced to pay for her mistakes.

What time was it? Would Kent be showing up soon?

Filled with a new urgency, Sierra hurriedly used the bathroom, splashed her face, combed her hair and gargled. When she started to open the door, she hesitated. She didn't have a single stitch on. He'd already noticed that, of course, so modesty now would be moot, not to mention silly. But still . . .

Ben tapped on the door. "Can I have a turn?"

Dumbly, Sierra opened the door and stared at him

some more. They hadn't turned a single light on yet, but she didn't need much light to appreciate how good he looked.

She stood eye level to his chest—and wow, he had such a great chest. Somewhat hairy, but not overly. Muscular and wide. Great pecs. She remembered how his chest hair had abraded her nipples when he'd moved over her the night before, deep and steady and hot . . . She shivered.

He had a really great abdomen too, hard and flat, with a happy little trail of silky hair leading down to his . . . her face heated with both embarrassment and interest.

He was hard.

Ben tapped her mouth shut. "Morning wood. It happens all the time."

Sierra forced her wide eyes up to his face—but she did so slowly, savoring the sight of him.

Gloriously naked, tall and strong and . . . perfect, he stood there in her doorway smiling. She loved his smile. She loved his body. She sighed in something of a lustful trance.

Ben stepped around her, patted her butt, and being outrageous, said, "How about you go arrange yourself on the bed? Maybe lay back with your pretty legs open. No sheets, okay? I'll be right there. And Sierra? Think about what I'm going to do to you."

"Do to me?"

"Yep. *After* we talk." He closed the door in her face.

Sierra stood there for a long moment, speechless, before stomping away. Wait for him naked? Not likely. She groped around in her dresser drawer until she located a large tee. The sleeves fell to her elbows and the hem landed just above her knees. After crawling into the bed, she pulled the sheet to her chin. She checked the clock, saw it was only five-thirty, and realized she had an hour and a half before she needed to be up, two hours before Kent would arrive to go to work with her.

True to Ben's word, she'd slept last night. Or more like she'd passed out. She barely remembered anything beyond the incredible wash of numbing pleasure. Experiencing an orgasm while Ben filled her up and touched her everywhere, was a part of her, went beyond mere pleasure.

She knew it was selfish of her, but she wanted more. Maybe they could use the rest of the morning to overindulge, *then* she'd be through with him.

Ben reappeared. He looked at her curled in the bed with the sheet covering her, shook his head, and said, "Spoilsport."

And he walked away!

Alarmed, Sierra scurried out of the bed to follow him. Since he was here, she didn't want him to leave. Not yet. Not when she knew exactly what he could do and how much she'd like it.

But he'd only gone to her phone. Here at the front of her home, the bright outdoor lights coming through the kitchen and living room window offered more illumination, but since they were closed and locked, this part of the house was very warm.

"What are you doing?"

He picked up the phone and dialed. "Ordering room service."

"We're not in your motel!"

He shrugged, and being that he was naked, it was quite distracting. "There are perks to being the owner."

When she started to reply to that, he held up one finger

to hush her and said into the phone, "Yeah, this is Ben Badwin." He grinned his teasing grin, making Sierra grind her teeth. "Well, good morning to you too."

Who had answered? One of the waitresses who no doubt wanted him? Which of the waitresses *didn't* want him?

"Could you get someone to run a pot of coffee and doughnuts across the street to me? Yeah, at the landscaping place. That'd be great. Thanks." He hung up.

Sierra felt hot with embarrassment and fury. "I can't believe you just did that."

He eyed her as he went past to the living room. "If you're not going to accommodate my first hunger, we might as well feed my second. And for that I suppose I'll need pants." He shook out his jeans and then stepped into them, but didn't bother with the zipper or snap. His shirt and briefs were still on the floor.

Somehow his wallet had gotten dumped so he scooped everything up and put it all back. He handed a ten to Sierra.

She looked at it. Though she should have been coming out of it a little, she still felt caught off guard. She imagined waking up naked in bed with Ben could rattle any woman. "Uh . . ."

"That's for the coffee and doughnuts—a tip. Not to pay for last night." He winked, and with his black hair mussed and his jaw dark with stubble, he looked like a pirate. "Course, if anyone got paid for last night it'd have to be me, right?"

She wadded up the bill and threw it at him, which only made him laugh. A tap sounded at her door and Ben went to answer it.

Naked beneath an oversized tee, Sierra hung back,

peeking around the corner. She saw Ben open the door with a warm greeting. "You're a lifesaver, Cathy."

"Anything for you Ben, you know that."

Sierra scowled, watching the little hussy with grim annoyance.

"Anything, huh?" Ben flicked the end of her nose. "Be careful or your beau might be after my ass."

She gave him a coy come-hither look. "Honey, your ass is so fine, he wouldn't dare."

Laughing, Ben balanced the tray on one palm and handed her the ten. "Here ya go, sweets."

"Wow, thanks." She folded the bill and stuck it in her pocket.

"Do me a favor and tell Horace I'll be over there in a couple of hours, okay?"

"Will do." She turned away and Ben closed the door.

Sierra stepped out in front of him, steaming mad. "Are you sleeping with her?"

He looked surprised by the question—and amused. "Naw. I don't fool around with my employees." Edging around her, he headed for the bedroom. Sierra followed in a furious stomp.

"You were coming on to her, Ben. I'm not blind."

"Wrong. We were just teasing. It didn't mean anything." His cavalier attitude set her teeth on edge, but then he set the tray at the bottom of her bed and shucked off his jeans without a care. Sierra tried to turn away, and he caught her arm. He tugged her close and fingered the hem of her T-shirt. "Let's get this off you, okay?"

Indignant, she clutched at the shirt. "Damn it, Ben. I'm serious."

Keeping his voice low and rough, he said, "Yeah, me too. I seriously want you naked in bed with me."

Sierra slapped at his hands, but he was in a teasing, playful mood despite her annoyance, and she was no match
against his good humor.

He won the tug of war over her shirt, and the next
thing she knew, she stood naked before him.

"Damn, you look good in the buff." His gaze touched
on her everywhere, nearly tactile in intent, especially
when he lingered at her belly. He stroked her abdomen
with the backs of his fingers. "I thought you looked cute
as hell in your work clothes too, but naked . . ." He whistled low.

Sierra was profoundly grateful that he hadn't turned
on a light. Not that she was shy about her body; she had
no reason to be ashamed or embarrassed. But she wasn't
used to being openly admired either, certainly not in a
sexual way, and most definitely not by a man like Ben.
The dim light and lengthy shadows lent some privacy
from his concentrated scrutiny.

He loosely held her hips and tracked his gaze up her
body to her face. Even in the shadows, Sierra saw the
flame in his dark eyes. "Now, if you're going to give me
hell, at least let's do it with a little caffeine in our sys-
tems, okay?"

She now felt so flustered, Sierra considered dumping
the coffee on his head. When she folded her arms under
her breasts, tapped her bare foot, and glared, Ben sighed.
"You're jealous over nothing, you know."

At his assumption, she gasped so hard she choked herself and felt doubly foolish. "I am *not* jealous, Ben Badwin."

"Right. Not jealous. Just pissed. Got it." Ben turned
away, but not before she saw his small smile. He stretched
out on the bed with his back propped on the wall, his an-

kles crossed, then patted the mattress next to his hip. "Care to join me?"

Sierra couldn't quite get her feet to move. The man was gloriously naked, semiaroused, and so appealing her tongue stuck to the roof of her mouth. Though he was naturally dark, she noted a lingering tan on his upper body and legs. Obviously he didn't cavort naked in the sun because his hips were paler, a stark contrast for the dark hair surrounding his penis.

She'd seen unclothed men before. Not that she had a lot of money to spend on entertainment, but she'd been to the movies, and she'd bought magazines on occasion. It was simply that most men didn't look like Ben, and most men didn't affect her as he did.

While she stared at him, he hardened more until he was fully erect, his penis long and hard, jutting upward. Sierra felt her mouth fall open, felt her heartbeat speed up until it felt as though she'd been running, she was so breathless. That part of him had been inside her and had brought her so much pleasure.

Ben made a low sound and her gaze flew to his face. He grinned at her, but his expression was strained. "I feel like a feast set before a starving woman." He reached down and touched himself lightly. "I'm starting to get used to a perpetual boner around you, but much more of that avid staring and I might just embarrass myself."

A faint buzzing sounded in her ears. She stared at him, unsure what to do, but knowing what she wanted to do. She wanted to devour him. Sex. That's all she could take from him and with Griff looming about, this might be the only time she could take it.

He again patted the bed beside him. "Come on, sweetheart. It'll be okay. Have a little trust."

His coaxing voice did her in. Nearly numb, Sierra went around to the other side of the bed and slid beneath the sheets. She pulled them high, covering her nudity. Then she just sat there. For the life of her, she couldn't think of a single thing to say.

Ben fixed her a cup of coffee and offered it to her, waiting until she'd finally slipped one hand from beneath the sheet and accepted it.

After she'd taken a cautious sip, he turned toward her. "First things first. Cathy is one of the few employees who doesn't try to coerce me into bed."

Feeling more in control now, Sierra slanted him a look. No way could Ben be that dense. "I saw her, Ben. She was flirting and so were you."

He shrugged. "There's flirting, and then there's flirting. The thing is, she's not serious about it and neither am I."

Needing something to do, Sierra reached for a dough-nut from the tray and sank her teeth into it, studiously ignoring Ben and his lame excuses. She didn't want him. *She didn't,* at least not for anything permanent or serious, so what did it matter to her if he slept with every woman he hired? It didn't. It couldn't.

But then again, damn it, it did.

"She's engaged, you know, happily so." Ben caught her chin and brought her face around. His dark eyes appeared very sincere, as if her trust mattered to him. "I've met her fiancé. A nice guy. They're in love, so when she teases with me, it doesn't mean a damn thing and we both know it."

Sierra considered that. When she'd been younger, she'd flirted and guys had flirted back. But that seemed a lifetime ago. She couldn't even recall the last time she'd noticed a man's interest. Excluding Ben, of course. "How can you tell the difference?"

To her consternation, Ben reached over and dipped beneath the sheet to touch her nipple with his middle finger. His expression was so concentrated, so intent as he circled her nipple and watched it draw tight, she felt chills race up her spine, followed by a wave of heat.

"I can tell." He captured and held her gaze. "It's in the eyes, in the way things are said. In the body language." That teasing finger slid down over her ribs to her navel, taking the sheet away from her breasts.

Sierra held coffee in one hand, a doughnut in the other, and she could do nothing to stop him. She didn't want to stop him.

"Some of the women have been very serious in their efforts." He trailed his finger back up her body, then touched her chin. "But as I said, I don't sleep with employees."

It took her a moment to gather her breath. "How . . . discriminating of you."

"Yeah." Ben set his mug aside on the nightstand and flipped on the light, temporarily blinding her. "Now, I want to talk to you."

Sierra didn't like the way that sounded. She'd hoped to make love with him again, but despite all his teasing and touches and hot looks, he didn't seem receptive to that idea. "I should be getting ready for work."

"There's time." He reached over and relieved her of her cup as well. He even took her last bite of doughnut from her, and set the tray on the floor. When he leaned back into the bed, he was all business.

The irony of it struck her, but she wasn't amused. She was too aroused and edgy and anxious for that. "I can't believe I'm in bed with you, and all you want to do is talk."

He sighed. "*All* I want to do? Not likely. But we have important stuff to discuss." He stroked the side of her throat. "When we're done talking, you can have at my poor body to your heart's content. Deal?"

She couldn't let him sway her with sensual promises. "We have nothing to talk about."

He groaned with his own measure of frustration. "Give over, Sierra. Things are different now and you know it. I have the right to ask a few questions."

"Because we slept together?"

"There's that." His normally teasing air was far too grave to put her at ease. "But there's also your ex-husband and the fact that I walked into something yesterday."

Her heart skipped a beat. "It's not your concern, Ben." Sierra had no doubt that if Griffin decided to ruin her business, he could. He could also do damage to Ben's motel. She wouldn't be able to live with herself if that happened.

"Bullshit." The word was harshly muttered, but his hand was gentle when he cupped her chin. "You've asked me to trust you, Sierra, and I do. Believe me, I know you're smart and I know you're more than capable of handling most situations."

"*All* situations."

His tone dropped, his brows gathered together. "I want to know what was going on yesterday, and I want to know if that bastard's ever hurt you."

Oh no. Sierra started to slide away, ready to leave the bed and the awful temptation Ben offered. She couldn't rely on him, couldn't confide in him. It was difficult enough having Kent at risk, but Ben . . . No, she wouldn't do that. It would only complicate her life, not make it easier.

Before she could apply action to intent, Ben caught her upper arms, halting her escape. He hauled her half over him, her face close to his. "*Goddamn it, Sierra—*"

Pain shuddered through her arms from where he gripped her, and she stiffened in surprise. In an instant, his hold gentled and he lowered her to her back, looming over her, his expression now carved in granite. "What is it?"

She couldn't tell him that Griff had manhandled her last night, that he'd bruised her arms with his casual cruelty. Not only did it shame her to admit to the type of man she'd married, but she didn't want Ben's pity. She absolutely didn't want his interference. She wanted sex, damn it.

She turned her head away.

Silence pulsed in the air between them. Ben's hands slid over her shoulders, her upper arms, caressing, searching— and she felt the awful stillness that came over him. "Jesus."

Sierra didn't need to look to know what he'd seen. She bruised easily, and Griff had deliberately squeezed her, wanting to mark her.

Ben's fingertips touched feather light over the bruises. He didn't physically hurt her, but emotionally she felt shattered. Sounding very grim, Ben asked, "He did this to you?"

It wasn't easy to swallow down the choking emotions and affect a nonchalant tone. Sierra wasn't at all sure she succeeded. "It's nothing."

As if he could heal the bruises with his touch, his fingers continued to gently coast over her. Tension radiated off him, and his voice went hoarse. "Meaning he's done similar things so many times you don't let it bother you anymore?"

Sierra forced herself to look at Ben. He sounded harsh with rage, but his eyes were nearly black and soft with concern. "Meaning it's none of your business."

She'd made her voice firm, detached, and she half-expected Ben to be angry at her direct rejection.

Instead, he leaned down and pressed a light, apologetic kiss to her mouth. "Sorry, sweetheart. Not this time."

Alarmed by the determination in his tone, Sierra tried to sit up but Ben sprawled over her until his warm hard chest covered her breasts and one hairy muscular thigh pinned down her legs.

She inhaled sharply at the touch of all that hard, hot male flesh against her. Her arms, her bruises, her ex were forgotten—until Ben spoke.

"This time," he whispered, "I'm making it my business."

Strain etched her features as Sierra stared at him. Her face was nearly white, her eyes liquid. "Get off."

Ben hardened his resolve. He had to reach her. "I'm not hurting you." He brushed a kiss to her jaw, to the side of her neck, under her chin where he'd already learned she was sensitive. Her pulse raced and he touched his tongue to her, leaving a damp spot against her throat.

He wanted to cherish her, and to do that he had to soften her first. Sierra never gave to him easily—she made him work for it.

And there only seemed to be one way around her reserve. Still placing those small, delicate kisses on all her sensitive spots, he whispered, "I'd never hurt you, sweetheart. You have to know that."

"Of course I know it, but . . ."

Her voice shivered with new awareness. Bless her, Sierra was so easy to arouse.

At least for him.

Trailing damp kisses over her shoulder to her arm, Ben soothed the ugly bruises with his mouth and wished like hell he could get hold of the man who'd done this to her. He'd take him apart, piece by piece. It wasn't easy, tamping down his rage, but Ben knew she needed something entirely different from him now.

Sierra shivered, and Ben asked, "Do you know what I want to do to you?"

"No." Her breath quickened. "Maybe." She squirmed, lifting into him. Since she no longer tried to shove him away, Ben moved a little to her side and rested his hand on her flat belly. His fingertips just touched her pubic hair.

Her breath caught and held.

"I want to kiss you everywhere."

Her eyes closed. "Yes."

She wasn't the only one turned on. Though grim resolve motivated him, no way could Ben touch her and kiss her without going a little crazy himself. She was so precious to him, so stubborn and quick-witted and independent. He could only reach her through sex, so he'd give her the best goddamned fucking she could imagine.

"Here?" He drifted his hand back up her body to her breast, circled her nipple, again and again.

With her bottom lip caught between her teeth, Sierra nodded.

"Do you like it when I suck on your nipples, sweetheart? Does it make you hot?"

Breathlessly, she replied, "You know it does."

"Then I will." Ben continued to lazily circle her until her nipple was flushed dark, puckered tight. "In a little while."

She groaned in impatience, making him smile. If he had to keep her aroused to make her agreeable, then he had no problem with that.

"What about here?" He kissed her parted lips, not a deep kiss, but a light, teasing kiss.

"Yes." Her mouth lifted into his, trying to catch him. Ben licked her bottom lip, nipped it with his teeth and just when she started to complain, he lightly pinched the nipple he'd been taunting. She groaned in pleasure.

"Does that feel good?" He kept the pressure just right, tugging a bit, rolling.

"Yes." She brought her arms up to hold him, and Ben saw the wince of discomfort from her bruising. His jaw locked until she pleaded, "Kiss me, Ben."

Despite his fury, he smiled and leaned down to her. "Whatever you want, Sierra." While kissing her long and slow and deep, he continued to toy with her nipple. Their tongues mated, their breath mingled.

He released her breast to caress her hip. "I want to kiss you here, too," he said against her mouth. "Your skin is so damn soft, it drives me crazy. And here." He touched the inside of her thigh, drawing small invisible circles, moving closer and closer to her vulva.

She moaned sweetly.

Keeping the touch light, he traced her triangle of hair. "And here."

"*Ben.*"

With his hand cupped between her thighs, he lifted up to watch her face. Her eyes were heavy and warm, her cheeks flushed. "Will you open your legs for me?"

She did so immediately, her thighs parting to give him better access.

He kept her pinned with his gaze as he parted the lips of her sex and worked his middle finger slowly inside her. Her internal muscles clamped down on him, as if to hold him captive.

"I care about you, Sierra."

Her eyes closed on a gasp, her hips lifting to bring him deeper. He held back.

"Look at me, Sierra. I want to see you."

It took her a moment, but she finally got her lids lifted. "That's right. Don't look away. Don't hide from me." Ben gently fingered her, watching her, gauging her responses. He kept the heel of his hand pressed to her mound, softly grinding, while his middle finger worked lazily in and out. She was hot, growing more so by the second, her breath coming faster and faster.

He pulled his finger out to tease her softly swelling lips, lower, making her gasp in shock, then back up again to push deep.

She moaned and again squeezed her eyes shut.

Near her ear, Ben whispered, "Think how this will feel when it's my tongue touching you, licking you, slipping inside you."

At the teasing of his own words, his muscles clenched. God, he'd push himself over the edge if he weren't careful. He was dying to taste her. He'd always loved pleasuring a woman with his mouth, hearing her raw moans and feeling her wild response. Women's bodies were so soft and sweet. But with Sierra, familiar desires were amplified because it wasn't just sex. It was Sierra. And she was his.

Sierra groaned and tightened her arms around him. "Make love to me, Ben, please."

"I will." He had to. He needed her more than he'd ever needed anyone.

Slow, steady, he pushed his finger in, teasing, plying her tender flesh, then withdrawing. She strained against him.

"Right here, Sierra." He used his rough thumb to rub over her distended clitoris. He was careful not to push her into a climax, careful to make it last. She looked beautiful in that moment, vague and excited and so hot. "I'll kiss you right here, curl my tongue around you."

Her panting breaths escalated, heat poured off her. Her gaze was locked on his as if she couldn't look away.

His mouth touched hers, and he whispered, "I'll suck on you."

With a harsh cry, she almost came. Ben quickly withdrew, holding her when she fought to come against him, soothing her.

"Shhh . . ." He stroked her hair, kissed her ear. "Easy now. Tell me you care about me, honey."

She sank her nails into his shoulders, opened her mouth against his chest. Bewildered, she asked, "Why are you doing this?"

"Do you mean the talking, or the touching?"

Her breaths were ragged, her body quivering, on the very edge of release. *"Both."*

"The touching is for your pleasure. It's only going to build and build, until you can't take it anymore." He licked her ear, drew her earlobe into his mouth. "Trust me."

"I . . . I need you. Now." Her belly rubbed his, her nipples prodded against his chest. "Please."

Ben fought the temptation to take her. He caught her hands as she reached down to encircle his erection. If she got hold of him there, he'd lose all control. "Tell me you care about me, Sierra."

She shook her head. "No . . ."

"Tell me."

"Ben. I can't."

"Tell me." He anchored her hands in one of his, then slid his hand back down her body. Her legs opened for him and he caught her clitoris between finger and thumb, just holding her, exerting the smallest bit of pressure. He could feel her heartbeat throbbing there.

She gave a small sob, clinging to him.

"Sierra?" He increased the pressure the tiniest bit.

"Yes." She swallowed, curled into him. "Yes, yes."

Desperation made her voice rough. Using his shoulders, Ben levered her back to the bed and held her there, his hand still between her thighs, his attention sharp on her face. "He hurt you, didn't he?"

Her eyes widened with sudden realization of his tactics. "You . . ."

Oh no, Ben wouldn't let her get distracted. Feeling ruthless in his determination, he pushed two fingers heavily into her. Her neck arched with a moan and Ben watched her stiffen, watched the wash of acute pleasure soften her anger. He had to push her. He had to know. "He hurt you, and you're afraid he'll somehow hurt me."

She squeezed her eyes shut and shook her head, refusing to answer.

Ben was intent on devastating her, on destroying her reticence. She was very wet now, very close, her flesh

swollen and sensitive. He teased her clitoris again, stroking, circling, tugging.

"*Tell me,* Sierra."

Her back bowed, her lips parted. The position forced
her breasts up and Ben couldn't resist briefly mouthing a
taut nipple. She shuddered as he softly drew on her,
flicked her with his tongue. "Tell me," he urged.

"*Oh God . . .*"

She tightened around his fingers, and it was beyond
Ben to stop her this time. He took her mouth, tasting her
excitement and swallowing her raw, broken moans. Wet
heat bathed his fingers as she climaxed and he felt the
convulsions of inner muscles, the rippling aftereffects of
her release. She cried out brokenly, rocking into him,
mindless in her pleasure.

In slow progression, she quieted, until finally she lay
still. Ben drew her half atop him, rocking her, holding her
to his heart. Damn it, that hadn't gone as he wanted. He
needed her to confide in him. He needed her to trust him.

Gradually, her fingers opened on his chest. Just as
slowly she pushed her head up to see him. Her reddish
hair hung in long tendrils around her face. Her green eyes
were dark, soft. Because she was still flushed, her few
freckles stood out across her nose and cheeks. Her lips
were rosy, swollen.

Ben waited, unsure what she'd do—unsure what he
should do.

She stared at his mouth and said, "One week after we
were married, Griffin hit me."

Chapter Twelve

Ben went rigid. He'd known, goddamn it, he'd known, but hearing her say it so casually ripped him apart. Hands shaking, agonized for what she'd gone through, Ben held her and waited.

Sierra shivered. She slid down to rest her cheek on his shoulder, snuggling in to get comfortable. To Ben, it seemed she was hiding, unwilling to face him as she made her confessions. He'd help her get over that, he decided. He'd make her understand that she had nothing to be ashamed of, and she need never hide from him.

"He didn't ease into it." Her voice was soft, a low whisper. "He didn't pretend it wouldn't happen again. He never apologized. Once he hit me, he decided there was no reason he shouldn't keep hitting me whenever he thought I deserved it, or whenever he got angry."

"Did he ever hurt you before you were married?"

She shook her head. "I wouldn't have married him if he had."

Ben hugged her to let her know he hadn't meant his question as an insult.

"He was always nice, very courteous. He complimented me and took me places. I realized later that he never really liked me, he just wanted to have sex with me. Men are nice to women they want to sleep with."

"Good men are nice to all women."

She nodded. "Like you."

"Like most of the men I know."

Sierra tangled her fingers in his chest hair, let out a long breath. "I honestly don't think he'd ever hit a woman before that. I remember he seemed as stunned by what he'd done as I was. He backhanded me, I fell, and he just stared at me, like he was in shock."

Ben swallowed hard, hating the picture that formed in his mind. The idea of anyone hurting Sierra made his stomach cramp with impotent rage. He hadn't even known her then, but he felt guilty that he hadn't been there to help her.

"He wasn't a happy man, but I thought at first that maybe he'd get over it."

"It?"

"Our . . . circumstances, because we'd had to get married."

"You were pregnant?" His whole body stiffened with that possibility.

"No. But we were found in a very compromising situation." She shook her head. "Looking back, I realize how dumb it was, that it wouldn't have even mattered if we hadn't lived in a small town, and if our fathers had been different, less important people."

Ben waited, rubbing her back, kissing her temple every so often just because he *had* to touch her.

"One of the local deputies caught us in the backseat of Griff's car, pretty much in the act. I was naked, Griff had his jeans around his knees." She shivered. "It was so humiliating. I can still remember the second that flashlight hit me in the eyes." She shook her head. "I don't think I'll ever forget it. Griff was twenty-one at the time, but I was underage, so the deputy hauled me home and presented me to my father."

Ben remembered when he'd been a teenager, all the lectures his mother had given him on sex and responsibility and how women should be treated. She'd never seemed overly uncomfortable with the discussions, but she'd also never walked in on him. That would disconcert anyone. "I can see how embarrassing that would be."

Sierra peeked up at him. "Dad was a minister for the biggest church in town. He was . . . very pious and righteous, not what anyone would call a softhearted man. Our house, his car, everything was paid for by the congregation." She shrugged again, as if it didn't matter when Ben knew it mattered a great deal. "Naturally, he was horrified. I mean, for the minister's daughter to be caught naked, making out . . . Well, it went against everything he preached on, every sermon he'd ever given."

Ben's heart wrenched, trying to imagine Sierra's guilt, and how her father must have felt. "What did he do?"

"He kicked me out. We'd had a rough time of it anyway, and that was just a little too much for him to tolerate. He told me I'd always been sinful, and he was tired of trying to deal with my shame."

Ben was thankful that she wasn't looking at him. He

didn't want her to know how her words hurt and enraged him. Some men didn't deserve to be fathers. "He over-reacted, honey."

"No." She nuzzled against him, rubbing his chest with her cheek. "He was naturally strict and I rebelled. Looking back, I don't know why I did it, why I always wanted to goad him." Sierra twisted to see him, and she looked so sad, so resigned. "He's gone now. He died not long after I left town. Because of me, he lost his church, his followers . . . he lost everything, and there's no way I can ever tell him I'm sorry, that I wish things had been different."

Ben's heart broke for the anguish he saw in her gaze. "He could have contacted you, Sierra. But he didn't."

"No. He didn't like me much." She resettled herself and Ben felt her soft sigh on his bare chest. "My skirts were too short, I cursed on occasion, and I liked boys." She gave a short laugh. "Obviously the wrong boys, huh? When I messed up that last time, he told me I'd made my bed and I'd just have to live with my bad choices."

Inadvertently, Ben tightened his arms around her, squeezing her too tight. She stroked him, trying to comfort *him*.

"I didn't really know what I was going to do. He was the only family I had. I didn't have anywhere to go, and I didn't have much money. But by the end of that day, half the town had found out, and everyone was talking about it, saying things about me, my father, and about Griff."

"Gossip is always hurtful."

She made a rough sound of agreement. "Griff's father was the sheriff, and he had me picked up in a patrol car. I was so scared, not knowing what he'd do. I wasn't going to be eighteen for another two months and I was dumb

enough that I thought maybe they were going to send me
to juvenile, or put me in a halfway house or something.
But when I got to the station, Griff was there, too."

She tightened against him, and Ben hugged her closer,
murmuring to her, wishing he could somehow remove the
past.

Her voice went flat, emotionless. "They took me into
the interrogation room, told me to sit in a chair, and then
pretty much ignored me. Sheriff Ross told Griff we had to
get married. They had an awful argument about it. Even
though the door was closed, I just knew everyone in the
station could hear them."

Ben ached for her, imagining her humiliation. It
sounded as though Griffin Ross had inherited his father's
cruelty.

"It was an election year," she went on, "and the sheriff
wanted to eventually run for mayor. He comes from a political background, with powerful relatives. He said . . .
some crude things."

"Tell me."

She drew a deep breath. "He said if Griff wanted to
poke the preacher's daughter, he could damn well do it
legitimately. He said he didn't care if I was a little slut,
that Griff should have thought of that before he got
caught screwing me in the damn car." She hesitated, then
added, "Griff was the first for me. I wasn't a slut. I flirted
a lot, but I hadn't . . . I hadn't gone all the way till I met
him. It seemed unfair for his father to say that to me, especially when he turned around and told Griff he should
have learned to keep his pants zipped." She snorted. "I
think Griff was the slut, not me."

"They were both wrong, Sierra."

"Griff argued that he shouldn't be punished just because my father was a bastard. It went on and on, but Sheriff Ross insisted. He told Griff he'd cut him out of the family if he didn't do the right thing. He told him he could divorce me in a few years, after he was mayor and I was older."

Ben ground his teeth together, appalled, enraged. Griff should have offered to take care of her, but not to save his father's career. He was older, a grown man while Sierra hadn't even been legal. Neither of them had shown any compassion. "The son of a bitch should have been in jail for taking advantage of you."

"His father mentioned that to him, too, and told him with so many people knowing what had happened, it was in his best interest to do the smart thing and marry me."

"Even after all that, you wanted to marry him?"

"What else could I have done? I had no family, no money, no place to go. I didn't have much choice."

Choices. Ben closed his eyes, knowing he, too, wanted to take away her choices. She wanted independence. She *deserved* independence—and he wanted a commitment.

Unaware of his personal turmoil, Sierra continued. She still spoke in a monotone, while Ben was choking on emotion. "I convinced myself that being Griff's wife would be better than living with my father. I thought maybe he'd get used to the idea and we could go on as we had been, having fun, laughing together, making out, and more. God, I was so dumb."

"Young, Sierra, and maybe a little naive. But never dumb."

She laughed. "Griff certainly thought I was dumb. He said I ruined his life and put him on bad terms with his father. He said the whole town was talking about him. There was no more teasing between us, no more laughter at all. It was like he despised me. He rarely wanted to have sex with me, and usually then only if he was angry. Our relationship, if you could call it that, went downhill from the day I said I do."

Absently, Ben stroked his hands up and down her narrow, silky back. She was a strong woman, but still slight and feminine. The thought of what she'd gone through left him raw. "You divorced him?"

"Yes. I had thought to wait, like his father said, but then I . . . just couldn't. When I first mentioned divorce, Griff got enraged. He told me he'd divorce me when he was damn good and ready, and not a second before. I was sort of stuck."

"Did you tell your dad that he was—"

"He knew. Everyone did."

Ben shook with a new rage. Her father had known she was abused but obviously hadn't done anything to help her. "Because of the bruises?"

"Yes. You can't know how humiliating that is, to have people, some of them near strangers, look at you with pity. Don't misunderstand, Griff never hurt me bad."

"He *hit* you."

"Slaps, mostly. I had bruises, a few split lips, a few black eyes . . ."

She must have felt his tension because she reared up to look at him. "I'm sorry, Ben. I don't mean to burden you with—"

"Hush. I want to know everything about you. It's just that I wish I'd been there. I wish you hadn't gone through it all alone."

Her small smile warmed him. "I didn't. When I finally worked up the nerve to leave, despite Griff's threats, I met Kent. He picked me up on the road and somehow we just became best friends in one afternoon. Like a guardian angel, he stuck close to me, keeping me safe, loaning me money until I . . ." Her smile faded, and she curled back into Ben, her hold tight. "After my father died, I inherited what property and savings he had. It wasn't a lot, but with a strict budget, it was enough to get me through school and help me buy this place. And now, I'm happy."

Ben smoothed her hair, kissed the top of her head, her ear. "You're skipping a lot."

"Yes." She sighed again. "A lifetime. But we are finally divorced now, and so I've left that all in the past. It doesn't matter anymore, not to me, and certainly not to us."

Us. Ben liked her wording, her small admission that they were in fact a couple. He continued to hold her, to cuddle her. "It can't really be over when he's still bothering you."

"Ben." She moved above him, leaving her breasts displayed over his chest. "You promised me you wouldn't get involved unless I asked you to."

She had to be kidding. With a straight face, he said, "Right. That's what I said."

Her eyes narrowed. "There've been enough people hurt."

"Meaning?"

"Meaning I do not want you tangling with him."

"Okay." *He wouldn't tangle. He'd pound him into the ground—they were two entirely different things.*

She thumped her fist on his chest, which made Ben start in surprise. "Damn it, Ben . . ."

Unwilling to fight with her now, Ben tumbled her onto her back. The need to join with her, to claim her again, to prove to himself and her that she belonged with him, took precedence over every other emotion. "Shhh. I know what I promised, Sierra. You won't regret confiding in me. But there's no damn way I'm going to let him hurt you again."

She started to shake her head, denying him, and Ben whispered, "Come to that, I made a lot of promises today, didn't I?"

"What are you talking about?"

"Sexual promises, and we still have"—he twisted to see the clock—"a good hour before either of us needs to be anywhere." He touched her upper arms where the colorful bruises showed stark against her fair skin. His voice turned gruff. "Are you okay? Do your arms hurt?"

"No."

He didn't believe her, but her pride was important to him, too, so he didn't push the issue. "I'm glad. So how about we spend our hour having fun?"

"I don't know."

Ben cupped her breast, and immediately felt her heartbeat tripping beneath his hand. "I can get you to agree."

Her eyes drifted shut, and she said with a hopeless groan, "I know."

Smiling, his own heart heavy, Ben kissed his way down her body, wanting to show her with touches what he couldn't yet tell her with words. "I love your breasts, Sierra. They're so sweet."

Her strangled laugh delighted him. "They're not real . . . bountiful."

"They're perfect." Ben held each soft breast in turn and slowly licked her nipples.

"Ben," she complained around a moan, trying to push him away, "I'm already too sensitive for that."

"Here?" He sucked her softly into his mouth, drew gently on her.

"Yes."

"By the time I'm done with you," he promised, "you'll be that sensitive all over." He caught her cautiously with his lips and tugged. She stiffened, and Ben held her still, ignoring her small pleas while flicking her with the tip of his tongue.

Holding her close when she automatically tried to draw back, he said, "I won't let you push me away, sweetheart. Ever." Then he sucked her deep.

She quit fighting him and pulled him closer.

Ben moved to the other breast and treated it to the same. Her fingers clenched in his hair while she writhed under him. Ben carefully caught her wrists and lifted her arms over her head. "I don't want you to hurt yourself. Lock your hands behind you."

"Ben . . ." She said his name as a broken moan.

"Do it, Sierra. Trust me."

Showing plenty of uncertainty, she laced her fingers together beneath her head. Her whole body was taut, braced for the unknown. "What are you going to do?"

"Make you wild." He stroked his hands over her, from her shoulders to the smooth undersides of her arms, to her breasts and her belly and down her thighs. She was small and sleek and silky. She was his.

Her eyes closed. "I'm already there."

"Not yet." Ben licked his way down her belly, watching her muscles twitch from the tickling caress. He dipped his tongue into her navel. "I love your belly."

Her hips twisted, and he had to catch her and hold her still. "Stop fighting me, Sierra."

"Then stop teasing me!"

Ben grinned. "I'm going to have to teach you some patience." He slid to his knees on the floor and pulled her around so that her calves dangled over the side of the mattress.

Sierra lifted her head to stare at him in confusion.

"Put your hands back behind your head."

Panting, she hesitated, struggled with herself, and finally complied. She dropped back against the mattress and stared at the ceiling, taut, uncertain.

"That's it." Ben smoothed his rough palms up and down her thighs to her hipbones and back again. Her stretched-out position made her belly more concave and emphasized the rise of her breasts, her sex—the places he wanted to devour. Hungry for the taste of her, he growled, "Now open your thighs. Wide."

With another small moan, she did as he asked. Ben helped her, easing her legs farther apart until she was spread before him, her knees bent. He looked at her, so damn pretty with her soft curls and pale thighs. Using both thumbs, he opened her, enjoyed the sight of her so vulnerable to him. His voice sounded hollow around the rushing of blood through his veins. "I love this, too, Sierra, knowing you're mine, every soft, pink, wet inch of you."

She shifted—and Ben covered her with his mouth.

With a broken cry, her hips lifted and Ben caught her small bottom in his big hands. He kept her arched high, his shoulders between her legs keeping her open while he tasted her deeply, thrusting with his tongue, sucking at her swollen lips, and finally drawing in her small, quivering clitoris for a long, soft, devastating suckle.

He loved her scent most of all, he decided minutes

later. He inhaled deeply as he ate at her, filling himself with her scent and taste. He couldn't get enough. She suddenly stiffened, made a small rough sound deep in her throat.

Ben felt the small tremors in her legs that signaled her rising orgasm. Her panting breaths turned to raw, guttural moans. He kept her steady, his heart rioting as she came. He kept the pleasure acute, going and going until she was weeping, drained. The second he released her, he rolled on a condom, moved over her body, and slid into her. She was very wet, tender, and she took him completely with that one deep push.

"Sierra."

She lay spent beneath him, still struggling for breath as he quickened his rhythmic thrusts. God, it wasn't enough. It'd never be enough.

Ben hooked his arms behind her knees and lifted her legs, spreading them wide, pushing them high so that she had no choice but to take more of him, all of him. He pressed forward to kiss her, stifling her small cry of surprise at the position. He thrust his tongue into her mouth just as his cock thrust into her body. She didn't fight him, even managed to kiss him back and all too soon, Ben was lost. He turned his face into the side of her neck and growled out his release, his whole body shuddering, words of love burning in his throat.

As his senses returned, Ben became aware of the fact that his fingers were tangled in her fine hair, his mouth open on her throat, and she was utterly still beneath him. He'd been rough, damn it. *He'd* been wild.

Alarmed, he carefully untangled her curls from his fingers and struggled up to his elbows, ready to apologize, to explain—and saw she was dead asleep. Again.

Her arms were still above her head, her palms up, fingers loosely curled. Slowly, with a bloom of happiness that made him feel whole, Ben smiled. But his smile soon faded.

God, he loved her so damn much it hurt, and another man had abused her.

He squeezed his eyes shut and fought for that last small thread of control. She didn't want him involved? Fuck that. In the normal course of things, he never lied to women. He'd never had any reason. But now, he'd tell Sierra whatever he had to, whatever she needed to hear, so that he could stay close.

And he'd do whatever needed to be done to see to her safety.

Suddenly her alarm went off with a shrill, ear-deafening ring that made Ben jump a good foot and curse like a madman. It was a wonder he hadn't hit the ceiling, he was so emotionally jarred.

Amazingly enough, Sierra slowly stirred awake. With a shake of his head, Ben crawled over and slapped the alarm off. "God almighty, Sierra, that thing about startled me out of my skin." He disposed of the condom, then rejoined her in the bed.

She yawned hugely and stretched. "Sorry. I'm a sound sleeper."

Watching her sluggish attempts to awaken brought back his grin. She really had been fatigued to fall asleep so soon again. He sat beside her. "Especially when you're satisfied."

"Hmmm." She touched him, her eyes still sleepy, the tension gone from her face. "What you did . . . I want to do that to you, too."

Ben froze as pictures of her on her knees in front of

him, taking him into her mouth winged through his already flogged brain. He dropped back on the bed with a groan. "You'll be the death of me, woman."

To Ben's astonishment, she laughed and tickled him and they ended up spending the next few minutes wrestling in bed. She was surprisingly strong, very agile and quick, and he had a heck of a time getting her gently pinned down beneath him. He liked this playful side of her and decided he could spend the rest of his life romping with Sierra, making love to her, and protecting her.

When she'd finally worn herself out and made to leave the bed, Ben asked her, "What do you have planned for today?"

Adorably naked, she padded to her dresser and located panties, jeans, and a shirt. "I've got errands to run, some grocery shopping to do, stuff like that. Then I'm going to your brother's new property to give him an estimate. Kent's going to your mother's to finish up her job. We should have an earlier day of it today."

"Then how about a date? A movie, dinner. Whatdya say?"

Smiling, she started to answer, and her phone rang. They both hesitated, staring at each other, but in the next second Ben slid out of the bed, determined to get to it before she could. She stopped him with her tone.

"Ben."

Damn it. He looked at her over his shoulder and his eyes widened at the sight of her. She wore her jeans, but hadn't yet put on her shirt. Bare from the waist up, breasts bouncing enticingly, she marched past him and snatched up the phone. "Hello?"

Ben rested a shoulder against the wall and watched her for any signs of distress. He saw the surprise that flickered in her gaze. She tucked her hair behind her left ear and fidgeted. "Oh, uh, hello." She looked at Ben with something close to helplessness, or maybe confusion. "Yes. Well . . . I don't see . . . No, I . . . All right." She glared at Ben, as if he'd done something wrong. "I suppose that would be okay. Just a second." She reached to a drawer in the kitchen and pulled out a pen and pad of paper. "Okay, go ahead."

Ben watched her jot down directions though he couldn't see what she wrote. A new job? But then why did she look so wary, so secretive? He knew it wasn't her ex; there was no fear or anger in her eyes, and for that reason, he didn't try to peek over her shoulder.

Sierra said a polite good-bye, hung up, stared at Ben a moment more, then tore the top note off the pad, folded it and tucked it in her fanny pocket. Damn, she was being secretive.

She gave him a sunny, totally false smile. "Now what were you saying? Oh yeah, a movie. How about we just watch something on cable? You have that at the motel, right? We could lounge out in your rooms and watch TV and I could get my turn to make you nuts." She licked her lips.

Ben's mouth fell open in combined shock and lust. He'd waited forever it seemed, to see that particular look of hunger and . . . *willingness* in her gaze.

He started to give his wholehearted agreement, then paused as he rethought things. He'd expected an argument to the idea of a date because that's what he usually got. Instead she'd offered a very tempting alternative and made it sound like she wanted to be with him. But since when? Then it dawned on him.

Sierra didn't want to be out in public with him for fear

her ex might find out. She expected to keep their relationship hidden, but she was smart enough to know he wouldn't like that idea. Hell, he loved her. He didn't want to sneak around as if they were doing something wrong. He damn sure didn't want to hide from her bastard ex-husband.

Oh, she was good, he'd give her that.

But he was better. After all, he'd had more practice. "I know what you're doing, Sierra."

She breezed past him, beguiling him with her attitude and her near nakedness. "Is that right?"

Ben followed. He wanted to grab her naked, too-proud shoulders and shake some sense into her. He wanted to insist that she share all her secrets with him. He wanted to drag her back to bed where they were usually in perfect accord, where she clung to him and gave him everything.

He wanted to marry her, to claim her legally as well as emotionally and sexually. Feeling taut from his ears to his toes, he growled, "Yeah, you're distracting me with promises of sex. Only it won't work."

Her look was sultry, sensually suggestive, her voice a low purr when she turned to him. "You don't want me to take a turn kissing you all over?" She glanced at his lap.

Ben stiffened, then clenched his jaw to swallow his groan. He was quickly getting hard again, but first things first. "Who was on the phone?"

The suggestive tone disappeared. "None of your business."

"The hell it isn't." He didn't mean to roar, but he was not going to go through this again. Naked, feet braced apart, hands on his hips, Ben got in front of her, blocking her way into the bathroom. "You said *us* before, remember?"

Her brows rose in bafflement. "What are you talking about?" She sidetracked around him and went into her bedroom instead.

Feeling like an idiot, Ben again followed and watched her pull on her bra and shirt, then shove her feet into socks and battered work boots. She sat on the side of the bed to tie up her laces. Watching Sierra dress was a distinct enjoyment, an intimacy that he wanted to share with her the rest of his life. They'd shower together, eat together, argue and love and . . .

He stationed himself in front of her. "*Us,* you mentioned *us* before, as in a couple." Why did he have to explain this to her? Most women he knew wanted to be involved with him. He didn't have to explain things to them, unless he explained that *he* didn't want to be involved.

But Sierra, the one woman he'd fallen irrevocably in love with, wanted to keep him an arm's length away.

That thought made him frown.

Sierra gave him a patronizing look and stood to tuck in her shirt. "There are two people, Ben, you and me, thus an us. Right?"

His eyes narrowed. It seemed there was only one way to deal with her. "I could get you to tell me." He took a step closer, lowered his voice. "We both know it."

Her head shot up. "Hold it right there, Ben Badwin!" She flattened a palm on his chest, then even gave him a small shove. He didn't budge. "I'm going on record right now as saying *no*, so don't even think of using your sex tricks on me."

"Sex tricks?" He tried to sound bewildered, innocent.

"You know exactly what I'm talking about." Her eyes were bright green and glittering. "I'm . . . susceptible to you and you like to use that against me. Normally I don't mind because, truthfully, I enjoy your efforts. But not this time."

Shit. He shouldn't have warned her.

Now annoyed, she marched past him and made it into the bathroom. Ben got right up to the door when she slammed it in his face. He heard the lock click and backed up.

Damned irritating, stubborn . . . He paced away and saw the pad of paper still sitting on the kitchen counter by the phone. He practically leapt on it. Sure enough, when he held the paper just right, he could read the impression left from her pen.

The address he saw made his blood boil.

His grandmother. Oh, she'd gone too far this time. If Aggie tried badgering Sierra . . . Ben decided he'd follow her there tonight. He'd be close at hand and he'd hear for himself what Agatha had to say. And if she hurt Sierra in any way, he'd . . . Well, he didn't know what he'd do. But he damn sure wouldn't let his formidable grandmother intimidate Sierra. He had enough obstacles without adding her to the equation.

Ben looked at the note, trying to see when they planned to meet, but he didn't see a time written down. Would she go after work? During a lunch break? She'd be meeting with Noah, so he'd notify his brother to let him know the second Sierra left him.

Ben shoved the notepad in the drawer and went to dress. Five minutes later Sierra came out of the bathroom with her hair in a high smooth ponytail and her face scrubbed clean. She looked like a teenage tomboy and still he wanted to drag her to the floor and ravage her.

Rather than risk hanging around and maybe saying too much, Ben pulled her to him, kissed her hard, and said, "I have to go." He slipped his hands down to her jeans-clad bottom and caressed her, hoping to soften her frown. "Let me know when you get home tonight, okay? We'll figure out a movie to watch then."

Confused by his quick turnaround, Sierra stared at him hard, but Ben just kissed her again and left. He had his own work, and he also needed to talk to Noah. His brother would know what needed to be done to protect Sierra. Once she was safe, Ben could decide what to do about Griffin.

He supposed he couldn't kill the man, but he'd definitely exact some retribution. He'd have to hit him at least once. Maybe twice. Ben rubbed his knuckles, thinking how much satisfaction he'd get out of bloodying Griff's nose. He even smiled.

Because Sierra was so touchy about it, so worried, he'd try not to do more than that. He respected her and wanted her to see that whenever possible he'd follow her wishes. But there were some things that couldn't be helped.

She was his now, and whether she liked it or not, he intended to take care of her. She'd see that loving him wouldn't be a hardship. She'd see that she could trust him.

Hopefully she'd see that she needed him too. Because God knew, he needed her.

Kent raked the remaining mulch into place, then stood back to admire the job. Lush green shrubs contrasted with flowering bushes and blended with precisely placed annuals and perennials. It looked great, if he did say so himself. Brooke would be pleased.

Of course, he'd worked at a leisurely pace, extending his time around Brooke. It had never taken him so long to finish a job that size, and she'd grumbled the whole time. To him. With him.

Being near her had made it worthwhile.

Kent grinned and swiped a bandanna across his sweaty forehead, then tucked it back into his pocket. Brooke Badwin did her best to make him think she wasn't interested. It did her no good. Ever since he'd started working on her yard, they'd indulged in several nice conversations, mostly because she couldn't seem to stay away.

She might be out of practice as far as dating and such, but her body language was right on target. She wanted him, not as much as he wanted her, but Kent figured once he had her in bed he could fix that. His instincts told him that Brooke would be as wild in the bedroom as she was sedate out of it. He could barely wait to have her under him.

Once, when she'd been sweet enough to carry him out an icy cold beer, he'd thanked her and then, casual as you please, stripped his shirt off. He wanted to see her reaction, and he hadn't been disappointed.

Eyes glued to his chest, Brooke had reeled back two steps, flushed to the roots of her hair, and then fled without a word. It had taken her two days to work up the nerve to face him again, and even then, Kent had needed to coax her back into conversation, into meeting his gaze. She'd never mentioned her over-the-top reaction to a man's chest, so Kent hadn't either.

No, he wouldn't mention it, but no way would he ever forget it, either.

He chuckled again just remembering.

"What's so funny?"

He turned and smiled in pleasure. "Brooke. When did you get home?" He leaned on his rake and devoured the sight of her.

Today she wore a long colorful sundress that hung straight from her bare shoulders to her trim ankles. The material was some soft, slinky stuff that draped over her breasts, her hips, her belly, and thighs. She looked elegant and sexy at the same time. Kent felt himself tighten in awareness. Damn, he was too old for this. His heart couldn't take it.

Dark sunglasses hid her eyes, and her mouth trembled the tiniest bit as she smiled. "I just pulled in and saw your truck still in the drive. Since you weren't out front, I came straight to the backyard."

Kent winked at her. "I'm in a good mood because your yard is done. Do you like it?"

Her head turned, taking in the landscaping. "It looks incredible."

You look incredible. "Thanks." Gold hoop earrings brushed her cheeks, and a slender gold watch on her wrist reflected the sunlight as she shielded her eyes.

Kent went on admiring her profile while she gracefully strolled forward, her sandals sinking into the lush warm grass. He saw her toenails were painted a frosty pink to match her fingernails. She wore a very slender ankle bracelet. She was so feminine, so classy, everything male within him just seemed to sit up and take notice.

He liked it that she made such a ladylike appearance. Every man saw her as proper. Kent wanted her to be improper with him. He'd have her naked, hot, straining under him with her hair and makeup mussed. Her legs would clench around his hips and her fingers would dig into his shoulders.

He shuddered, watching her with narrow, intent concentration. Her gait remained slow and leisurely, and she stepped over a trowel, around an empty container.

"I'll get this stuff picked up and put away before I go."

She glanced sideways at him. "No rush."

Such a simple statement and his heart raced, his guts churned. No, once he got Brooke in bed, he wouldn't rush. He'd take his time tasting and touching her.

She moved beyond him and Kent stared at her heart-shaped ass beneath the dress. His palms twitched with the need to touch her. Maybe he'd take her from behind, so he could grip that lush ass, hold her tight to him. Had Brooke ever had sex doggy style? Somehow, he doubted it.

Voice husky and low, he murmured, "You look nice today. Business?"

She slanted him another look. Kent wished he could see her eyes.

"Lunch."

He followed behind her, closing the gap. "Women's afternoon out?"

His attempt to subtly discover if she'd had a date was met with resistance.

She bent to touch a soft pink azalea. "No."

When she stood, he was close enough that they nearly touched. "Quit teasing me, Brooke. Were you out with a man?"

She started to step back and Kent caught her arms above her elbows. Her skin was very soft, very smooth, warmed by the bright sunshine. "Easy." He brought her closer to his torso. "You're about to land in the bushes."

Her hands fluttered, then flattened on his chest, her brows rising above her glasses. Her mouth, very kissable in shiny pink gloss, opened in a small *oh*.

Kent steered her to the side and the second she was clear, she pulled away from him. He let her go, but kept close to her.

"May I ask you something, Kent?" She stepped up to the back patio, under the shade, but didn't sit in any of the thick padded chairs.

Kent relaxed his stance, crossed his arms over his chest. "Shoot."

"Does Sierra care about my son?"

He'd been expecting—hoping—for something entirely different. But he shouldn't have been surprised. Several times now, Brooke had used her son to start a conversation. She acted as though she had no life except what centered around him.

He gestured at a chair. "Mind if I sit?"

"No, of course not. Can I get you something to drink?"

"That'd be great."

She gave him her patented polite smile and slid the patio doors open to disappear inside. In her absence, Kent stewed. And plotted. He had to have her tonight. He couldn't wait any longer.

Within minutes, she'd returned with two frosty glasses of lemonade. "Will this do?"

"Perfect. Thanks." He accepted the glass and downed half of it in one long gulp. Brooke sat across from him in another chair, knees together, spine straight, sipping her drink. Eyeing her, Kent asked, "Sierra and Ben, huh? That's what you want to talk about?"

She'd slid her glasses to the top of her head and her eyes were direct, concerned. "He's not acting himself with her."

"I take it he doesn't befriend a lot of women?"

"Of course he does. Ben is friendly with everyone. But . . . this is different. He usually keeps those friendships less . . . involved."

Kent had to admit even he was surprised at how much fortitude Ben had shown. Kent could practically see Sierra falling under his spell.

He admired Ben for a variety of reasons, but most of all because he helped Sierra smile. Kent felt better about her living alone, knowing Ben was close at hand and watchful. He had a strong suspicion that Ben would wear her down soon.

"He strikes me as a young man used to being chased by the ladies, not the one doing the chasing."

Brooke smiled with a dose of indulgent mother's love. "He's very handsome, but he's also very nice. I suppose it's a potent combination."

"You raised him right."

Pride shined from her dark doe eyes, making her all the more appealing. "Thank you."

"He looks like his father?"

For a single instant, Brooke went still. Casually, as if he hadn't just thrown her, she set her glass aside and relaxed in her seat. Her long legs crossed, drawing his attention. Kent had the feeling she'd meant to do that, to distract him with her body. He smiled, enjoying her ploy.

"I asked you a question, which you've answered with more questions. Is there something about Sierra that you're hiding from me?"

"You're a suspicious little mother hen, aren't you?"

Trying to mask her impatience, she swung one foot. "Yes, and you're evasive."

Kent laughed. "All right, I suppose I feel as protective

of Sierra as you do of Ben. The difference is, where he was lucky enough to have you his whole life, she's been pretty much on her own."

Sympathy overshadowed her annoyance. "How so?"

"Her dad was a pious hypocrite, her ex-husband an abusive bastard."

Brooke looked startled by that disclosure. "Oh, I'm sorry. I hadn't realized."

"Sierra is very private. She doesn't tell much about herself." Kent tilted his head, took a chance, and said, "You know, you and Sierra might have something in common."

"Really? Other than an affection for my son?"

He liked it when she teased him, but God knew, she usually only did so with Ben as the topic. Her love for Ben made him a safe subject. "You were both mere children when you got involved with the wrong guy."

Alarmed, Brooke came to her feet in a rush. "More lemonade?"

Slowly, Kent stood to face her, blocking her escape. "It's great that Ben's willing to give Sierra so much time. Do you think it's a sign of real interest on his part?"

As Kent had intended, his new question helped her relax. The stiffness left her shoulders, and she conceded the possibility with a nod. "I believe he's in love with her." Then, a mother to the bitter end, she added, "But I don't want to see him hurt."

"The way you were hurt?"

Her laugh was forced, humorless. "Ben is strong and confident and self-reliant. He's not a young girl. He's not . . ."

Kent halted her spate of words by touching her mouth. "Not you?" Her lips were slick with the pink gloss and he wanted to lick it away, to taste her naked mouth.

She didn't move, but her eyes darkened, a pulse quickened in her slender throat. Kent slid his finger back and forth, tracing her bottom lip. "First things first, okay? Sierra is a total sweetheart. She's reserved because of things that have happened to her, but she would never deliberately hurt anyone, so don't worry about Ben. I have a gut feeling those two are going to work everything out without our interference. Probably sooner than you think."

She remained silent, but she did nod.

"Now, for another thing." He stepped closer, moving slow so he wouldn't take her by surprise. He slipped one foot between hers, enjoying the contrast of his big boot enclosed by her slender, strappy sandals. He wrapped one arm around her waist so she couldn't retreat.

Lifting his finger to his mouth, he tasted her and with a small smile, said, "Cherries. You little tease."

She inhaled, her lips parting, and Kent bent down to take her mouth. He didn't rush her, just moved his mouth over hers, gently, easily, parting her lips more so he could touch her teeth with his tongue, explore just inside her mouth.

She tasted hot, tangy with the lemonade. Deliciously shy, but responsive.

Kent leaned back an infinitesimal amount, opened his eyes, and caught her wary, smoldering gaze. "Brooke?"

She swallowed, staring at his mouth. Her breathing was harsh. "I . . . I hardly know you."

Kent's blood surged. She sounded accepting, willing. "We'll go slow." So slow, he'd have her begging for release.

"You're younger than me."

He grinned. She was reaching for excuses—and coming up short. "We're both all grown up, sweetheart, and we know what we want. We can do whatever we damn well please." His voice dropped to a growl. "And getting you under me will please me a lot."

She looked down at his sweaty chest, inhaled slowly, and touched him. Kent watched the progress of her soft, delicate hand with the manicured nails, against the front of his sweaty, dirty shirt. Christ, it turned him on. The contrasts of his rugged maleness against her soft femininity were strong.

"I'm too old for silly infatuations."

Kent nudged his hips into hers. "You're never too old for this, believe me."

"I should be smarter by now. You'd think I would have learned . . ."

That gave him pause. "Being with me wouldn't be smart?"

"I don't know." She glanced up, licked her lips. "I don't know you."

"You know I want you." Kent stroked her back, her bottom. "What else is important?"

Confusion made her eyes darker, softer. "Everything."

Damn. He didn't want to get into long discussions now. He made an exasperated sound.

Brooke stiffened. "I'm sorry. I'm not very good at this."

His dick was so hard, he hurt. "You're doing great."

"I want to kiss you." After she made that sudden admission, she stared up at him, then shook her head and added in a rush, "No, I feel like I *have* to kiss you. I think about it all the time. It's making me nuts—"

Kent hauled her close, uncaring now about the sweat or dirt, and fed off her mouth. She moaned, clung to him and when he kissed her jaw, her throat, she tipped her head back to give him better access.

His jeans felt ready to burst.

Brooke shivered with excitement. "I . . . I need you."

"Hell, yes." She'd said wanting him wasn't smart, but she still wanted him all the same. Later, he'd explain to her that she had no reason to be wary. "Invite me in, Brooke."

Indecision warred with need, but Kent saw the need win. Brooke smiled—and then they both heard the rustling of grass. Kent released her and took a hasty step back, then had to catch her when she slumped toward him. He hauled her up to his side, keeping her steady, and turned to see who had invaded their privacy.

A little old lady drew to a regal halt and stared at him. Slowly, her gaze moved to Brooke and she scowled. "What is this awful propensity you people have for public displays?"

Brooke jerked away from Kent, gaping at the intruder. "Oh dear."

Kent was slower to react, his mind still churning on the fact that Brooke had been about to ask him into the house and into her bed.

He drew one breath, then another, before he felt ready to deal with the slender gray-headed woman piercing him with her censuring gaze.

"Well, young man? What do you have to say for yourself?"

Young man? Annoyed at the untimely interruption, Kent demanded, "Who the hell are you?"

Brooke touched his arm. She was wide-eyed and shaken. "She's Ben's grandmother."

Chapter Thirteen

Brooke watched as Agatha thrust her nose in the air. "Exactly, not that Ben puts any stock in the association." She narrowed her eyes at Brooke. "With that being the case, and I assure you it is, it appears I'll need your assistance to make him see reason."

Brooke blinked, totally bewildered by the demand. *Agatha Harper wanted her help?* When she remained mute with surprise, Agatha huffed. "Yes, well, since Brooke appears somewhat tongue-tied, I suppose I'll do the introductions." She thrust out her thin, blue-veined hand toward Kent. "I'm Agatha Harper. And you are?"

Very gently, Kent enfolded her fragile fingers in his own much larger paw. "Kent Monroe."

"You're acquainted with my grandson, Ben?"

She still held Kent's hand, and he shrugged. "I know him."

Her attention darted back and forth between Brooke and Kent. "You met my grandson through this . . . liaison?"

Her blatant snooping startled Brooke, but Kent didn't appear offended. "Actually, Ben's seeing the woman I work for. I met Brooke through Ben."

Agatha's gaze turned sharp and astute. "You say you work for Sierra?"

"That's right. You know her?"

She ignored Kent's query. "Doing what, exactly?"

Brooke had always been a bit intimidated by Agatha Harper, a reaction no doubt left over from her youth when Pierce Harper had informed her in no uncertain terms that she would never fit in with his life. He was of the elite and she was beyond common. He'd told her to do whatever she wished with the baby but not to expect him to further involve himself. She'd been a conquest, nothing more, appetizing enough for a brief diversion, but certainly nothing more.

Whether Agatha had known about Ben all along, Brooke couldn't say. It didn't seem likely that Pierce would have told her, because she hadn't been important enough for him to mention. Once Agatha had met Ben, she'd offered Brooke money as a way to hedge being sued for back child support, which Agatha claimed would have damaged the Harper name.

Brooke had flatly refused her, partly because by then, she'd had no desperate need of the money, and partly because she didn't want the Harper family to have any financial claim on her son. She'd also explained to Agatha that she had no intention of slandering anyone. She had her son, and in that she knew, she was far more blessed than Pierce had ever been. Pierce had died without ever realizing what an incredible young man he'd sired. Brooke had almost felt sorry for him.

She definitely felt sorry for Agatha.

She'd never mentioned the incident to Ben, choosing to let him draw his own conclusions. She'd been determined that his relationship with Agatha would grow or falter through no fault of her own.

Far from being intimidated by Agatha, Kent appeared arrogantly amused. He pulled his hand free and smiled. "I don't have any specific jobs I do. Depending on where we're working, things change from day to day. Sierra can pretty much handle anything there without me, so I just pick up the slack, fill in wherever she tells me to, doing whatever needs to be done."

Agatha tucked in her double chin. "You're a lackey?"

His smile widened. "If that's what you want to call it."

Agatha looked him over again, from the top of his dark blond head to the tips of his big dirty work boots. Brooke thought there was a lot of man in between those points, too much man to be wasting his life on a dead-end job.

"I see." Agatha couldn't quite hide the scorn in her voice. "Not much ambition, huh?"

Brooke straightened in agitation. She might have been thinking the exact same thing, but she wouldn't allow Agatha to insult Kent. He was her guest, at her house. "Mrs. Harper—"

Kent silenced her with a touch on her arm. "I can't see that my ambition is any concern of yours."

"Well! I certainly—"

"Haven't learned any manners? I can see that." Kent slanted a tender look at Brooke. He even winked, and Brooke had the awful suspicion he'd read her mind, that he knew she'd had the same thoughts as Agatha.

Her suspicions were confirmed when he answered. "But because Brooke might be interested, too, I can tell you that I don't need to work. I've done well enough in the stock market and through investments that I could retire today and be comfortable. Working for Sierra is just for fun."

Shocked, Brooke blinked at him. The stock market? *Working for fun?*

"I adore Sierra and I enjoy keeping busy." He flexed his broad shoulders. "The heavier work also keeps me in shape, which sometimes works in my favor."

He smiled at Brooke again and she felt like melting. Oh, he was definitely in shape. She'd felt the strong, bulging muscles under her palms just moments ago. Kent Monroe was a man in his prime.

Agatha sniffed. "Yes, well, I admire a man who disdains indolence."

Kent laughed at that. "Since you've interrupted my attempts at wooing Ms. Badwin, I suppose I should be on my way." He turned his back on Agatha. "Brooke, will you walk me to my truck?"

Brooke was quite shaken. It seemed she'd been fighting against Kent for all the wrong reasons, and now that she knew more about him her legs felt like noodles. Kent wasn't irresponsible, wasn't indolent. Just the opposite, it seemed.

He wanted her, and there wasn't a single reason Brooke could think of to deny him or herself.

Not anymore.

She cast a quick, apologetic glance at Agatha. "Mrs. Harper, if you'll excuse me just a moment?"

Agatha waved a hand at her. "Go, go. I'll await you inside, out of this dreadful sun." She marched across the patio and in through the patio doors as if she'd had a written invitation.

Brooke shook her head. The old woman's nerve was astounding.

Kent slipped his arm around her waist and led her away. "What the hell was that all about?"

"I have no idea." Brooke shook her head, confused by Agatha's visit, and thrilled by her new revelations on Kent. His hold now was casual, polite, but even so, it excited her. Now she knew they'd eventually end up in bed, and she could barely wait.

Brooke cleared her throat. "She's never been to my home before. As to that, she's barely ever spoken to me. I can't imagine what she's doing here now."

Kent picked up his tools on the way, holding the long handles easily in one big hand. "Want me to hang around?"

The offer surprised her. And pleased her. "Thank you, but no. I'll be fine."

"Will she give you a hard time?"

"I don't really know her well enough to say. She and Ben aren't on the best of terms. He . . . Well, he's protective of me."

"He's your son." Kent said that as if it explained everything, and Brooke supposed it did. They'd reached his truck—a new, expensive truck, Brooke realized for the first time—and Kent stored the tools inside.

They both noted the limousine parked at the curb, partly hidden behind one of the large elms that grew all along the street. A driver sat patiently inside. Kent raised a brow. "Agatha's?"

"I assume so. She's very wealthy."

"She's also pushy, old, and," Kent added with a grin,

"blessed with hideous timing." He hesitated, then asked, "Agatha's son is Ben's father?"

"He was, yes. He died some time ago, when Ben was still a teenager." Feeling somewhat defensive for the foolish child she'd once been, Brooke folded her arms around her middle. "Ben had never met Agatha until then. Pierce wanted nothing to do with either of us. The day I told him I was pregnant is the last time I ever saw him."

Kent leaned on his truck. The sun gilded his hair, made his blue eyes seem brighter, more intense. "His loss."

Pleased that Kent shared her outlook on that, Brooke smiled. "That's exactly how I've always seen it."

Kent's lounging position against the truck put him at a tilt, with his long legs stretched out before him. He looked very good in his snug, worn jeans.

Brooke imagined he'd look even better out of them.

When he caught the back of her neck and dragged her closer, she willingly fell into him, practically lying against him with his legs outside hers, caging her in. She went breathless and warm in a single heartbeat. His callused hand cupped her cheek and tipped up her chin.

Their eyes met.

"We're going to burn up the sheets, Brooke, you can count on that."

She shivered, and her breathing deepened.

"But you should know up front, I want more than just sex."

Startled, Brooke said, "You do?"

"Damn right."

"Why?" She'd only just resigned herself to the idea of an affair with him. It was a huge step for her, certainly not something she normally did. She'd had a few discreet relationships, never serious enough for Ben to know about because she'd always known the men were temporary. The resulting sexual encounters had come about naturally.

This was the first time she'd walked into an affair with her eyes wide-open, with sex as the intent.

With so much anticipation.

They were at the top of her long driveway, hidden by large shrubs. Kent held her face and gently kissed her, leaving Brooke wanting more.

"Damn," he said, sounding frustrated. "This isn't the best time or place, so I'm going to make it brief."

"Make what brief?"

"My explanations." He pulled her into his chest and held her there. Brooke could feel his heartbeat against her cheek, and she breathed in his sun-warmed, rugged scent. "After I lost my wife, it took me a while to get on with my life again, and even then, women didn't mean much to me other than a warm body when I needed to get laid."

His bluntness continued to shock Brooke—and sometimes excite her. But she didn't want to hear about him with other women. Not even his wife.

"You don't have to—"

Kent kissed her before she could deny him. This kiss wasn't gentle. He took her mouth possessively while pressing his erection against her belly. He felt huge and hard, so much a man that he made her feel more like a woman.

She couldn't stop the moan, or the shivers that chased through her.

His forehead to hers, his jaw locked, Kent said, "You're different, Brooke. It's not just about the sex, though God knows, when I get inside you, it's going to be so fucking good."

Brooke moaned again, because she knew he was right.

"But I want more than one night, more than one week. More than temporary."

Brooke shuddered—and carefully moved away. Her chest rose and fell and for an instant, she could barely think.

Kent caught the back of her neck, keeping her near. "You'll like it fast, sweetheart. Fast and hard and deep."

"Yes."

He was silent a moment, hesitating, then resigned. "When I met Sierra for the first time, she had a black eye and more bruises than I could count."

Brooke gaped at him. He'd thrown her with that statement, dropping it on her cold and she couldn't think of a single thing to say.

"I'd been dead inside, mourning my wife, and then one day I was driving past this small town and there she was, a battered suitcase in her hand, trudging along the damn highway. She didn't want a ride, but I was afraid she'd collapse any second she looked so defeated. I talked her into getting into my truck, then talked her into sharing lunch and . . ." He rolled his shoulders and stared up at the clear blue sky. "It's strange, because Sierra thinks I saved her, when really she saved me. I'd been floundering, unable to think of anything except my loss, and she gave me a new purpose."

"Dear God." Brooke's heart softened and swelled. Kent was the antithesis of Pierce. Ben's father had turned his back on her when she'd needed him most; Kent had gone out of his way to befriend and assist a woman he didn't even know. Her smile came, wobbly and uncertain but filled with hope.

"Yeah, it hasn't been easy for her." He stared at Brooke, his look concentrated, hard. "Her ex is a coward and I should have taken care of him long ago."

Brooke touched his jaw. "Why didn't you?"

Strangely enough, Kent looked pleased by her question. "He has a knack for knowing what will hurt Sierra the most. And he has a lot of powerful relatives with far-reaching influence. He can't hurt me, and he knows it, but if I went after him, he could make it impossible for Sierra to ever get a loan, and he can buy existing loans and call them in. That's what he did to her father, and the man lost everything."

"Is that legal?"

"Other than his personal abuse of Sierra, everything he's done is aboveboard. And even the abuse would be hard to prove. His father was the sheriff, then the mayor."

"Which gave him certain immunity?"

"That's about it. Sierra thought moving farther away was the answer, and since there was no place in particular I wanted to be, I came with her. She's so happy here now, so content—except for Griff." He looked at her and admitted, "He's followed her here."

"Well, we have to do something!"

Kent grinned and hugged her close. "I knew you'd understand. And yeah, I agree. I'm just not sure yet what to do. Sierra is so damned adamant about not involving others."

"I'll speak with her."

"I'd rather you didn't. She'd be upset if she knew I'd told you."

"Oh." Brooke worked things through her mind. "Maybe Ben . . ."

"Shh. I'm keeping an eye on things, and I'm hoping like hell Sierra will tell Ben herself, that she'll trust him enough to let him know what's going on."

"If this cretin could hurt my son, then I have to warn him."

Kent rubbed the backs of his fingers over her cheek. "Will you let me handle it? Please?"

She didn't want to, but she also knew that Sierra wouldn't welcome her interference. Brooke settled on a compromise. "For now, I'll trust you."

"Thank you." He gave her a quick, hard kiss. "And now you know that Sierra is very special to me, but I don't want her, not in the way I want you."

The way he wanted her gave her pause. "Not for a brief fling?"

"There won't be anything brief in our dealings together, Brooke."

A shiver of sexual awareness nearly took her breath.

"I'll be back tonight when we can have a little privacy. Seven o'clock?"

The evening seemed too far away. "Yes. All right."

Kent reached for her but she stepped back. She had to collect herself before she went back inside. "I have to go. I don't want to keep Mrs. Harper waiting."

His lopsided grin almost made him look boyish.

Almost. "Meaning you don't like having her snoop through your house."

Brooke smiled too, a genuine smile this time. Kent wasn't just a devastatingly handsome, sexy man. He was a very good man as well. "Exactly." She touched his chest. "Don't be late."

His eyes widened at the wicked way she whispered that, and then his slow smile made her heart turn over.

Brooke hurried away. Oh God, it was going to be all too easy to fall in love with Kent Monroe.

Agatha ducked away from the window when she saw Brooke heading for the house. She didn't blame Brooke for being swept away. Why, if she were forty years younger, she'd have been lured by the impressive Kent Monroe herself.

She was seated demurely in a soft padded chair when Brooke rushed into the living room. "I'm sorry to have kept you waiting."

Agatha sniffed, but deep inside, she was amazed by Brooke's continued politeness. She'd given her little enough reason to be polite and no reason at all to be kind.

Agatha went straight to the matter of her visit. "I want Ben named in my will, but he insists he'll discard anything I leave him."

Brooke slowly sat across from her on a matching sofa. "I see." She gave her a look of apology. "He's a grown man, Mrs. Harper, and he makes his own decisions without my help."

"Nonsense. He loves and respects you. That's apparent enough to one and all. He'll listen to you."

Brooke started to shake her head but Agatha continued. "He deserves his share of the inheritance. I want him to have it."

Brooke stared at her a long moment, then she sighed and her voice gentled. "Perhaps what you want to give him is not what Ben really wants from you."

"Then what? I've named him for property, stock, cash . . ."

"Love?"

Agatha drew herself up. "I beg your pardon?"

"Respect? Affection?"

Damn it, she was too old to get flustered, but she still found herself muttering without her usual decisive tone. "The scamp knows I care about him."

Brooke smiled, and in that smile, Agatha saw a resemblance. "Does he? How often have you told him?"

To Agatha's consternation, she felt herself blush. It was unbearable so she came to her feet and began to pace. "I'm nearly eighty years old, you know. I need this matter settled."

"Then I suggest you settle it."

Agatha would never have imagined that stern tone from Brooke Badwin. The few times she'd been in the woman's company, she'd been as timid as a mouse. Agatha gave her a sharp look. "You're berating me?"

"Don't sound so surprised, Mrs. Harper. You were a mother yourself. You know that there are times when you must be stern. And Ben's always been a rascal. He's kept me on my toes."

That hurt. Agatha sank back into her seat and made an admission that she hadn't given to anyone else. "I wasn't much of a mother, I'm afraid." She didn't dare look at Brooke but kept her gaze trained on a distant wall.

Silence stretched out, painful, making her old bones ache, making her want to relax her shoulders, even slump back in her seat. Then she heard Brooke stand up. Seconds later Brooke sat beside her and took her hand.

Agatha was so startled by the gesture, she had the

awful feeling her mouth hung open. If she wasn't careful, she'd lose her partial bridge.

"We all do the best we can." Brooke gently squeezed her fingers, offering her comfort when Agatha knew she'd never deserved it. "Sometimes as mothers, we make mistakes that haunt us forever, and sometimes we come to brilliant conclusions. Unfortunately, it's tough to know which is which until the child is older and we can see the results."

Agatha swallowed her pride, and gave Brooke a truth she should have given her years ago. "You made some brilliant conclusions concerning Benjamin. He's quite the remarkable young man."

Brooke smiled, and Agatha realized exactly how lovely she was. It made it easier for her to understand how her son could have been taken with her, but not why he would have been so reprehensible in his duty.

"Thank you, Mrs. Harper."

Agatha mustered her gumption and sat a little straighter. "Bosh. Enough of that ridiculous formality. You'll call me Agatha."

"All right. Agatha, have you ever told Ben that you're proud of him?"

"He doesn't exactly make it easy." No, Agatha thought. Anytime she was around him, Ben put up his defenses and either argued with her or made everything a joke. "His wit is quite entertaining, but he also uses it to distract me when he doesn't want to come right out and insult me." Agatha shook her head. "He's a charmer, and he knows it."

"If you want a closer relationship with Ben, you'll have to be honest with him."

Agatha focused on Brooke with shrewd intent. "I thought perhaps I'd enlist you and his young lady, Sierra, to aid me."

"Aid you how?"

"He cares about you both. When Noah was giving me fits, it was Grace who brought him around."

Brooke shook her head before Agatha could finish. "Oh no. You'll have to work through your personal relationship on your own."

"You're refusing to help me?" Agatha had deliberately made her voice strident, commanding.

Brooke pushed to her feet. "Not once have I ever tried to turn Ben against you or your son. Don't expect me to do the opposite now. Ben is a grown man, intelligent and fair and kind. If you want his respect and affection, you'll have to give him yours in turn."

"Perhaps Sierra . . ."

"I know my son, Agatha. I wouldn't suggest you attempt to use Sierra. It's possible Ben is in love with her and I can tell you, he's very protective of those he loves."

Agatha wanted to argue, but God knew she'd spent her life giving orders and now she was old and mostly alone. She pushed to her feet. "I'll have to think this over. You won't say anything to Ben?"

"About your visit? Not if you don't want me to."

Agatha smiled. "You really are an honorable young woman aren't you?"

Brooke's own smile slipped into place. "I'm forty-five, hardly all that young."

"Comparisons, my dear. Comparisons. To me, you're a baby."

This time Brooke laughed. Her laughter died, however, when Agatha said, her eyes a bit watery, "I'm very sorry for all you went through. My son was . . . a disappointment in many ways."

Brooke's smile was gentle and understanding. "But still your son, and so you loved him, and you'll never stop missing him."

"Yes."

"I understand. And I'm sure if you speak as candidly with Ben, he'll understand as well."

"Thank you."

Brooke took her by surprise with a hug. "Try putting a little faith in Ben. You won't be disappointed, I'm sure."

Flustered, pleased, near tears, Agatha blustered her way through the awkwardness of her own emotions. "Yes, well, he has good genes." She knew she had to go before she entirely disgraced herself. But she paused in Brooke's doorway. Keeping her back to the other woman, she said, "Sierra asked me about big family get-togethers. I hadn't thought about it much," she lied, "but since she mentioned it, do you think for one of the holidays, perhaps we could all . . ."

"It sounds lovely."

Damn it, she *was* going to cry. All Agatha could manage was a stiff nod, thanks to the emotions now choking her. She strode out, her head held high, her back rigid, and inside her heart felt ready to shatter. She had a family, a large loving family, but she knew she'd done nothing to deserve them.

That was about to change, by God. She now understood what needed to be done.

Ben would be pleased. At least, he'd better be.

Chapter Fourteen

Sierra accepted the cell phone that Noah handed her. He shrugged an apology when she gave him a quizzical look. "It's my grandmother."

She wanted to groan. She was supposed to meet the woman an hour from now and had been running late. Noah's condos were far larger and more complex than she'd ever imagined. It would prove to be her biggest and most impressive job and she should have been excited.

Instead, Ben owned her thoughts.

He had thoroughly invaded her life in the most wondrous ways. She'd even helped him by spilling out details of her past. It had been a selfish thing to do, and Sierra regretted it but wasn't sure how to handle it.

God, the truth was awful. She hadn't been able to handle Ben at all. He touched her and her brain turned to mush.

Her voice was a little harsher than it should have been when she said, "Hello?"

"There's been a change of plans, my dear. I'm afraid I need to cancel our visit."

"Oh?" Relief washed over Sierra. That was one worry she could put aside.

"Yes, but I'll see you tonight. What time will you be returning home?"

Sierra rubbed her forehead. She'd had a headache all day, which nearly matched her heartache. Concentrating on what would need to be done to Noah's new condo complex wasn't easy. Now this. "I'm not sure . . ."

"I'll wait for you in Ben's diner. His cook really is quite competent, isn't he?"

"Yes. Quite." Sierra was aware of Noah watching her, making it impossible for her to roll her eyes. She dropped her voice and turned her back on Noah. "I thought you didn't want Ben to know that you'd contacted me."

"I've changed my mind about that. My grandson and I will have a nice visit and you can let me know when you get in. I trust that will work for you?"

Before Sierra could reply, Agatha said, "Good. I'll look forward to seeing you soon, then. Good-bye." She hung up and Sierra all but choked the phone.

Smiling, Noah relieved her of it. "Everything okay?"

"Just dandy."

Noah laughed. "You look ready to spit. My grandmother has that effect on everyone, you know."

Sierra stared up at Noah. He was a massive man, no two ways about it. His stance was casual, his expression calm. But behind his blue eyes lay a barely banked savagery. He didn't scare Sierra. He was Ben's brother and therefore trustworthy. "It's amazing that you and Ben are related to her. She's so small."

"Ben says she's wiry."

Sierra laughed at that, losing some of her tension. "He would. He seems to enjoy provoking everyone."

"You included?"

"Me most of all."

Noah startled Sierra by reaching out and tipping up her chin. He studied her face until her heart felt ready to slam through her chest. Then he shook his head. "You're exhausted. We should have done this another day."

"No, I'm fine . . ."

"Ben's been keeping you up late, hasn't he?" That appeared to amuse Noah, given his wide smile. "What did my grandmother want?"

He slipped that question right in there, making it seem the safer of the two topics, and Sierra just naturally answered. "She just wanted to visit me."

"Ah." Noah appeared resigned, and annoyed. "She's plotting again. Ben's going to have a fit."

"That's nothing new. He's always having fits about something or other." Sierra walked away to the other side of the complex, examining the soil, the direction of the sun, the existing shrubbery. "He's impossible."

Noah strolled behind her. "You know, you're the only woman I've ever heard say so. As to him having fits, that must be reserved just for you, because usually he finds humor in every damn situation. He likes to laugh."

"And he likes to flirt." Sierra winced at the acrimony in her tone. She kicked the toe of her work boot against a small rock. "We'll be able to use some of these existing shrubs. With a few contrasting evergreens and some texture, some colorful flowers, it'll all come together. What's here isn't a total waste. That ought to save you some money, but getting it all healthy will take about a month—"

"You love him, don't you?"

Sierra nearly tripped over her own feet. She whipped around to face Noah. Her heart was slamming again, her mouth dry. "I never said that!"

"So you don't love him?"

A trickle of sweat chased down her spine. She had a hard time swallowing. Love Ben? Oh God. She knew she admired and respected him. She knew she loved his sense of humor and the way he treated his mother, his honor and his stubbornness.

And she loved his touch, too, the way he made her feel so much. He was gentle and kind and strong and intelligent and . . .

She'd been standing there staring at Noah, and she shook her head, dumbfounded, shaken. "I . . ."

Noah stepped up to her. "Forget I asked. I didn't mean to scare you to death."

"You didn't scare me," she lied, "it's just that . . ."

His smile said he didn't believe her, but he was willing to drop it—now that he'd planted the thought in her head.

"You're diabolical."

"Yeah." He slipped his arm around her shoulders and led her back toward the drive where their vehicles were parked. "Have you seen enough to give me an estimate?"

"Yes." Attempting to pull herself together, Sierra glanced at her notepad where she'd written dimensions, ideas, what would be needed, what could be salvaged. "I can let you know something tomorrow. Will that be soon enough?"

"That'd be fine." They walked along in silence and

Sierra was acutely aware of Noah beside her. She knew he was just waiting for the right moment to throw her off guard again. Still, she actually flinched when he said, "Ben's never been in love before."

Oh God, he wasn't going to let it drop after all. "Oh?"

"He is now, though."

Sierra gulped, and trembled. Her emotions seemed to be on a roller coaster ride. She knew it was dangerous, yet the idea that Ben might love her . . . Well, it made her want to laugh out loud with the joy of it.

"It's tough on a guy." Noah patted her shoulder and released her so she could open her truck door. "I hope you'll cut him a little slack."

Sierra knew she should get in her truck and drive away. Instead, she felt compelled to explain. She didn't know Noah well, but she felt a kinship with him. He'd been alone most of his life, too. She met his glacial blue eyes and drew a breath. "I don't want to see Ben hurt."

"You'd hurt him?"

"No, of course not."

"Then who?"

She shook her head, unwilling and unable to tell him anymore. His loyalty was to Ben and he'd repeat anything she said.

Noah was quiet a long time before asking, "Do you trust anyone Sierra?"

"Trust doesn't have anything to do with it."

"Trust has everything to do with it. So tell me, is there anybody you trust completely?"

She thought about it, then nodded. "Kent."

Noah laughed at that and rubbed his face. "Your assistant, right?"

The way he said that nettled her. "And a dear friend."

"Yeah, that's what Ben told me, that you and Kent were just friends. Very special friends." Noah leveled a look on her that nearly knocked her to her knees. "Well, if Gracie had trusted another man more than she did me, it would have eaten me up inside. I think I'd have been blind with jealousy. But Ben apparently respects Kent, even likes him. You know what that means?"

"That Kent's a very likable guy."

"I think it means that *Ben* trusts *you.*"

Noah's comments, along with his tone, felt like a very thorough set-down. Sierra's face burned and her stomach twisted into knots.

"Ben's grown up with the knowledge that his father— *our father*—walked out on him the day he found out Brooke was pregnant. She was only sixteen, alone, without a job. It wasn't easy, but they managed, mostly because Brooke loved Ben so much. Maybe it's because of that, I don't know, but Ben's extra-sensitive to women. He wants to protect and cherish them all. He loves you, so of course he'd feel especially strong about helping you." Noah tipped his head, his expression intent. "What you see as interference is an instinctive reaction for Ben."

Sierra didn't know how to admit it, but she didn't really feel as though Ben's involvement was interference, not anymore. She enjoyed him too much to do anything other than welcome his time with her.

She . . . God, she loved him.

Sierra covered her face and groaned.

Noah nodded again, and said, "You might just want to keep that in mind, okay?"

Feeling very solemn and thoughtful, Sierra got into the truck and closed the door. Noah leaned in through the window. "You heading straight home?"

"Yes. I'm done for the day." She glanced at him, very unsure of his mood. He was the protective older brother, so she didn't fault him. In fact, he'd pushed her into some eye-opening conclusions. "I thought I'd work on your estimate."

"And talk to Ben?"

"Yes." She bit her lip, then said, "Thank you."

Noah's smile was identical to Ben's and made her smile in return. "You're welcome." He rapped on the roof of the truck and stepped back. "Drive carefully."

Sierra was anxious to get home where she could sort through her thoughts. She wanted to see Ben, and she wanted to kiss him. When he touched her, there was no room in her mind for doubts or worries or second thoughts.

Yet when she turned the key, the truck wouldn't start. She frowned, pumped the gas a few times, and tried again. The truck was as dead as road-kill. "Well, hell."

Noah leaned back in. "Won't start?"

"No." Sierra glanced at her watch, closed her eyes in exasperation, and turned back to Noah. "Could I use your cell phone?"

"For what?"

"To call a tow truck."

He opened her door and gently hauled her out. "Nonsense. I'll drive you home, pick up Ben, and we'll check it out. We're both handy with motors."

"But . . ."

He held up a finger. "I insist, and Ben will, too."

In short order, Sierra found herself hustled across the parking lot, settled in a spacious Land Rover, and on the road heading home. All the while Noah continued to sing Ben's praises.

It was unnecessary, at least as far as the praise went.

She already knew what an extraordinary man Ben was. In fact, the more she thought about it, the more she knew Noah was right. Ben deserved her complete and total trust.

Actually, he already had it.

She wouldn't have told him about her past otherwise, but the words had just tripped out. She'd been comfortable, happy inside, and she'd wanted to share with Ben. Sierra sighed. He deserved everything from her and from here on out, he'd get it.

Noah parked in her lot and walked around to open her door for her. "Grace is working today. Give me just a few minutes to chat with her and to locate Ben, then I'll be back. If Ben's not too busy, we can take a look at your engine now. I've got the rest of the day free."

Sierra started to thank him, when his attention got diverted. Agatha Harper had just been driven up to the diner's front door. Noah shook his head. "Then again, we might all be busy for a few minutes."

At the sight of Ben's grandmother stepping from the limo, Sierra couldn't help but smile. True, Agatha scared her a little, but she knew from her brief conversation with her that she loved Ben and only wanted to get closer to him. If Sierra could help her do that, she would.

"I'm going to go in and change and clean up a little. Will you please tell Mrs. Harper that I'll join her shortly?"

Noah turned back to her. "Of course."

"And Noah?" Sierra hesitated, then because she couldn't stop herself she went on tiptoe and hugged him. "You were right."

His brawny arms went around her and he returned her embrace. Sierra could tell he was smiling. "About what?"

"I do love him."

* * *

Sierra took extra care getting ready after her tepid shower. It wasn't every day she told a man that she loved him, and as unfamiliar as it seemed, she wanted to look her best.

She left her hair loose after blow-drying it into long smooth curls. Ben seldom saw her hair unconfined, except after sex when it was horribly tangled. Sierra wondered what he'd think, if he'd like it or if he'd even notice. Probably not, she decided, but it still made her feel more confident.

Next she got dressed, choosing a sleeveless white blouse and tan shorts. Her sandals were a little scuffed, but they definitely looked better than her work boots or ratty sneakers. When she surveyed herself in the mirror, she smiled. Not that she looked that great, but she was excited.

She'd changed a lot about her life, set herself on a better course. But she still allowed the past to rule her, specifically her involvement with Griff. Avoiding him had seemed wiser, easier, and much safer than fighting him, but no more. Come what may, she'd get Griff out of her life once and for all. If that meant a court battle, if it meant she had to start over again, she would do it.

Because she wanted to be free for Ben.

With that decision, her heart felt lighter than it had in ages, and her body tingled in anticipation because she knew she'd end up in bed with Ben. And that's where she wanted to be.

The early evening sun was a gigantic red ball when Sierra stepped outside. A humid breeze blew over her, carrying the scents of fresh mulch and topsoil. She stared toward Ben's diner across the street. It appeared to be in full swing with the front door standing open and music, along with a few guests, spilling out to the walkway.

As Sierra started across the lot, she saw Ben dance past the front door. He wasn't alone.

No, he held Molly in his arms, his hold gentle as if she were a fragile flower. Their laughter was contagious and Sierra smiled. She'd met Molly, a fifty-something truck driver who adored Ben, a few weeks ago. She was nearly as tall as Ben but . . . boxier, with broad, sturdy shoulders and an enormous bosom. Ben treated her like a princess, swirling her, kissing her cheek.

Oh yes, Ben flirted—with everyone. It was an integral part of him and Sierra loved him for it. He made all women feel special, but if Noah was right, then she was more special than the rest.

She was still smiling, her stride anxious, when she stepped up onto the walkway in front of Ben's diner.

That's when she heard the laugh.

Sierra froze for a single moment. Then with iron determination and a new outlook on life, she turned. She spotted Griff just getting out of his Camaro, which he'd parked next to the curb. She'd been so intent on getting to Ben, Sierra hadn't noticed him at all.

She stepped away from the diner, approaching Griff, hoping to have this new confrontation without disturbing the guests of the diner and motel. She really didn't want an audience if she could help it. "What do you want, Griff?"

"Just visiting, baby." He leaned against the roof of his car and slipped off his expensive sunglasses. His smile was smarmy, his leer more so. "But you know, you don't look happy to see me. Why is that?"

When she stood only six feet away from him, Sierra

braced herself. Griff hadn't moved from the side of his car. He looked cool and relaxed in khaki slacks and a button-down short-sleeve shirt. "I'm only going to tell you this once, Griff. Stay away from me."

Giving a shout of surprised laughter, Griff pushed away from the car. "Yeah? Or what?"

From behind Sierra, a strident voice sounded. "Sierra, who is this young man? I don't like his tone at all."

Sierra groaned. Mrs. Harper stood rigidly at her back, her chin elevated, her eyes cold and unwavering.

Griff gave her a dismissive glance. "Mind your own business, old lady." He continued to casually close the distance until he was a mere breath away from Sierra.

Agatha gathered herself, moved to Sierra's side before Sierra could stop her, and pointed an imperious finger right in Griff's face. "Now see here . . ."

Griff swatted her hand away, making Agatha gasp with pain. "Get lost, bitch."

Sierra moved fast, motivated by a deep rage that burned through her blood. It was one thing for Griff to give her hell, but she would never allow him to mistreat Ben's grandmother.

She put herself in front of Agatha, shielding her with her body. Her words came out from between clenched teeth. "I'm telling you for the last time, get out of here and don't come back or you'll be sorry."

"You've got that wrong, Sierra. You're the one who's going to be sorry."

Sierra laughed without humor. "I'm already sorry, you ass. Sorry I ever met you, and twice as sorry that I ever married you."

Griff's hands curled into fists and he leaned closer so that his angry breath pelted her face. "You humiliated me, you little whore. Everyone knew I was going to divorce you, everyone knew you were a damn ball and chain around my neck." His voice rose to a shout, drawing the attention of other people in the lot, the diner. "Everyone understood my predicament, until you crawled away in the middle of the damn night like a whipped dog."

Agatha was quiet now, too quiet, but Sierra couldn't spare her a glance. All her attention was trained on Griff. "That's what this is about? I hurt your feelings? I *embarrassed* you?" Sierra laughed again. "God, that's pathetic. I left with only a few clothes. You got everything, Griff."

"Not the satisfaction of divorcing you."

She rolled her eyes. "So lie. Tell everyone you kicked me out. I don't care, as long as I don't ever have to see you again."

Griff's face was mottled with rage and he grabbed Sierra by the upper arms, jerking her toward him. She almost stumbled, and he yanked her upright, crushing her, deliberately hurting her.

Agatha gasped in outrage. "Unhand her this instant."

"Fuck off, old lady."

Sierra started to struggle, thinking to bring her knee up into Griff's groin, when suddenly a fist shot past her face. It landed dead center on Griff's nose. His hold went slack as he was knocked back and just barely managed to stay on his feet.

Ben stepped around Sierra, a solid wall of tense, angry, protective male. He cast her a cautious glance, then said to Griff, "You touched my grandmother."

Sierra gawked at him.

Griff, swaying just a bit, held his bloody nose and groaned. "What in God's name are you talking about?"

Agatha shook a thin brittle fist at him. "You heard him,

you miscreant. You touched me. I'm his grandmother." She gave a nod of satisfaction, patted her gray hair, and muttered, "Ben is outraged over your audacity."

Ben stood looking at Griff with his fists on his hips, his legs braced apart, every inch of him tense and ready and willing. He glanced at Sierra again, and she thought he looked a little apologetic although she had no idea why.

From behind her, Sierra heard Noah say, "Kick his ass, Ben."

Agatha said, "Oh, I think he will. Won't you, Ben?"

Ben nodded. "Damn right."

Attempting to straighten up, Griff wiped his wrist across his nose, smearing the blood all over his cheek. He looked incensed, his eyes red, his face swollen and starting to bruise. "How the hell was I supposed to know the old harpy was your grandmother?"

Agatha said, "Benjamin?"

"Yeah, Aggie?"

"He just insulted me."

Ben smiled. This time he hit Griff in the stomach. "You can't insult her either."

Because Griff was bent double, holding his guts and wheezing, Ben spoke to the top of his head. "Sierra has forbidden me to touch you on her behalf, and I love her, so I'm respecting her decision." He glanced at Sierra. "Though God knows it's not easy." Then to Griff: "But my grandmother is another matter entirely. She hasn't forbidden a damn thing."

Sierra stared at Ben. Her heart galloped madly, her chest felt too tight to breathe, and her eyes were filling with hot tears. It was a strange sensation, because she also had to fight the urge to laugh out loud.

She now understood Ben's apologetic look when he'd

first slugged Griffin, and she also understood Agatha. Oh yes, Ben's grandmother was positively beaming under his attention. She was a bloodthirsty old woman and she didn't appear to mind one bit that Ben had used her to retaliate. Just the opposite, in fact.

Griff looked up at Agatha, his eyes bleary and his nose grotesquely bent. Agatha hooked her arm through Sierra's elbow. "Ben protects those he loves, isn't that right, Ben?"

"That's about it. Now stand up, you bastard. Fight me."

"No." Shaking his head, Griff backed up. "I'll call the police. You'll pay for this. Sierra will pay. I'll make you all sorry."

"Yeah?" Ben cocked a brow, and a new energy seemed to hum through him. "How exactly are you going to do that?"

"Tell him, Sierra," Griff taunted, still backing away. "I know people, powerful people. When I finish with you, you won't have a fucking penny to your name."

Ben stared at Sierra. "You believed this? It's why you didn't want me involved?"

With so many people looking at her, Sierra felt self-conscious. She shrugged. "I'm so sorry, Ben. He closed loans on my friends, destroyed my father's reputation in the church . . ."

Ben's smile was wicked, full of promise. "Don't be sorry, sweetheart. Just let me beat him to a pulp, okay?"

His mood so surprised Sierra, she said, "Well . . ."

Agatha raised an imperious hand. "Now Ben, I will handle this."

Ben sighed. "Stay out of it, Aggie."

"But don't you see, this is what I can do. He thinks he knows powerful people? Ha." She rubbed her hands together in something akin to glee. "I'll show the scoundrel some powerful people. When I'm through with him, his people won't want to mutter his name, much less acknowledge him."

Noah laughed. "Let her help, Ben."

Sierra took in the small crowd of Ben's family. Not a one of them appeared disgusted by her past mistakes and disreputable ex. Agatha was in her element, as staunch as a four-star general planning a strategic attack. Noah had Grace hugged up to his side, and they both appeared to be enjoying the show, if their smiles were any indication. Many of the guests and employees from the motel and diner had gathered around, urging Ben on, heckling Griff.

Overwhelmed by it all, Sierra slumped back against the wall of the diner. Everything would truly be all right, she realized. She loved Ben and she found his family fascinating and endearing. She hadn't known family could be that way, blindly supportive, cheerfully defensive.

More tears filled her eyes, but they were happy tears.

"My father is a mayor," Griff snarled. "My uncle is a senator. My family is in banking, we . . ."

"You're about to cause your family a horrible embarrassment, and I can tell you right now, they will not appreciate it one bit." Agatha spoke with conviction—and eagerness. Her smile was not pleasant, not by a long shot.

Sierra sniffed around a giggle.

Ben glanced at his grandmother, amused by her expression. "Sure, why not? He's yours, Aggie. Do your worst."

She gave a small nod. "I'll make the necessary calls right away."

Sierra decided things had gotten well out of hand. She pushed away from the brick wall and gently touched Ben's upper arm. His biceps were bunched and hard, his body fairly buzzing with anger. "Ben, none of this is necessary."

He absently patted her hand while watching Griff, who looked haunted and suddenly uncertain. "I didn't break my word to you, Sierra. But he did touch Aggie."

"He did," Agatha confirmed. "And naturally Ben would defend my honor. Isn't that right, Ben?"

Ben shook his head. "I already told you that it is, Aggie. Hell, I might argue with you, and God knows you love to irritate me. But you are my grandmother. No one is allowed to insult you but me."

Agatha beamed. "I love you, Ben."

Her announcement at such an inauspicious moment had everyone coughing and snorting. Ben's face went blank, then immediately turned bright red. He scowled at her. "Damn, Aggie, do you really think now is the time?"

She laughed—and damn if her laugh didn't sound just like Ben's.

Bemused by that, Sierra cleared her throat and got her brain back on track. "But Ben, I was going to handle it. I was about to—"

An approaching police siren splintered the air. Noah explained, "I called the cops."

Ben winced, and he curled his fingers around Sierra's, giving her a squeeze. "I'm sorry, sweetheart. I didn't have a chance to tell Noah that you didn't want—"

"I was going to call them myself."

Ben faltered. "You were?"

She nodded and peered around at their audience. The guests and employees of the motel watched her with avid curiosity. Noah winked at her and Grace was positively beaming. Agatha looked very satisfied with herself, while Ben showed his confusion.

Griff had collapsed against a telephone pole. He was making an awful mess, what with his bloody nose and all.

Sighing, Sierra looked up at Ben and managed a smile. "I want to be with you."

He breathed a little harder. "With me?"

She nodded. "I decided you were plenty strong enough and smart enough to deal with Griff if he tried anything against you. Of course I didn't know you had Mrs. Harper as a secret weapon."

Agatha preened.

"Sierra?" Ben's hands shook as he cupped her face.

The damn tears threatened again, and she swiped them away. "Griff had me so . . . so worried, that I was afraid to confront him. I didn't know what he might do, especially to you." Her heart lodged in her throat. The sirens were getting closer. Everyone had closed in around them so they could eavesdrop on their private conversation. "Damn it, Ben. I didn't want him to cause you any trouble, so I tried to stay away from you. Only you wouldn't let me, and then I decided being with you was worth any trouble. I hope you feel the same because—"

Ben hauled her close, silencing her with a kiss.

The crowd cheered.

A police cruiser pulled up to the curb.

Vaguely, through a pleasant humming in her ears, Sierra heard Agatha say, "Officer, I can explain everything. I'm Agatha Harper and this reprobate attacked me."

Her voice faded away with Ben's laugh. He nuzzled Sierra's chin, her cheek, her mouth again. "God, I love you, Sierra."

The tears overflowed. "Ben." She shook her head. "What am I going to do with you?"

He glanced around. "Well, when this crowd clears away, I have a few ideas." He grinned shamelessly.

Sierra wrapped her arms around Ben. "I love you, too."

He squeezed the breath right out of her. Then said, "Sweetheart, did you do something different with your hair?"

Two weeks later

Ben walked into the diner and saw Agatha, Sierra, Grace, and his mother all sitting together at a round table, laughing, drinking coffee. Plotting. He stopped and stood in the doorway, his heart content. All the women he loved, together.

Damn, life was good.

Noah sauntered up to his side and handed him a steaming cup of coffee. "They're planning an engagement party. A huge, fancy affair if Agatha gets her way."

Ben nodded. "Whatever Sierra wants."

Noah laughed. "You're more lovesick than Kent."

Ben looked at Kent, seated at the bar not three feet away. His hair was mussed, his face unshaven, and he was busy looking at the women. Or more specifically, he was looking at Brooke. There was a sharp satisfaction about him, a mellow edge to his mood. Ben rolled his eyes and smiled.

Sierra noticed Ben and left the table. The second she reached him, she said, "Morning," and kissed him warmly on the mouth.

Damn, Ben thought, having Sierra openly love him was almost more than his heart could take. He hooked an arm around her until she was hugged up to his side, then took a drink of coffee. After spending all night making love to her, he was a little sluggish, a lot tired—and very satisfied.

Kent gave a low rumbling growl, like a lion's purr, and everyone turned to him. Noah chuckled. "He's been doing that all morning."

Sierra snickered. "That's the way Kent always acts after he's spent the night in a sexual marathon."

Because Kent was looking at Brooke, Ben spewed his coffee and promptly choked.

Laughing and commiserating at the same time, Noah thwacked Ben on the back. "Get over it Ben. Brooke is beautiful. Men are bound to notice."

Ben continued to wheeze. "I'm choking to death here," he rasped. Kent ignored him.

Sierra hugged Ben. "I think it's sweet."

Having overheard that comment, Kent growled again. "It is that. Very sweet."

Noah held Ben back when he reached for Kent, but he was laughing.

Then Kent turned all businesslike. He faced Ben, his expression resolute. "You might as well know, I'm going to marry her."

Ben held his head with his free hand and groaned. "Did she say yes?"

"Haven't asked her yet, but she will."

While the others laughed, Ben muttered, "Your conceit is unbearable."

Brooke waved Kent over. He grinned and started away, saying, "That's because she gives me good reason for conceit."

Ben waited until Kent was out of earshot to laugh. "Kent's a good man. My mother deserves him."

"*You're* a good man," Noah said. "You deserve Sierra."

"Damn right." Ben kissed her temple, then asked, "Do you have to get to work soon?"

Sierra started to answer, and Noah raised a hand. "Since she's still working for me, and I'm in no dire rush, I can safely say that she has the morning free."

"In that case . . ." Ben sat his coffee aside, took Sierra's hand and led her away.

Sierra laughed. As Ben hauled her back to his rooms, she waved to Cathy in the kitchens, then to Wendy and Gary who were manning the front desk of the motel.

In the two weeks since Griff had been stuffed into the back of the patrol car, Ben had watched Sierra grow comfortable being in his motel. Ben liked showing her off, and his employees loved teasing her, almost as much as his customers did. Molly was forever trying to give her lewd advice on how to keep Ben happy.

Ben tugged her into the room and into his arms. Sierra definitely didn't need any help in that department. She kept him very happy, indeed.

With her pinned to the wall, his hips pressed closed to hers, Ben kissed her. "I heard from Griffin's lawyers today."

She stiffened, but only a little bit. Griffin couldn't hurt her anymore. "Yeah?"

"Yup."

Nuzzling his chin, Sierra asked, "What did he have to say?"

"He told me that Griffin will effectively drop out of your life if I get my grandmother to drop the harassment charges. I refused."

"Ben." Sierra pressed back a little to see his face. "All we want is to be left alone."

"Wrong. I still want to pound him into the ground. Those few measly punches didn't make me feel a bit better. Thrilled the hell out of my grandmother, but I'm still pissed."

Sierra had to fight hard to keep from laughing. "Agatha is very proud of you."

"That she is. She's driving me nuts, acting like we've got this long-standing history of affection." He shook his head. "I think my mother put her up to it. The two of them seem to get along very well now."

"They both love you."

Ben slowly smiled. "And what about you? You love me, too, sweetheart?"

Sierra pinched him. "Every woman loves you and you know it."

"Will you still love me when I tell you that I've filed for a restraining order?"

Sierra dropped her forehead to his chest. "Ben, is that really necessary?"

"Yes, because I want Griff, his father, and his lawyer to all understand that if he comes near you again, I'll see him in jail. Hell, I'll probably wring his neck, *then* see him in jail."

"I'm sure he knows that already, Ben. But they are influential people and I'd hate for you to have any problems with them."

Ben snorted. "Aggie's lawyers assured me that stalking is one of those politically incorrect crimes. You get caught doing it, no one is going to want to reach out and help you, no matter how influential they can be. It looks really bad for anyone in the public eye, or with political aspirations. Get a speeding ticket and know some officer who will help you—no big deal to most. Get caught stalking your ex-wife, and people will leave you out to hang.

"With the restraining order, Griff will know the law is keeping a close eye on him. One mixup and his ass is in jail."

Sierra wrapped herself around Ben. "As long as he leaves us alone, I don't care what happens to him."

"Good, because you'll need to sign some papers for the lawyer."

She nodded, kissed his chin, and started to stroke her hands down his body.

Ben wasn't ready to get distracted yet. "Did you ladies come up with a date for the wedding?"

"Mmm. Seven months from now." Her fingers drifted over the front of his fly.

Ben caught her wrist. "*What?* No, now wait a minute. No way in hell am I waiting seven months . . ."

Sierra pulled her hand free. "You told us to do whatever we wanted. Agatha needs that long to get the guest list organized and the invitations together, and your mother needs that long to get the church and hall reserved."

"Forget it! I want . . ."

"Me to touch you, right now. Isn't that right, Ben?"

He blinked at her. "Yeah." Then he shook his head. "But I'm not waiting seven months."

Sierra found his growing erection through the material of his jeans. Ben was gasping when she whispered, "Besides, I need that long to get my business going before I take off on a honeymoon."

"Honeymoon?" His eyes closed when she slid his zipper down.

"Agatha is sending us to the Bahamas." Sierra began gently nudging him toward the bed. When the back of his knees hit the mattress, she pushed him into a sitting position, then gracefully dropped to her knees.

Ben stared at her with hot eyes, barely able to think beyond wondering why she might be positioned that way and what she might be going to do to him. "The Bahamas?"

"Hmm. She wanted us to go to Paris, but we're not Paris-type people."

He cupped the back of her neck. "Whatever you want, Sierra."

"I know." Her smile made his heart melt. "Now lift your hips so I can take these jeans off you."

"Hell of an idea." Ben immediately complied, but when she curled her small hand around him, he again thought to protest. "Anything you want, except a seven-month wait."

"That's the date, Ben. Accept it." Before he could find his voice, Sierra leaned forward and kissed him.

"Oh God."

"Shhh. Relax back. Let me have some fun."

Ben lay back, but said again, "We're not waiting seven damn months and that's that."

"We are." Her mouth slid over the head of his erection and she gently sucked.

Ben shouted, his hips jolting off the bed and his muscles all clenching tight.

Her rough velvet tongue was magic, licking, tasting. She drew back and smiled up at him. "I already approved the date." Then she went back to driving him to distraction.

"Sierra . . ." Ben felt dangerously close to coming already. Her mouth was hot, wet, drawing on him, teasing him. *"Sierra."*

She took more of him into her mouth until he nudged the back of her throat. She moved back and forth, her tongue stroking the underside of his cock; then she gently cupped his testicles in her palm. Ben lost the struggle for control. His heart slamming hard, his breath raging, he came.

He was staring at the ceiling, his mind numb, trying to focus when Sierra scooted up to lie alongside him. He could feel her smile when she kissed his shoulder and rested her hand over his heart.

"Seven months, Ben."

"Yeah. All right. Whatever." He could barely breathe, damn it. "But you're sleeping here with me until then."

"Of course."

Rational thought slowly returned and Ben gave her a suspicious look. "Are you laughing at me?"

"No, but I'm happy." She grinned up at him and there was a mischievous light in her green eyes. "I like controlling you with sex. I can see why you do it to me so often."

Very slowly, Ben's smile came. "Is that what you just did?" He pulled her atop him and laced his hands over the small of her back.

"Yep." And then, more seriously, "I like the way you taste, Ben."

"You know what I think?"

Sierra kissed his chin. "What?"

"I think you should do it again."

"Take you in my mouth?"

He shuddered at the eager way she said that. "No, control me. Only this time, I want to be inside you." He nudged his fingers under the hem of her shorts and teased her warm silky cheeks.

Sierra tried to roll away. "Ben, we have guests in the diner."

"Just family. They'll understand."

Sierra laughed even as she tried to wriggle free of his hold. "Ben, no. Ben, stop that. Ben!"

"You like it," he growled, and pushed two fingers inside her.

"Ben . . ."

"I can get you to agree," he said with some satisfaction.

Sierra gave a long sigh and stopped fighting him. "I know."

Ben turned her beneath him. She didn't look bothered by her confession. No, Sierra was smiling, her face flushed. Beautiful.

She was his. "I love you, Sierra."

"I love you, too, Ben. Forever."

Out in the diner, Agatha shook her head in disgust. "Ben's dragged the poor girl off and now we won't be able to finish making plans. How can I organize a wedding of this size if he won't cooperate with me?"

Brooke was about to commiserate with Agatha when Kent leaned down and whispered in her ear. With an apologetic, and shaky, smile, Brooke excused herself. The two of them dashed out the front door like teenagers skipping school.

Agatha rolled her eyes. Ben came by his lustiness legitimately, it seemed.

She turned toward the bar where she'd last seen Noah

and Grace, ready to call them over—then had to pause when she saw they were playing kissy-face right there at the bar for all the world to see. It was downright shameful.

In a huff, Agatha stood up and gathered her purse. She put enough money on the table to cover the tab, left an extra-generous tip and headed for the door. She tried to look stern, she really did.

But damn it, the smile broke free, quickly followed by a rusty laugh. She had more money than she could ever spend, but that wasn't what made her rich. No, it was so much more than that. It was Noah and Ben, Grace and Sierra, Brooke and now even Kent.

They were a loving, wonderful bunch of people.

They were her family, and that made her the wealthiest woman alive.

Don't miss UNEXPECTED by Lori Foster,
available now!

She'd already signed the contract.

Backing out now would blow her reputation with the agency, and besides, this mission would be a piece of cake. There was no reason to drag her feet. She needed the money, she was free at the moment, and it'd be a routine run, nothing more, nothing less. It'd be easier now than in the past. Everything had changed.

Herself included.

She shook her head at that errant thought. True, she was older now, wiser, more settled. But at the core, she was the same—unacceptable to most, invaluable to others. Her skills, an innate part of her, were still finely honed. She knew what she could do, and damn it, she'd do it. Hell, she'd *missed* doing it.

So why, when she pushed the door open and stared into the dim, smoky room of the bar, was her heart so heavy in her chest? It wasn't the depressing gray cloud that hung thick in the air, not only from cigarettes, but from disgust and ambivalence and antagonism. This was far from a happy place, but then, she'd known it wouldn't be. By necessity, it was an obscure hole in the Chicago slums where meetings like this one, with people like her, could be handled with discretion.

It was stupid to borrow trouble or dwell in indecision. Doing so undermined her credibility, so instead, she'd concentrate on getting this over with fast and easy, with no complications.

She had everything planned out.

Flipping her bangs off her forehead, she strode into the room, ready to get things started.

Several heads turned her way, scrutinizing her, making note of her appearance. Calculating. For much of her life, she'd gotten undue attention for one reason or another, most of the reasons uncomplimentary. She'd long since gotten used to the stares and the whispers. She ignored them all, and with luck, they'd show her the same courtesy.

Peering through the obscuring smoke, she scanned the tables and booths, searching out each darkened corner. Country music blasted through tinny speakers, vying with the boasting and bragging of drunken men. It was the typical atmosphere of a seedy bar. Without thinking, she rubbed her stomach, sick with a rush of vivid memories that never failed to surface.

Then her gaze locked onto his. Wow. The past faded away under the impact of the present—*his* impact. She felt . . . invaded.

Bright hazel eyes, radiant in the otherwise dismal interior, held her captive. She stared at him; he stared back.

Never before had she seen such intense emotion in a man's expression. For a moment, it knocked her off guard. Without moving, he appeared turbulent, frustrated, filled with determination and impatience.

Because of his situation, or because she'd arrived late?

She watched him a moment more, taking his measure. He was bigger than most of the men she knew or had worked with. And he had a more self-assured air. That he'd be trouble she didn't doubt—he pretty much screamed it with a capital T. But how much trouble, that's what she needed to know.

Lounging back in his chair, he allowed her perusal, and even took the time to look her over, too. But then, amazingly enough, he dismissed her by giving his attention back to the entrance of the bar.

Cynical amusement nudged away the lingering nervousness. He hadn't realized her identity? She wasn't what he'd been expecting? Typical. And for a second there, she'd thought he might be more astute than the others.

Anticipating his reaction when she introduced herself, she started toward him. He sat at a solitary table at the far end of the room, his back to the wall so he could face the bar, a rear exit to his right. It was a guarded position she would have chosen, but probably just a coincidence for him.

She wove her way around tables, drunks, and proffered drinks without once taking her eyes off him.

As was her usual habit at such meetings, she'd dressed in plain black clothes. It made it easier to disappear if necessary, and didn't draw added attention that more complimentary clothes might have.

Her long-sleeved tunic hung to midthigh, loosely fitted so it wouldn't impede her movements should she need to take physical control of the surroundings. Her jeans were slim, her low-heeled boots only ankle high. She never wore jewelry—in fact, she didn't own any—but she did carry a black briefcase. The case was an annoyance, but it usually proved necessary to have it handy.

When she stopped in front of him, his gaze came to her face, arrested for only a moment. Then slowly, very slowly, he looked her over again, his attention lingering in certain places like her chest, below her waist, her thighs. His look was so intimate, so personal that it brought on a mélange of sensations—outrage, disgust, and strangely enough, heat. Surely not embarrassment, she told herself. She was too old and far too jaded to be disconcerted by the likes of him.

His visual inspection was appreciative and felt like a tactile touch. Damn it, she didn't like being touched, not without permission.

Her eyes narrowed, prompting him to a softly uttered, reluctant rejection. "Sorry, honey. It's unfortunate, but I'm already busy tonight."

The nerve. Despite her exceptional control, antagonism bristled to the surface. Her every movement rigid, Ray hooked a chair and drew it out. She seated herself, placing the briefcase at her feet for safekeeping.

He cocked one dark brow upward and braced his forearms on the rough, scarred table. The new position emphasized the width of his shoulders, the brawn of his arms. She'd expected another wimpy, slim *GQ* look-alike, but this man could be a barroom bouncer. He wasn't bulky, just big and hard and solid.

Added to the fine physique were the eyes of a predator, now filled with annoyance. He leaned toward her with a scowl.

"I'm Ray Vereker," she drawled, stopping him in his tracks.